Birnbaum's

Walt Disney World®

WITHOUT KIDS

W9-DBO-268

Wendy Lefkon
EDITORIAL DIRECTOR

Jill Safro
EDITOR

Michael Farmer
DESIGN DIRECTOR

Frieda Christofides
DESIGNER

THE OFFICIAL GUIDE

Jody Revenson
CONSULTING EDITOR

Alexandra Mayes Birnbaum
CONSULTING EDITOR

Disney EDITIONS

ISBN 0-7868-5547-9

Printed in the United States of America

Other 2006 Birnbaum's Official Disney Guides:

Disneyland

Disney Cruise Line

Walt Disney World

Walt Disney World Dining

Walt Disney World For Kids, By Kids

A Word from the Editor

When you stop to think about it, a Walt Disney World guide for grown-ups makes a lot of sense. After all, how many kids do you know who have been there alone? As it happens, Disney has been catering to adult sensibilities for a long time—since 1955, to be exact. That's when Disneyland first opened its gates and a generation of grown-up kids was unabashedly hooked. Now, as Disney's original park continues to mark its 50th anniversary—aka "the happiest celebration on earth," its theme park siblings are celebrating, too. As are several generations of folks who continue to crave a side of whimsy with their grown-up getaway.

Editor Jill Safro consults with Minnie and Mickey, the ultimate Walt Disney World insiders.

The parks of Walt Disney World are by no means the exclusive domain of small fry. In keeping with the spirit of the World that Walt built, there are no age limits here. The Disney-MGM Studios is a veritable haven for movie buffs. The Magic Kingdom sprinkles guests with pixie dust and transports them to the giddy, fantasy-filled days of their youth. Disney's Animal Kingdom, a lush celebration of all creatures great and small, is sure to lure the nature lover out of even the most buttoned-down sophisticate. Add to the above a hopping nightlife district and a sports complex, and you have proof positive that the World has expanded in precisely our direction. Chic resort hotels and restaurants, world-class golf courses, and sensuous spa treatments only add to the allure.

But there's also another, more subtle level on which Walt Disney World has always appealed to grown-ups. We're referring to the little jokes, both visual and verbal, that keep popping up where you least expect them. More than ever before, Disney's creative

3

efforts are crossing over to the grown-up side of the street. Lots of adults are descending on the parks with notions that are vastly different from those of the parental persuasion.

This book, unlike *Birnbaum's Official Guide to Walt Disney World*, is by no means comprehensive. Rather, it skips the flat-out kid stuff and delivers the goods on the grown-up amusements Disney has to offer. And because this guide is updated every year, we have spent the past twelve months debating which of the attractions, hotels, and restaurants—both new and old—continue to merit special attention by adults. Final decisions were reached after making countless trips to Florida and putting everything to the test.

Even with research aplenty, this book would never have seen print were it not for the assistance of many other people. To begin, we owe a thank-you to the people who run Walt Disney World. It is their willingness to explain operations in the most accurate way possible that makes this the Official Guide. However, it is important to note that while the folks at Walt Disney World help us to ensure factual accuracy, they do not determine what we do and do not cover in the guide. *All editorial decisions are made by the editor.*

In the listing below, I've tried to acknowledge Disney staffers who contributed their time, knowledge, and experience to this edition. In addition, I want to extend a deep bow to Linda Warren, Darlene Papalini, Laura Simpson, Jeff Titelius, and Dave Herbst for the care and effort they've put into this project.

We Couldn't Have Done It Without . . .

Jim Bourhill	Christi Erwin	Kristi Koester
Katie Brandon	Bebee Frost	Mark Peters
Pam Brandon	Richard Gregorie	Rosely Piraino
Mike Carroll	Karen Haynes	Frank Ritti
Michelle Coley	Mark Jaronski	Anna Rivera
Stacey Cook	Carrie Matson	Rick Sylvain
Craig Dezern	Sarah Morris	Dara Trujillo
Debbie Dizon	Mike Nesmith	Pamela S. Weiers
Mark Drennen	Heather Keroes	

For their key roles behind the scenes, we salute Monica Mayper, Diane Hodges, Sue Cole, Janet Castiglione, William Feik, Guy Cunningham, and Michelle Magenheim.

Special kudos to those for whom doing Walt Disney World research is truly a labor of love. The class of 2006 includes Irene Safro, Roy Safro, Joy Safro, Amy Safro, Margaret Verdon, Linda Verdon, Trace Schielzo, Heather Pommerencke, Judith Lagano, David Sabino, and Liliana Lovell.

Of course, no list of acknowledgments would be complete without our founding editor, Steve Birnbaum, as well as Alexandra Mayes Birnbaum, who continues to be a guiding light and a careful reader of every word.

Finally, it is important to remember that Walt Disney World is constantly changing and growing, and with each annual revision, we refine and expand our material to serve your needs even better. For the present edition, though, this is the final word.

Have a great visit!

Don't Forget To Write

No contribution is of greater value to us in preparing the next edition of this book than your comments on what we've written and on your own experiences and discoveries at Walt Disney World. Please share your insights with us by writing to:

Jill Safro, Editor
Birnbaum's Walt Disney World Without Kids 2006
Disney Editions
114 Fifth Avenue, 12th Floor
New York, NY 10011

Table of Contents

9 Planning Ahead

First things first: lay the groundwork for an unforgettable vacation by timing your Disney visit to take advantage of the best weather, crowd patterns, and special goings-on. We set forth information about package and ticket options, offer time- and money-saving strategies, and present the keys to the World's transportation system. Our custom-designed sample schedules will help you plan your days and nights. And a round of specialized advice offers the promise of a hassle-free trip.

When to Go 10
The Logistics 15
Getting Around 20
Sample Schedules 23
Customized Tips 28

39 Checking In

Whether it's elegant, rustic, whimsical, or romantic digs you're seeking, you'll find them among Walt Disney World's 22-plus resorts—including the new Pop Century Resort and Saratoga Springs Resort & Spa—and two island-bound cruise ships, themed as only Disney knows how. Choose from hotels whose architecture and ambience evoke such locales as Africa, New Orleans, Martha's Vineyard, Polynesia, or an early 1900s mountain lodge. Within our listing we explain the big draws of and grown-up appeal of all the resorts located within Walt Disney World borders.

Walt Disney World Resorts 40
Disney Cruise Line 74
Resorts on Hotel Plaza Boulevard 76

81 Theme Parks: The Big Four

Enchanting, engaging, entertaining . . . overwhelming. The Magic Kingdom, Epcot, Disney-MGM Studios, and Disney's Animal Kingdom can rekindle even the most sluggish sense of wonder. But where to begin? Right here. We've devised strategies to help you make the most of each day. We've also provided detailed theme park walking tours that highlight the most alluring stops for adults; a primer on Fastpass, Disney's time-saving service; and lists of touring priorities that rank every attraction. From "Don't Miss" to "Don't Knock Yourself Out," we've scoped out the grown-up fun quotient.

Magic Kingdom 82
Epcot 93
 • **Future World** 97
 • **World Showcase** 107
Disney-MGM Studios 118
Animal Kingdom 130

141 Diversions: Sports, Shopping, and Other Pursuits

Because the World's attractions extend way beyond the theme parks, so does our guidance. Here, discover the options, including five first-rate 18-hole golf courses, tennis, boating, fishing, and biking. Shoppers will have a field day checking out our favorite shopping spots. For those who prefer soaking and sliding, we plunge into the water parks. Our in-depth report on romantic (and private) sunset and fireworks cruises reveals the creative essence of this adult-minded retreat. We also visit the natural realms of Fort Wilderness, and indulge in the sinful splendor of Walt Disney World's spas.

Sports 142

Shopping 162

Other Pursuits 171
• Water Parks 171
• Natural Distraction 174
• Romantic Excursions and
  Specialty Cruises 176
• Spas 178

183 Dining & Entertainment

Here's your insider's guide to adult best bets for full-service restaurants and casual eating spots in the theme parks, resorts, and elsewhere in Walt Disney World. We've found dining rooms with prime views, cheap eats, sweet treats, afternoon tea, wines by the glass, and hearty microbrews. After dark, you'll know where to go to watch the big game, hear cool jazz, join in a rollicking sing-along, and dance the night away (to disco, country, or hip-hop), as well as how to navigate the newest Downtown Disney hot spots, find a dinner show or a comedy club, or catch a theme park spectacular.

Restaurant Guide 184

Nightlife Guide 206

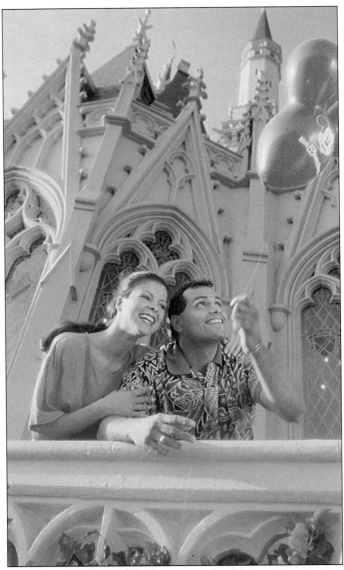

Anyone can have a magical time at Walt Disney World with advance planning.

Planning Ahead

There are plenty of hotels, restaurants, and theme park attractions for everyone at Walt Disney World. So why sit down with a book to plan ahead? Because a little attention to detail beforehand—we like to think of it as shopping for fun insurance—pays big dividends once you arrive. Just ask the couple who had the foresight to book a table at the deluxe Victoria & Albert's dining room before they left home. Or the friends who arrived with tickets in hand and avoided the line at the entrance to Epcot (they also saved time and money by purchasing tickets in advance). Or the golfers who were able to snag a coveted mid-morning tee time during their Easter visit.

Our point: You can't be assured of the vacation experience you want without knowing which of the gazillion ways to enjoy Disney World most appeal to you—and how to make sure these potential highlights don't become missed opportunities.

This first chapter not only provides the framework for a successful visit but also establishes a vital awareness that helps the information in subsequent chapters fall right in line.

On the following pages, you'll find insight on when to visit; advice on tickets, packages, reservations, and how to save money; information on how to get around the World; flexible adult-oriented touring schedules; and tips for older travelers, couples, singles, and guests with disabilities. In short, it's a handy guide to all the magic of Disney—and a whole lot more.

This chapter is a straightforward planner that you'll return to again and again—no doubt with greater purpose than the first time through, when you're still eager to learn about Disney's hotels, theme parks, dining, and nightlife. So go ahead and give it a quick skim if this is your first read, but don't forget to come back.

WHEN TO GO

Much tougher than the (rhetorical) question of if you want to visit Walt Disney World is the prickly matter of when. In addition to your own schedule, there is the weather to consider; you would also like to avoid the crowds, although you'd love to get a gander at the Christmas parade or that flower festival you read about in the newspaper. You want to experience Disney World at its best. But when?

Weather and crowd patterns are charted in this section, along with other factors, such as extended park hours, so you can see how possible vacation dates stack up. Timing your visit to meet all expectations may be impossible, but our experience does suggest certain optimum times. Mid-January through early February, late April through late May, September through early November, and the week after Thanksgiving through the week before Christmas stand out as particularly good times to find oneself in the World.

Taking things one step further, we like to underline the period from the Sunday after Thanksgiving to the week before Christmas as the ultimate timing for a WDW visit. This is a chance to savor Walt Disney World during one of its least crowded and most festive times of year. The place is wrapped in wonderful holiday decorations, and there are scads of special goings-on, from parades to parties.

WDW WEATHER

Average:	High (F)	Low (F)	Rain (inches)
January	71	49	2.3
February	73	50	3.0
March	78	55	3.2
April	83	59	1.8
May	88	66	3.6
June	91	72	7.3
July	92	73	7.2
August	92	73	6.8
September	90	72	6.0
October	85	66	2.4
November	79	58	2.3
December	73	51	2.2

If your travel dates fall outside the above-mentioned ideal, don't despair. Walt Disney World makes a spectacle of itself year-round. This listing highlights holidays and happenings that— for their fanfare, crowd-drawing potential, and, in some instances, accompanying package deals— are worth factoring into your vacation plans.

NOTE: We've provided 2006 dates when available, but specifics are apt to change.

For current details about listed events and vacation packages, call 407-824-4321, or visit *www.disneyworld.com* up to three months before your visit.

Holidays & Special Events

WALT DISNEY WORLD MARATHON (January 7–8): Marathoners lace up for a 26.2-mile race through scenic areas of Disney World on January 8. Bands, Disney characters, and hot-air balloons inspire some 13,000 runners to stay the course. There's a half marathon, too (on January 7)—with similar fanfare and number of participants. Both events are extremely popular, so plan ahead. (There's a 5K race, too.) For details, call 407-939-7810. Vacation packages are available.

ATLANTA BRAVES SPRING TRAINING (March): Some of Major League Baseball's greatest gather at Disney's ballpark to get a jump on the upcoming season. Packages (800-892-7687) and single-game tickets (407-839-3900) are available.

ST. PATRICK'S DAY (March 17): On this day, impromptu shindigs sprout like shamrocks in the more spirited corners of the

All in the Timing

Consider the following WDW trends before settling on vacation dates. For details on park hours and attraction refurbishments, call 407-824-4321.

Shortest Lines, Smallest Crowds: The second week of January through the first week of February; late April through late May; the week after Labor Day until Thanksgiving; the week after Thanksgiving through the week before Christmas.

Longest Lines, Biggest Crowds: Presidents' week; the third week of March through the third week of April, especially Easter week; June through Labor Day, particularly the Fourth of July; Christmas through New Year's Day.

Potential Pitfalls: The water parks and certain WDW attractions sometimes close for renovations (most often during winter months). Spring break (between February and mid-April) lures many students, as do Grad Nites (weekend events in late April and early May).

Extended Hours: The two weeks surrounding Easter; summer; Thanksgiving week; Christmas through New Year's Day.

World. Raglan Road, Pleasure Island's Irish pub, is rather festive on this occasion.

EASTER (April 16): Extended hours—and monumental crowds—at the parks make for a hopping Magic Kingdom. It's one of the busiest times of the year.

EPCOT INTERNATIONAL FLOWER & GARDEN FESTIVAL (mid-April–early June): This flowery, annual event—a fragrant affair featuring some 30 million blossoms—not only makes a glorious perfumery of Epcot, but also allows gardeners to learn a trick or two from the folks who care for 10,000 rosebushes and then some.

In addition to character topiaries and elaborate display gardens, guests can take part in workshops, behind-the-scenes tours, dining, and a nightly concert series featuring acts from the '60s and '70s.

STAR WARS WEEKENDS (May–June): Galactic good times can be enjoyed as Disney-MGM Studios salutes the ever-popular *Star Wars* saga with celebrities and characters from the movies, autograph and photo opportunities, trivia contests, and more.

FOURTH OF JULY CELEBRATION (July 4): Double-fisted fireworks at the Magic Kingdom, Epcot,

What to Pack

- Comfortable shoes (2 pairs)
- Sunglasses and sunscreen
- A bathing suit
- Insect repellent
- T-shirts and shorts for day
- Casual separates for evening (jeans are okay)
- Lightweight sweaters or jackets for summer evenings and air-conditioned rooms; warmer clothing for evening (and often daytime) from November through March
- A jacket for men and a dress or comparable outfit for women for dinner at Victoria & Albert's
- Suitable togs and equipment for tennis, golf, fishing, jogging, or gym workouts (racquets, clubs, balls, golf shoes, and poles are available for rent)
- Lightweight rain gear and a folding umbrella

and the Disney-MGM Studios are a glorious salute to our nation's birthday. The parks often have extended hours to mark the occasion. But you pay a price: It's the busiest day of the summer.

FUNAI CLASSIC AT WALT DISNEY WORLD RESORT (October): In this tournament, now in its 36th year, top PGA Tour players compete alongside amateurs on two Walt Disney World venues: the Palm and Magnolia courses. The drama builds until the final day, when the Magnolia's fickle 18th hole has been known to twist the fates of more than a few players. For information, refer to the "Golf" section in the *Diversions* chapter, or call 407-824-2250.

EPCOT INTERNATIONAL FOOD & WINE FESTIVAL (October–November): The temptation to eat and drink your way around World Showcase is intensified by cooking demonstrations, plus samples of a host of exotic specialty dishes, international wines by the glass, and worldly desserts (about $2 to $6.50 per taste). Special five-course dinners sponsored by various vintners are also a highlight (to book the aforementioned dining experience, call 407-WDW-DINE). There is a nightly concert series and a "Party for the Senses" each weekend.

ABC SUPER SOAP WEEKEND (November): Soap fans will think they've died and gone to Pine Valley at this annual Studios event. Meet actors from the ABC daytime dramas *All My Children*, *General Hospital*, and *One Life to Live*.

Question-and-answer sessions give die-hard fans the chance to interact with the stars. For more information, contact the Super Soap Hotline at 407-397-6808 or visit *www.abc.com*. Note that this is a popular event.

Hot Tickets

Here are a few numbers to add to your pre-vacation Rolodex.

- Consider that a recent month brought such acts as Elvis Costello, David Allan Coe, and B.B. King to House of Blues. Call 407-934-2583 a good month ahead to reserve seats.

- To make a sure thing of witnessing Cirque du Soleil at Downtown Disney, call 407-939-7600 for tickets up to six months ahead.

- Advance planning also pays off when Disney's Wide World of Sports complex hosts, say, the always popular Atlanta Braves. Call 407-939-4263.

FESTIVAL OF THE MASTERS

(November): One of the South's top-rated art shows, the three-day event at Downtown Disney draws upward of 150 award-winning exhibitors from around the country. It tends to be least crowded on Friday and Sunday mornings.

DISNEY'S MAGICAL HOLIDAYS (Late November through December):

The whole wide World is positively aglow with holiday spirit, and it doesn't stop at decorations: Tree-lighting ceremonies are held in three theme parks.

The Magic Kingdom celebrates the season with Mickey's Very Merry Christmas Parade and Mickey's Very Merry Christmas Party, a special-ticket event held on several nights during late November and the first three weeks of December that includes hot chocolate and cookies, plus a dusting of snow on Main Street.

Epcot invites guests to enjoy a candlelight procession and a choral celebration of holidays around the world (inquire about dinner and show packages).

The Disney-MGM Studios

Cost-Cutting Tips

- Consider accommodations with kitchen facilities to save on food costs, or stock your refrigerator (available for free at deluxe and moderate WDW resorts or for a $10 nightly fee at value resorts).

- Compare lunch and dinner menus. The same dishes may be cheaper by day.

- Buy a WDW resort mug good for unlimited refills (of soft drinks) at the hotel during your stay; save time, too—just swipe the bar code on your mug past the reader at the self-service dispenser and fill 'er up.

- Keep a refillable water bottle with you on steamy summer days.

- When choosing a place to stay, don't break the budget for a resort packed with amenities you won't have time to enjoy. Also realize that often the only difference between the least and most expensive rooms in a hotel is the view, and decide how often you'll be looking out that window.

- If you plan to stay at Walt Disney World for more than a week, or make multiple visits within a year, get an annual pass. Ownership nets many discounts, including savings on merchandise and room rates.

- Membership in organizations such as AARP and AAA often come with a few Disney perks as well. Check with your member representative to see if there are any special privileges for you to take advantage of.

- The Disney Visa Card holders can take advantage of exclusive theme park discounts and money-saving opportunities.

mesmerizes with the Osborne Family Spectacle of Lights—an enveloping display featuring some millions of twinkling lights. Vacation packages are available; for details, call 407-828-8101.

Animal Kingdom presents Mickey's Jingle Jungle parade.

NEW YEAR'S EVE CELEBRATION (December 31): The theme parks are open after midnight, attracting huge throngs and presenting high-spirited fun and entertainment.

Though all of the theme parks are decked out in full holiday regalia, Animal Kingdom does not offer pyrotechnic displays (for obvious reasons). Many of the resorts have special celebrations. Double-size fireworks are launched in the skies over the Magic Kingdom, Epcot, and the Disney-MGM Studios.

Pleasure Island unleashes its own New Year's Eve spectacular in a special-admission blowout.

The Logistics
Should You Buy a Package?

Vacation plans put forth by Disney are known as Magic Your Way packages. The goal is to encourage you to tailor your vacation to your own needs,

"Extra Magic Hours"

New perk alert! The "Extra Magic Hours" program (which has allowed WDW resort guests occasional visits to a theme park before it opens) has been expanded. Now, if you're staying at a WDW-owned-and-operated resort hotel (plus the Swan, Dolphin, or Hilton on Hotel Plaza Blvd.)—and have the right kind of ticket—you'll also have the opportunity to play in your favorite theme park for three hours *after* it has closed to the general public.

In a nutshell, one park opens its doors an hour early or stays open three hours late on any given day for guests bearing a resort ID and the right park ticket. It allows you to visit some (but not all) attractions and hobnob with Disney characters.

What's the right kind of ticket, you ask? If you have a ticket with "park-hopping" privileges, you're in no matter what. If you have a Magic Your Way base ticket without the park-hopping feature, you must visit the park offering the "Extra Magic Hours" that particular day. Check with your lobby concierge for the "Extra Magic Hours" schedule and procedures or visit *www.disneyworld.com*. At press time, it was free.

wants, and budget. The components of the base Magic Your Way package include accommodations at a WDW resort (any price category, excluding the Swan, Dolphin, and resorts on Hotel Plaza Boulevard) and an upgradable Magic Your Way Base Ticket. Guests may also include the

Disney Dining Plan (see page 190). There is such a thing as a Magic Your Way Premium Package, too. This comes with many of the most popular add-on options, such as park-hopping, golf, fishing, water sports, admission to Cirque du Soleil, tennis, and more.

The Disney Cruise Line can combine a visit to Walt Disney World with a cruise vacation.

For details about Magic Your Way packages, call the Walt Disney Travel Company, call 407-828-8101 or go to *www. disneyworld.com*. Note that you must pay for vacation packages in their entirety up front. *Cancellations must be made at least 45 days in advance in order to receive a full refund.*

Other operators with plans featuring Walt Disney World include American Airlines Vacations (800-321-2121), and Southwest Vacations (800-243-8372). Online tour operators offering Walt Disney World packages include GoGoWorldwideVacations (*www.gogowwv.com*), Travelocity (*www.travelocity.com*), and Vacation Outlet (*www.vacationoutlet.com*), or call 800-690-2210).

If you think you might be interested in buying a package, call for brochures. And keep in mind that the right package: (1) saves you money on the type of lodging, transportation, and recreation you want; (2) includes meaningful extras, as opposed to fluff like welcoming cocktails or so-called privileges that are actually services available to all guests; (3) its like a glove; no matter what the sale price, you wouldn't buy gloves that were too big, nor should you buy a package that encompasses more than you can reasonably expect to enjoy.

Ticket Tips

- All admission tickets and passes are non-transferable. The new "Ticket Tag" system enforces it. (See page 18.)
- Multi-day tickets expire 14 days after first use—unless the "no expiration" option is purchased.
- At the end of your visit, note the number of unused days on a multi-day ticket. Write it on the ticket itself. (Provided, of course, that you purchased the "no expiration" option for the ticket.)
- Any ticket can be upgraded within 14 days of first use (even if there are no days left). Tickets with the "no expire" option must be upgraded within 14 days of first use, too. Adjustments must be made on WDW property.
- If you want to visit more than one theme park on a single day you need to buy the Park Hopper option, or an annual pass.

Money Matters

A few points of interest related to green matter and its plastic counterparts: Traveler's checks, American Express, Visa, MasterCard, Discover Card, Diners Club Card, JCB, Disney's Visa Card, Disney dollars, and Disney gift cards are acceptable for most charges at WDW. While restaurants in the parks accept credit cards, some refreshment stands accept cash only.

Disney resort guests who leave a credit card imprint upon check-in may use their hotel ID card to charge meals at all restaurants and most food carts, purchases at shops and lounges, and recreational fees. These guests also receive the benefit of Express Check-out—an itemized bill is slipped under their door on the day of departure—a nice perk when that morning rolls around and last-minute to-dos await.

As for banking, there are a slew of ATMs accessible for a $2 service fee. There are locations in all four theme parks; the Transportation and Ticket Center; Pleasure Island; Downtown Disney Marketplace and Disney West Side; and the lobbies of all WDW resorts. For full-service banking, there is a SunTrust opposite Downtown Disney Marketplace, at 1675 Buena Vista Drive (407-828-6103 or 800-786-8787); hours are 9 A.M. to 4 P.M. weekdays (until 5:30 P.M. Thursdays), with drive-in teller service from 8 A.M. to 5 P.M. (if you have an account with them).

That's the Ticket

Admission tickets may be purchased at Disney's stores at the Orlando International Airport, theme park entrances, Guest Relations at Downtown Disney, any WDW resort, any hotel on Hotel Plaza Boulevard, and the Transportation and Ticket Center (offerings vary at each location). WDW resort guests may charge tickets to their rooms. Cash, traveler's checks, personal checks (with presentation of driver's license and major credit card), Visa, MasterCard, American Express, Discover Card, Diners Club Card, JCB, and Disney's Visa Card are also accepted.

Multi-day tickets can be bought at some Disney Stores; by phone at 407-824-4321 or online at www.disneyworld.com (allow two to three weeks for processing); or via mail order (allow three to four weeks). Get annual passes at theme park entrances, at a Disney store through WDW's Web site, or by mail. To get tickets by mail, send a check or money order (including $3 for handling) payable to the Walt Disney World Company to: Walt Disney World; Box 10140; Lake Buena Vista, FL 32830-0030; Attention: Ticket Mail Order.

Disney's "Ticket Tag" System

As a means of enforcing the non-transferability aspect of all WDW tickets, Disney has devised a system to trace each ticket to its rightful owner, both at the turnstiles and in the event that a ticket is lost or stolen. It's simple in theory: After signing the back of the ticket, you slip it into the machine at any park entrance. While the machine is crunching the data encrypted on that mysterious magnetic strip, you will be asked to make a "V" with your middle and forefinger and slip into a little gizmo perched on the ticket-grabbing device. Afterward, your newly personalized ticket should pop out the other side and give you the green light to enter. You'll have to do this every time you use the ticket. The good news is, if you lose it, you can have it replaced (keep your receipt, too). The downside? It slows the park-entering process—so allow extra time to get in.

Admission Options

With the exception of annual passes, all admission media are called Magic Your Way Tickets. They are available for one to ten days. The goal is to let guests custom build their tickets, based on individual schedules, wants, and budgets. In a nutshell: you purchase a Magic Your Way Base Ticket. The first decision you need to make? Number of days. After that, you have a selection of different "add-ons" to choose from (each one comes at an additional cost). They include: park-hopping privileges, a "no expiration" option, and the "water parks & more" package. You may add any or all of the aforementioned options as you purchase your base ticket. What's more, you may "upgrade" by adding one of these elements after you buy the base ticket, provided that you do so at Walt Disney World within 14 days of *first use.*

After a little number-crunching, it becomes clear that "per day" price comes down as more days are added to the base ticket. It may also be possible to save $7 to $11 per ticket on 5- to 10-day tickets with "Park Hopper" and/or "Water Parks & More" add-ons if you purchase in advance, outside Florida prior to arrival at Walt Disney World. Keep in mind that all tickets are non-transferrable.

NOTE: For the purposes of this section, the term *parks* means Magic Kingdom, Epcot, Disney-MGM Studios, and Animal Kingdom. Prices were correct at press time and do not include sales tax.

"Water Parks & More" add-on options may include admission to Typhoon Lagoon, Blizzard

Beach, Pleasure Island venues, Disney's Wide World of Sports, and DisneyQuest. Call 407-824-4321, or visit *www.disneyworld. com* for updates.

MAGIC YOUR WAY BASE TICKET: Good for 1- to 10-day admission to one theme park per day only. No park hopping allowed. Days used need not be consecutive, but remaining days expire 14 days after first use. The cost for this ticket: $59.75 for one day; $119 for two days; $171 for three days; $185 for four days; $193 for five days; $196 for six days; $199 for seven days; $202 for eight days; $205 for nine days; and $208 for ten days.

NO EXPIRATION ADD-ON: Not sure if you will use all your theme park days? Consider purchasing the "no expiration" option. Think of it as a kind of insurance. If you buy this add-on, it means any unused days on your ticket *never expire*. (Without this add-on, unused days expire 14 days after first use.) It's not available for one-day tickets, for obvious reasons. Prices for 2- to 10-day tickets are: $10 for two days; $10 for three days; $15 for four days; $35 for five days; $45 for six days; $55 for seven days; $100

for eight days; $100 for nine days; and $100 for ten days.

PARK-HOPPING ADD-ON: Allows you to "hop" from theme park to theme park within a single day (*i.e.* spend the morning at Magic Kingdom, hop on the monorail, and spend the evening at Epcot). It's available for 1- to 10-day tickets for the flat rate of $35, regardless of the number of days on your base ticket.

WATER PARKS & MORE ADD-ON: This package provides admissions to water parks, Pleasure Island venues, DisneyQuest, and Disney's Wide World of Sports complex. It may be added to *any* base ticket (1–10 days) for $45. The specific number of admissions depends upon the number of days on the base ticket: a 1- to 3-day ticket yields two visits; 4- and 5-day tickets get three visits; and bearers of 7–10-day tickets are entitled to five visits.

THEME PARK ANNUAL PASS ($395; $355 for renewal): Valid for unlimited admission (during regular operating hours) to all four theme parks for one year from the date of purchase; includes unlimited use of WDW transportation and free theme park parking.

PREMIUM ANNUAL PASS ($515; $465 for renewal): Valid for admission to the four theme parks, the water parks, Disney's Wide World of Sports complex, Downtown Disney Pleasure Island, and DisneyQuest for one year from purchase date; includes unlimited use of WDW transportation and free theme park parking.

NOTE: Both types of annual passes may net discounts on WDW resort rooms (depending on the season and availability), dinner shows, and more.

Medical Matters

Although medical care is readily available at WDW, travelers with chronic health problems are advised to carry copies of prescriptions and ask their physicians to provide names of local doctors. Diabetics should note that Walt Disney World resorts will provide refrigeration for insulin. More generally:

Report emergencies to 911 operators or to Sand Lake Hospital (407-351-8550).

Each of the theme parks has a First Aid Center staffed by a registered nurse.

For nonemergency medical care, Centra Care (407-239-6463) offers 12-hour-a-day house calls. Doctors On Call Service (407-399-3627) offers 24-hour house-call-only medical service.

Another nonemergency medical care option is Centra Care Walk-In (407-351-6682), located at 12500 South Apopka-Vineland Road, open 8 A.M. to midnight weekdays and 8 A.M. to 8 P.M. weekends.

For referral to a pharmacy or to find out how to have medication delivered, call Turner Drugs: 407-828-8125. (It's located next door to Centra Care.)

GETTING AROUND

Before you can find your way around WDW, you must have a firm sense of where you are (and where you are not). Disney World is actually about 22 miles southwest of Orlando in a much smaller community called Lake Buena Vista.

The most important (and congested) highway in the Orlando area is I-4, which cuts through the southern half of Disney World. All the area's other major highways intersect I-4.

Among the more frequently traveled is Route 435 (or Kirkman Road), a route that links I-4 to the major hotel and business thoroughfare called International Drive, known locally as I-Drive.

Should You Rent a Car?

Will you need a car during your stay? It's a tough call. Most area hotels offer buses to and from Walt Disney World. Disney's own resorts and parks are serviced by buses, monorail trains, and boats, which provide efficient (though very time-consuming) means of traveling within WDW borders.

This transportation is available to visitors staying at WDW resorts and those with a multi-day park ticket or an annual pass. If reliance on mass transit will cramp your style, by all means rent a car. It'll often get you from point A to point B in a fraction of the time (provided that you're familiar with the terrain). If you plan on exploring the many WDW resorts—and the great dining opportunities they offer— we recommend a car, or committing some of your travel budget to taxi rides (more on that later).

Disney's transportation is reliable (departing from most areas every 15 to 20 minutes), but it can accommodate only limited spontaneity. If you decide to drive, note that parking at any of the theme parks costs $8 per day (it's free for WDW resort guests).

We find it's easiest to rent a car from one of the airport's on-site

Disney's Magical Express

Flying to WDW via Orlando International Airport and staying at a Disney owned-and-operated resort? You may be eligible for "Disney's Magical Express"—a new perk that allows guests to check their specially tagged luggage at their originating airport, skip baggage claim in Orlando, board a free shuttle bus to their WDW resort, and have their luggage delivered to their room *free of charge*. On the final morning of the trip, guests flying on participating airlines bid adieu to luggage at their resort and get airline boarding passes at the same time. At press time, participating airlines included American, Continental, Delta, Song, United, and Ted.

The system, which was introduced as part of the Happiest Celebration on Earth, should remain free in 2006. At press time, you could be booked on any airline to get round-trip shuttle service. For guests who don't plan to rent a car, it can be a real money saver. But, buses aren't direct, so you may stop at a few resorts along the way. (If you'd prefer door-to-door service, consider taking a taxi or a car service. See page 22 for details.) Since bags may arrive many hours after you do, you should pack everything you'll need for that afternoon or evening in your carry-on.

Note: Guests staying at the Swan, Dolphin, Shades of Green, or on Hotel Plaza Blvd. are not eligible for Magical Express service.

companies (Alamo, Avis, Budget, Dollar, and National). You can rent a car after you've arrived at WDW, too. Inquire at your hotel.

Once inside the resort, you can rely on buses, the monorail, boats—or, in some cases, your own two feet—to get you wherever you're going. Not all destinations can be reached directly; you may have to transfer several times. Information and schedules are available at WDW resorts.

Our Take on Taxis

Disney's transportation system is vast and cost-efficient. That said, it can also chew up time and, at times, can be flat-out confusing.

Getting from a Disney resort to any theme park is a no-brainer. It's also relatively easy to "hop" from park to park. The options always include buses and choices such as monorail or ferry.

However, as we've traveled the

Getting to WDW from Orlando Airport

During rush hour take the airport's South exit, and follow the Central Florida Greeneway (Route 417) to State Road 536, which leads right to WDW; tolls total $2. The distance is about 22 miles. For the shortest route, take the airport's North exit, head west on Route 528 (aka the Beeline Expressway) to I-4 west, and turn off at the appropriate WDW exit; tolls are $1.25.

- **Exit 64:** Magic Kingdom, Disney-MGM Studios, Fort Wilderness, Grand Floridian, Contemporary, Polynesian, Wilderness Lodge, Palm and Magnolia golf courses, or Celebration
- **Exit 65:** Disney's Wide World of Sports complex, Animal Kingdom, Blizzard Beach, Pop Century, Coronado Springs, All-Stars, or Animal Kingdom Lodge
- **Exit 67:** Epcot, Typhoon Lagoon, Old Key West, Caribbean Beach, Swan, Dolphin, BoardWalk, Yacht and Beach Club, Port Orleans Riverside and French Quarter, or Downtown Disney
- **Exit 68:** Resorts on Hotel Plaza Boulevard
- **For those without wheels:** Florida Towncar offers direct service to Disney resorts for $95–$105 round-trip for up to five people. Call 407-277-5466. A Selective Limousine, Inc. will transport up to four passengers in a Town Car for about $100 to $105; call 407-854-7503 or 800-730-0211. Mears Motor Shuttle, though time-consuming and often frustrating, is economical. Operating 24 hours, Mears serves area hotels at $17 one way or $29 round-trip, per person. Taxis are also a viable option. For info, call 407-423-5566. (For details on taxi transport, see "Our Take on Taxis" above.) Last, but certainly not least, guests staying at one of WDW's deluxe resorts may take advantage of Disney's Magical Express (see page 21).

World over, we have come across a few trouble spots. In each case, we've solved our transportation woes simply by hailing a cab. The only drawback? It'll cost ya.

Traveling between resorts usually involves at least one bus transfer. If you ask bell services to call a cab (be sure it's authorized, with regulated fares), you'll get to your destination in a fraction of the time. Trips generally cost about $5–$20 plus tip.

Buses to and from Downtown Disney are plentiful. However, when all is said and done (often in the wee hours of the morning), it's nice to hop into a waiting cab. The trip shouldn't set you back too much (in the $10–$18 range), depending on the destination.

Cabs are an efficient means of getting to and from Orlando International Airport. Taxis can take up to 9 passengers. Rates are one-way. Trips to Magic Kingdom resorts cost $50, Epcot resorts $43, and Hotel Plaza Blvd. resorts $37 (plus tip and tolls). The wait for taxis here is shorter than for the Mears Shuttle and the trip is direct. (We tend to shy away from Mears shuttle buses, having had to wait between 30 minutes and *3 hours* the past several times we tried to use them.)

Tips for Drivers

- Florida state law requires use of headlights in the rain or fog and at dusk.
- There is a gas station at the Magic Kingdom Auto Plaza , opposite Pleasure Island, and near BoardWalk. They are all open 24 hours.
- Be alert to slippery roads when it rains, as a fine layer of oil accumulates between drizzles.
- It's legal to turn right at a red light anywhere in Florida, unless a sign is posted.
- Call 407-824-0976 for free AAA towing at WDW. The Auto Plaza's AAA Car Care Center provides service (407-824-0976). Off-property, call Riker's Wreckers for 24-hour towing (407-855-7776) and repairs (407-238-9800), or call AAA if you're a member.
- For traffic, news, and weather reports, tune to 580 AM.

DAY-TO-DAY SAMPLE SCHEDULES

A Day at the Magic Kingdom

- Plan to be in the parking lot at least 30 minutes before the park is scheduled to open. Grab a guidemap and times guide once inside.

- If you haven't booked a table in advance, make reservations at City Hall. (We recommend Tony's Town Square for lunch and Cinderella's Royal Table for dinner.)

- When the park opens, grab a Fastpass (see page 83) for your personal "must-sees." Don't miss Splash Mountain, Big Thunder Mountain Railroad, and Pirates of the Caribbean. After exhausting Adventureland, head for The Haunted Mansion, followed by a cruise on the *Liberty Belle* Riverboat. Resist the urge to sprint through the park, and move at a comfortable pace.

- After pausing for lunch when your reservation time arrives or hunger calls, begin a second sweep of the park, targeting such attractions as Mickey's PhilharMagic and the Country Bear Jamboree. Check out any shops and entertainment en route that catch your eye.

- About 20 minutes before the afternoon parade (daily at 3 P.M.), either camp out on Main Street or skip it and head for Fantasyland to see as many key attractions—Peter Pan's Flight, The Many Adventures of Winnie the Pooh, Mickey's PhilharMagic, and It's a Small World—as possible before the crowds swell back to normal.

- Phobic about long lines? The Walt Disney World Railroad, Tomorrow-land Transit Authority, and The Hall of Presidents all tend to keep wait times to a relative minimum. And take advantage of Fastpass as much as possible!

- Breeze through Mickey's Toontown Fair. Then head over to Tomorrowland and experience one of the biggest thrills the Magic Kingdom has to offer—Space Mountain—before taking a jaunt through toyland on the zany Buzz Lightyear's Space Ranger Spin.

- Spend the rest of the day tying up loose ends on your touring checklist and perusing the shops on Main Street.

- Consider having dinner at a restaurant accessible via monorail (perhaps California Grill or Narcoossee's). Return to the park in time to watch the evening parade. If there are two runnings of the parade, aim to see the later one, when the crowds are apt to have dwindled and better viewing locations can be had. And do not miss Wishes—the nighttime fireworks spectacular.

A Day at Epcot

- Guests are often permitted to enter the park a half hour before the opening time, though the attractions may not be up and running.

- Stomach growling? If you haven't had breakfast or need a quick java jolt, slip into Fountain View Espresso and Bakery.

- If you don't have reservations for dinner (see page 185), you can stop at Guest Relations or Innoventions Plaza to book a table at one of the restaurants of World Showcase. We enjoy Les Chefs de France, in the France pavilion, and Germany's Biergarten.

- Fight the urge to see Spaceship Earth (the lines are lighter later) and head to Test Track, the Imagination! pavilion (if you miss Honey, I Shrunk the Audience, you will probably live to regret it), and finally, The Land's Soarin' attraction the Living with the Land boat ride, and "Turtle Talk with Crush" at The Living Seas.

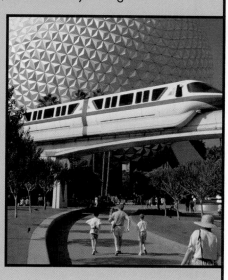

- This should take you up to (at least) noon, which is about when World Showcase opens. Consider grabbing a bite at The Land's Sunshine Seasons before crossing into World Showcase.

- View O Canada! at the Canada pavilion. Then wander through the shops, gardens, and pub at the United Kingdom before fully exploring France. (There's a lovely movie here, too.)

- Walk toward The American Adventure to catch the extraordinary live performances and the star-spangled Audio-Animatronics show, stopping to take in art galleries and other sights along the way

- Don't forget about making reservations for dinner. Keep in mind that many restaurants can accommodate walk-ins.

- After dinner, pop into Mexico and then hightail it back to Future World to visit Spaceship Earth and Innoventions.

- Plan to get to the World Showcase Lagoon at least 30 minutes ahead to secure a spot to watch the evening's performance of IllumiNations—Reflections of Earth.

A Day at the Disney-MGM Studios

- Arrive before the posted opening time, as doors often open early.

- Pick up a complimentary guidemap and times guide; many attractions have set showtimes, and some don't open until later in the morning. Study the layout of the park—it has been known to confuse even the most skilled navigators.

- Haven't had breakfast yet? Consider stopping by the Starring Rolls Cafe for a quick croissant and a cup of coffee.

- If you were unable to book a table for dinner before leaving home, just stop at the kiosk at Hollywood Junction (the corner of Hollywood and Sunset boulevards) and make reservations for the 50's Prime Time Cafe, Sci-Fi Dine-In Theater, or the Hollywood Brown Derby. This plan assumes a quick lunch taken whenever your personal lunch bell rings (good bets include Sunset Ranch Market and Backlot Epress).

- If you're up for some early morning thrills, head to The Twilight Zone Tower of Terror, but be sure to do so before you eat. For something much tamer, you might try the Great Movie Ride, followed by Magic of Disney Animation and MuppetVision 3-D.

- Stroll over to Mickey Avenue where you'll go behind the scenes via the Disney-MGM Studios Backlot Tour. Afterward, try your luck at Who Wants to Be a Millionaire—Play It! Note: The Disney Stars and Motor Cars parade passes through each afternoon.

- Make time for Sounds Dangerous starring Drew Carey. The Indiana Jones Epic Stunt Spectacular; Lights, Motors, Action! Extreme Stunt Show; and Star Tours all merit a look-see—as do the Voyage of the Little Mermaid and Rock 'n' Roller Coaster (provided that you're comfortable being flipped and shaken like James Bond's martini).

- Between attractions, check out the shops on Sunset and Hollywood boulevards. For a relaxing breather, slip into the Tune-In Lounge.

- Note when the Beauty and the Beast—Live on Stage takes place and be sure not to miss it.

- Get a spot for Fantasmic! at least 60 minutes before showtime. This evening spectacle wraps up the day nicely. (Though the bleacher-style seating can be tough on tired backs.)

A Day at Disney's Animal Kingdom

- Arrive about 15 minutes before the park's posted opening time, and prepare to bond with others waiting to enter.

- Pick up a guidemap and times guide and check schedules for shows you may want to see, such as Flights of Wonder or Festival of the Lion King. Arrive about 45 minutes before the Lion King show begins, and up to 30 minutes for the show at Theater In the Wild.

- Resist the urge to conduct an informal wildlife census in the Oasis and head straight for the bridge to Discovery Island (the path on the right offers the most direct route). The animals will be here all day. Minimal lines for your biggest priorities—Expedition Everest, Dinosaur, Kali River Rapids, and Kilimanjaro Safaris—won't be around for long.

- Give the Tree of Life a quick once-over, but don't stop to inspect it now. Instead, head to the first brachiosaurus skeleton on your right. In DinoLand U.S.A., make the acquaintance of Dinosaur, a bumpy, bouncy thrill ride.

- Next, go to Asia and ride the drenching Kali River Rapids. Afterward, walk through the Maharajah Jungle Trek and explore the tiny village of Anandapur. While you're in the area, consider taking in Flights of Wonder (check your times guide for the schedule).

- Grab a quick bite along the way to Africa (we suggest Tusker House in Harambe). Then make tracks for Kilimanjaro Safaris. Afterward, dally on the Pangani Forest Exploration Trail to watch the gorilla family at play.

  - When afternoon crowds descend, hop on the Wildlife Express and get your fill of all the interactive exhibits at Rafiki's Planet Watch.

    - Make your way to Camp Minnie-Mickey in time for the next Lion King staging.

      - Now it's time for It's Tough to be a Bug! in the Tree of Life. Be sure to check out the amazing animal carvings on and around the tree.

    - No fireworks here (imagine the stampede). As an alternative, experience dinner as entertainment at Rainforest Cafe (or, hop to Epcot for IllumiNations).

CUSTOMIZED TIPS

Guests with Disabilities

Walt Disney World has long earned praise from guests with disabilities because of the attention paid to their special needs. Still, familiarization with the World as it relates to one's personal requirements is essential, and to this end, the theme park guidemaps can be of tremendous help. And the *Guidebook for Guests with Disabilities* is certainly required reading, too. It is available at all wheelchair rental locations (as well as City Hall in the Magic Kingdom and Guest Relations at Epcot, Disney-MGM Studios, and Animal Kingdom). However, we recommend getting this publication before leaving home. To receive a free copy of the *Guidebook for Guests with Disabilities*, send a written request, well in advance, to Walt Disney World Guest Communications, Box 10000, Lake Buena Vista, FL 32830, or call 407-939-6244.

Those interested in guided tours should note: The Society for Accessible Travel & Hospitality (347 Fifth Ave., Suite 610, New York, NY 10016; 212-447-7284; *www.sath.org*) can provide a list of travel agents who are knowledgeable about travel for people with disabilities. To receive the listing, just call (there may be a $5 fee).

If you prefer to connect directly with a tour operator who specializes in travel for the disabled, consider Flying Wheels Travel (507-451-5005) or Accessible Journeys (610-521-0339). The following advice is an indication of WDW facilities and services:
• Accessible parking is available at the theme parks (inquire at the Auto Plaza upon entering).
• All monorail stations are accessible to guests in wheelchairs. Most (but not all) Disney buses are equipped with wheelchair lifts.
• Life jackets for guests with disabilities are available at the water parks.
• Most theme park attractions are accessible to guests who can be lifted to and from their wheelchairs with the assistance of a member of their party, and many can accommodate guests who must remain in their wheelchairs.

Consult the *Guidebook for Guests with Disabilities* or a guidemap, or ask a host or hostess for additional guidance.

Note that all hotels listed in the *Checking In* chapter offer rooms specially equipped for guests with disabilities. Walt Disney World resorts are easily explored by wheelchair. While guestroom and bathroom configurations vary from hotel to hotel, lending themselves better to guests with certain needs, all resorts offer roll-in showers.

For assistance in selecting a Disney hotel whose public areas and rooms best serve your specific requirements, ask to speak to someone in the Special Reservations Department when you call Central Reservations (407-934-7639 voice; 407-939-7670 TTY). Confirm any special requests before you arrive.

Most Disney resorts have a small number of free wheelchairs (with a $250 refundable deposit). Request one when reserving your room and confirm it before you arrive. You may use the wheelchair across Disney property for your entire length of stay.

In the Evening Hours

Here's more than a week's worth of activities for your consideration. For more information on after-dark amusements, refer to *Dining & Entertainment.*

- Attend a dinner show. All require reservations, and the Hoop-Dee-Doo Musical Revue calls for more forethought than any other.

- For a relatively cheap thrill (about $8 per person) and an early night, take a wagon ride at Fort Wilderness. Or enjoy a slightly more extravagant carriage ride for about $30 for four people.

- Play the coolest tennis at Walt Disney World. There are a few courts lighted for night play. Swan and Dolphin courts are open 24 hours a day.

- For dining as a special event, book a table at Artist Point, California Grill, Cítricos, Shula's Steakhouse, Victoria & Albert's, or Jiko—The Cooking Place.

- If ready-made nightlife appeals, go club hopping at Pleasure Island—one stop, many different venues (check out Raglan Road, the Adventurers Club, or 8TRAX). Or swing by Downtown Disney West Side, Pleasure Island's neighbor, to see who's playing at the House of Blues.

- Take a wine tour. California Grill at the Contemporary resort, Jiko—the Cooking Place at Animal Kingdom Lodge, and Cítricos at the Grand Floridian take crushed grapes seriously and pour wines both by the glass and in pairings suggested by the sommelier.

- Prefer the grain to the grape? Beer lovers' hangouts include BoardWalk's ESPN Club; Crew's Cup lounge at the Yacht Club resort; and The Laughing Kookaburra Good Time Bar at Wyndham Palace Resort and Spa.

- For a nostalgic evening, stroll the boards at BoardWalk, where everything from saltwater taffy to a dance hall and a sing-along piano bar awaits.

Wheelchairs are available for rent at each of the theme parks, as are Electric Convenience Vehicles (ECVs). At the Magic Kingdom, the rental area is inside the entrance on the right; at Epcot, rentals are available inside the entrance plaza on the left, at the shop to the right of the ticket booths, and at International Gateway; at the Disney-MGM Studios, rentals are handled at Oscar's Super Service, just inside; at Animal Kingdom, the site is Garden Gate Gifts near the entrance.

Wheelchair rentals cost $7 per day plus a $1 refundable deposit. Guests planning to visit more than one park on the same day may get a replacement at the next park with no extra charge or deposit (save your receipt and return the wheelchair by the end of the day). ECVs can be rented at the parks for $30 (plus a $10 refundable deposit) per park per day. Equipment may not be taken out of the park from which it is rented.

Due to the limited number of ECVs, they usually sell out soon

Know Before You Go

- If you want to see a dinner show—especially the Hoop-Dee-Doo Musical Revue—reserve a table when you book your hotel. Reservations are taken up to one year ahead; call 407-939-3463.

- Arrange for reservations at WDW restaurants (up to 90 days in advance) by calling 407-939-3463 (WDW-DINE). Refer to page 185 for details.

- The elite and popular Victoria & Albert's—the biggest grown-up splurge on property—may be booked up to 180 days ahead.

- Call 407-824-4321 or visit www.disneyworld.com to confirm park hours in effect during your visit, and use the schedules provided in this chapter.

- If you're a golfer, reserve tee times as far in advance as possible. Golf reservations may be made four months ahead or 90 days if you've purchased a golf package or if you're staying at either a WDW resort or a resort on Hotel Plaza Boulevard, 60 days ahead if you're not, to secure your preferred time(s) and venue(s). Lessons may be reserved up to 90 days ahead. Call 407-WDW-GOLF (939-4653). Also see "Sports" in Diversions.

- Note that tennis lessons and guided fishing trips may be booked up to 90 days in advance. Call 407-WDW-PLAY (939-7529).

- A few days before you leave home, make a quick round of calls to confirm all arrangements and reservations.

- You must dial the area code for all local calls.

after the parks open. To avoid disappointment and to have the freedom to use your scooter or wheelchair everywhere, consider renting from ScootAround (888-441-7575), which provides standard and electric wheelchairs as well as scooters; pickup and delivery is available to all hotels in the Walt Disney World area. Wheelchair Getaways (800-242-4990) and Rainbow Wheels of Florida (800-910-8267) both rent wheelchair-accessible vans and offer pickup and delivery for most hotels in the area.

Certain spots along most parade routes and at nighttime show areas are marked for guests using wheelchairs. Arrive early, as these areas are filled on a first-come, first-served basis. See park maps for locations.

A limited number of wheelchairs is available in theme park disability parking areas. Guests with limited mobility may use them to travel between their vehicle and the wheelchair rental area. These courtesy wheelchairs are intended for park use. For guests with visual disabilities, the theme parks offer audiocassettes designed to accentuate enjoyment of each park through detailed description. A $25 refundable deposit is required for use of a tape recorder.

Pay phones equipped with Text Typewriters (TTYs) are available throughout the Disney World Resort. For more information, call 407-824-4321 (voice) or 407-827-5141 (TTY).

Assistive Listening devices, which amplify attraction sound tracks, are available (with a $25 refundable deposit) at City Hall in the Magic Kingdom and at Guest Relations in Epcot, the Studios, and Animal Kingdom. Scripts are also available for guests with hearing disabilities at most attractions. For live performances, sign language interpretation may be available for certain shows; call 407-824-4321 (voice) or 407-827-5141 (TTY) for schedules.

Also, Reflective Captioning devices that project dialogue onto a panel placed in front of guests are available for use in some theater shows. Inquire at Guest Relations.

disneyworld.com

Log onto *www.disneyworld.com* to receive an interactive preview or update of WDW's offerings.

Among its more valuable features: ticket sales, customized resort recommendations, a reservations desk, maps, details about special events, and park hours during your stay.

Older Travelers

Walt Disney World is a friendly
and welcoming place, but its
sheer enormity and energy level,
and its mere heat, particularly
during the summer, have the
potential to overwhelm.

While knowing what to expect
is half the battle, planning
accordingly is just as important.

Important Numbers

AMC Theatres: 407-298-4488

Behind-the-Scene Tours:
407-WDW-TOUR (939-8687)

Central Reservations:
407-W-DISNEY (934-7639)

Dining reservations:
407-WDW-DINE (939-3463)

**Disney's Wide World of
Sports Complex:**
407-939-1500

**Florida Hospital Celebration
Health:** 407-303-4000

Golf Reservations / Lessons:
407-WDW-GOLF (939-4653)

Lost and Found: 407-824-4245

Recreation:
407-WDW-PLAY (939-7529)

Sand Lake Hospital:
407-351-8550

**Walt Disney Travel
Company:**
407-828-8101

**Walt Disney World
Information:** 407-824-4321

Weather: 407-824-4104

The keys to an enjoyable,
relaxed visit apply to everyone.
Our suggestions:

Plan your visit for one of the
less crowded times of year. That
will make for shorter, less har-
ried days. In the parks, eat early
or late to avoid mealtime crowds.

Florida residents can net discounts year-round. Call 407-824-
4321 for details. Also, some off-
property hotels offer discounts to
AARP members.

Take frequent rest stops (for the
best locales in each park, see the
"Quiet Escapes" lists in the margins of the *Theme Parks* chapter).
Know that if you are overcome at
any point, each park has a first-
aid station with a friendly and
certified staff.

Don't underestimate the dis-
tances to be covered at Epcot and
Animal Kingdom. These parks
are huge, and visitors often log a
few miles in a full day of touring.
Lots of older travelers who enjoy
walking around the other parks
choose to rent a wheelchair or
Electric Convenience Vehicle at
these two (they're available at the
park entrances).

No matter how you're getting
around, take it slowly. Broken
into small increments with plenty
of air-conditioned and shaded
breaks, it's not so tiring. The

FriendShip launches that cross World Showcase Lagoon in Epcot provide a nice break for weary feet.

Not all of Pleasure Island's clubs are inundated with exuberant twenty-somethings. Stop at Raglan Road for an authentic dose of the Emerald Isle and eavesdrop on tall tales told by weary world travelers at the Adventurer's Club. Don't miss the four-star tribute to Hollywood's heyday that is the Disney-MGM Studios. The Art Deco architecture, retro restaurants, and Technicolor tributes to Tinseltown make for a day of nostalgic amusement.

Single Travelers

While Walt Disney World may not exactly be the last word for singles, the fact is, unattached guests and independent travelers can have an absolute blast here. Some ideas:

Pleasure Island's clubs typically attract lots of locals on weekends. The restaurants and lounges at Downtown Disney West Side, particularly the concert hall at House of Blues, also attract a fun-loving crowd.

Try eating at the Teppanyaki Dining Rooms and the Biergarten restaurant at Epcot, where smaller parties are seated together, creating a social setting.

At all of Walt Disney World's 18-hole golf courses, company is a given; players are assigned to a foursome when tee times are allotted.

Some of the World's more compelling restaurants have an area with counter seating, which helps take the sting out of dining solo. These noteworthy spots include Flying Fish Cafe,

For Woofers & Meowers

No pets other than service animals are permitted in the parks. Travelers may lodge Fluffy or Fido in one of WDW's five air-conditioned Pet Care Kennels: near the TTC; at the entrances to Epcot, the Disney-MGM Studios, and Animal Kingdom; and at Fort Wilderness. WDW resort guests pay $9 for overnight stays, including food; others pay $11. Day rates are $6 and include one feeding. For an extra $2.50 per day, they'll walk your dog for you (though guests may do the walking themselves). Pets must have proof of vaccinations. Accommodations are available on a first-come, first-served basis. For hours and information, call 407-824-6568.

Narcoossee's, Cítricos, Fulton's Crab House, Wolfgang Puck Cafe (the sushi bar), and Portobello Yacht Club.

The casual atmosphere along the BoardWalk makes it a fun place to people-watch, and the eateries, shops, and clubs provide interesting diversions. The Jellyrolls' piano bar never fails to entertain.

Another favorite, and a great destination for sports fans, is ESPN Club. The environment is conducive to frenzied rooting for your home team, as well as calmer discussions about the intricacies of the game with fellow fans.

Tour programs are engaging alternatives to exploring Epcot solo (see page 116 for details).

Rainy-Day Advice

The sun will come out tomorrow (or maybe in a few hours). In the meantime, here are some great ways to pass the time:

- See a movie with all the comforts in the 24-screen AMC Theatres at Downtown Disney.

- Sink into a sofa in the lobby of the Grand Floridian and listen to the graceful music. Or curl up by the fireplace at Wilderness Lodge.

- Pick up a rain poncho (about $6) and head for Epcot, which has more places to escape rain than any other park.

- Experience the high-tech interactive arcade games at Downtown Disney's DisneyQuest.

- Get a massage. Disney spas offer myriad treatments that can be blissful excuses to stay dry.

- Take afternoon tea at the Grand Floridian's Garden View lounge.

Couples

There is a place for lovebirds at Walt Disney World. Actually, there are many spots in the World perfectly suited to those with romantic intentions.

The Magic Kingdom's carousel-and-castle combo invokes enchantment in true fairy-tale tradition. Epcot's World Showcase has the aura of a whirlwind tour (and inspiration for a future trip?), with countries as exotic and far-reaching as Japan and Morocco. The Disney-

MGM Studios recaptures an era of starry-eyed elegance. And what could be more enjoyable than sharing a safari through Africa at Animal Kingdom?

By day, there is romance in the theme parks for couples who are already inclined to hold hands; by night, the parks sparkle with an intensity that inspires sudden mushiness in those who never considered themselves the type, and that's before the fireworks.

As Disney's themed resorts go about transporting guests to various times and places, they make quite a few passes through settings straight out of everyone's fantasy textbook.

From the endearing Victorian charms of the Grand Floridian to the exotic island getaway that is the Polynesian, it's safe to say that Disney definitely has romantic notions (if not in the form of heart-shaped tubs).

You won't find a more inspiring backdrop than that at the wondrously rustic Wilderness Lodge, marked by geysers, waterfalls, steamy hot springs, and the grandest stone fireplace you've ever seen.

At the nostalgic BoardWalk resort, unique surrey bikes are available for romantic rides along the waterfront. You can pedal all the way to Epcot's International Gateway. And a romantic stroll around Crescent Lake is an undoubtedly lovely way to cap off the day.

For those too lovestruck to think about taking pictures themselves, there's the Romance Photographic Session. For $295, a photographer follows you and your sweetheart around the park of your choice (for one hour), clicking away. For more information, call 407-827-5099.

Couples with bigger things in mind, like perhaps tying or re-tying the knot, might consider "I do"–ing it here. Each year, more than 2,000 couples exchange their vows here.

Why this place? For some couples it's a matter of mutual Disney admiration; for others it's a convenient answer to the dilemma posed by the bride being from one area of the world and the groom from quite another (why not make a vacation of it for everyone?). Stick around for a while, and you've got an instant honeymoon!

While no one yet has likened Mickey Mouse to Eros, newlyweds have beaten such a path to Mickey's doorstep over the years that Disney World rates as one of the most popular honeymoon destinations in the country.

WEDDINGS: In these parts, the sky truly is the limit. Intimate weddings for up to eight guests start at about $3,500; for larger affairs, figure $7,500 minimum during the week, $10,000 on Fridays, Saturdays, and Sundays. Coordinators work with couples from three months to a year in advance to create a wedding tailored to their needs—from elegant affairs without a hint of Disneyana to the sort in which the bride arrives in Cinderella's coach and Goofy "crashes" the reception. These wedding gurus can handle any detail and a litany of unimaginables.

Nuptials in the theme parks (which range from $7,500 in Epcot to $55,000-plus in the Magic Kingdom) take place before and after park closing and allow couples to take their vows in front of Cinderella Castle in the Magic Kingdom or in an English courtyard in Epcot's World Showcase, among other places.

For an extra $15,000, a free-spending couple gets pixie dust and a personal fireworks show.

Then there's the Wedding Pavilion, a structure reminiscent of a Victorian summerhouse, which sits on a landscaped island between the Grand Floridian and Polynesian resorts. Surrounded by roses, palm trees, and beaches, the pavilion seats 250 and offers a prime view of Cinderella Castle, which is framed in a window

Religious Services

Protestant services are held on Sundays at 10:30 A.M. at Celebration Presbyterian Church at 635 Celebration Avenue, Celebration, Florida (for schedule, call 407-566-1633), and at River of Life Presbyterian at 83 Sand Lake Rd. (407-351-4333) and at 9:30 A.M. and 11 A.M. at Lake Buena Vista Baptist Church at 11551 County Rd. 535 (407-239-6030). Catholic masses are held at Mary, Queen of the Universe Shrine at 8300 Vineland Ave. (407-239-6600; call for mass times).

Jewish visitors may attend Conservative services at Temple Ohalei Rivka at 11200 Apopka-Vineland Rd. (407-239-5444), or Reform services at the Congregation of Liberal Judaism at 928 Malone Dr. (407-645-0444). Muslim services are at Jama Masijid at 11543 Ruby Lake Rd. Call 407-238-2700.

behind the altar. Picture Point—a trellised archway set among the pavilion's gardens, with the castle in the background—is also available for intimate ceremonies.

For couples in the planning stages, the on-site wedding salon—known as Franck's Bridal Studio—is like a three-dimensional bridal magazine.

Ceremonies can be held at many WDW resorts. The garden gazebo at the Yacht Club, Sunset Point at the Polynesian, Sea Breeze Point at BoardWalk, and Sunrise Terrace at Wilderness Lodge are all popular spots for weddings or vow renewals.

Packages vary depending upon the type of ceremony and reception and can include discounted tickets and rates at certain resorts for guests attending the wedding. When booking a package, the bride and groom get a complimentary room for the first night. For more information about Disney weddings, call 407-828-3400; *www.disneyweddings.com*.

HONEYMOONS: Most Disney resorts have designated suites for just-marrieds. Special honeymoon packages offer keepsakes and pre-arrival services. For information, call 877-566-0969; *www.disneyhoneymoons.com*.

Did You Know?

Walt Disney World encompasses 47 square miles, an area about twice the size of Manhattan.

The Most Romantic Places in the World

RESORTS
Animal Kingdom Lodge
BoardWalk
Grand Floridian
Polynesian
Port Orleans Riverside and French Quarter
Wilderness Lodge
Yacht and Beach Club

RESTAURANTS
Artist Point
Bistro de Paris
California Grill
Cinderella's Royal Table
Cítricos
Le Cellier Steakhouse
San Angel Inn
Victoria & Albert's

LOUNGES
Belle Vue Room at BoardWalk
Crew's Cup at the Yacht Club
Martha's Vineyard at the Beach Club
Matsu No Ma at Japan

THEME PARK SPOTS
Magic Kingdom's *Liberty Belle* Riverboat
All of Epcot's World Showcase

At Walt Disney World, there's a hotel to suit every taste, budget, and mood.

Checking In

Like a photograph whose mood changes depending upon the frame in which it is displayed, a Walt Disney World vacation is colored by the context in which it is experienced. Guests have quite a variety of frames—rather, resorts—from which to choose, and each yields a unique perspective on the World.

Some hotels imbue the mousedom with surprising elegance; others render it especially whimsical, homey, or romantic. Looking for grand seaside digs or a home base straight out of New Orleans? They're here. Something Polynesian? No problem. From campsites to villas, economy-priced rooms to suites, there are accommodations in Cinderella's neighborhood to suit most every taste and billfold.

If you're the sort who favors a gilded frame for your vacation, you'll find the chandelier quotient you're seeking—and a rich Victorian aura—at Disney's turreted Grand Floridian Resort & Spa.

If rustic romance is more your style, your ultimate roost is the Wilderness Lodge, which patterns its grandeur after National Park Service lodges of the early 1900s.

To stretch your vacation dollar, do try the All-Star and Pop Century resorts. Starting at $79 a night and augmented by three-story cultural icons, they're the brightest dwellings you'll ever call home.

If you're not sure what you want, that's fine, too. We've covered all of the Disney-owned-and-operated resorts and their favored siblings, the Swan and Dolphin, plus the Disney Cruise Line.

When it comes to the resorts that line Hotel Plaza Boulevard (seven properties that are within Disney's borders but independently managed) we've included our top three choices for adults.

So think about what's important to you in a Walt Disney World resort. Then read on for all the information you'll need to choose the perfect frame.

WALT DISNEY WORLD RESORTS

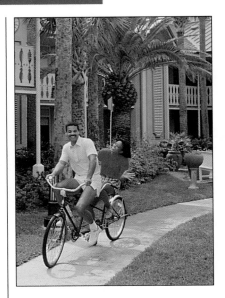

As an example of the meticulous theming that is a hallmark of the Disney resorts, consider Port Orleans French Quarter, a moderately priced resort designed to evoke the Big Easy's most famous neighborhood. As you check in, you might catch the aroma of fresh beignets wafting over from the resort's food court, decorated as a Mardi Gras warehouse. The lobby has French horns for light fixtures and restrooms with such great jazz coming over the speakers they could almost impose a cover charge.

In addition to compelling theming, Disney's resorts are often marked by staffs trained to bend over backward to ensure guests' happiness, and well-kept, comfortably furnished accommodations comparable in size to those found outside Walt Disney World borders. There are also many practical advantages to staying on-property. Chief among these benefits are convenience and easy access to Disney services. Other privileges enjoyed by WDW resort guests include use

The Last Word On . . .

Reservations
Book at least six months in advance by calling 407-934-7639 or visiting *www.disneyworld.com*. A deposit (one night's lodging or $200) is required within 10 to 14 days of the time a reservation is made. The deposit will be refunded only if a reservation is canceled at least five days before the scheduled arrival. Packages must be paid in full.

Checking In
Check-in time is 3 P.M., except at BoardWalk Villas, Disney's Old Key West, Beach Club Villas, and The Villas at Wilderness Lodge, where guests register after 4 P.M., and Fort Wilderness, where it's 1 P.M. Checkout time for all these properties is 11 A.M.

of WDW transportation; guaranteed admission (with ticket) to the theme parks (including the "Extra Magic Hours"—see page 15); discounted golf fees; and the option to reserve tee times on Disney golf courses up to 90 days prior to their check-in date. At all WDW resorts except the Swan and Dolphin and resorts on Hotel Plaza Boulevard, amenities also include Disney's Magical Express Service (see page 21), package delivery, and the ability to charge meals, merchandise, and recreation fees to one's room.

This resort listing is organized according to price tiers—Deluxe, Moderate, and Value. Note that Disney no longer uses the term "Home Away from Home" to describe accommodations. The category was replaced by "Disney Vacation Club and Camping."

These categories are consistent with Disney's rating system for its resorts (explained on page 42). But consider location as well as price, especially if you'll be spending a lot of time touring a particular theme park. The "Vital Statistics" section of each entry will help you place the resorts on the World map. You'll notice that certain hotels are earmarked as "sister resorts"; these are adjacent properties that feature complementary designs and shared facilities. With the exception of Port Orleans Riverside and Port Orleans French Quarter, whose greater separation and distinct identities we feel merit individual attention, sister resorts' descriptions are combined.

We've packed in as much detail as possible about the offerings at each resort; to learn even more about restaurants and lounges, see our recommendations in the *Dining & Entertainment* chapter. For details about Walt Disney World transportation, consult *Planning Ahead*. For more on recreational opportunities available at the resorts, turn to the "Sports" section of the *Diversions* chapter.

Amenities Checklist

While there are significant differences in the amenities offered at Disney's Value and Deluxe properties, certain conveniences are provided at all WDW resorts. Namely: voice mail, TVs with the Disney Channel and ESPN, clock radios, in-room safes, guest laundry facilities, dry-cleaning service, an ATM, and either room service or more limited food delivery options.

Deluxe
Animal Kingdom Lodge

The zebras, ostriches, and Thomson's gazelles out back are neither mascots, nor exotic props, nor escapees from the nearby Animal Kingdom theme park. They and their hoofed and feathered comrades—about 200 animals in all, mostly African expats—live on the resort's carefully plotted pasturelands, giving round-the-clock credence to its claims as Florida's only African wildlife reserve lodge. Of course, this ambitious theme is not carried entirely by the storks and giraffes whose habitat comes within thirty feet of guests' domain. Hardly. The lodge's hut foyer opens to an immense thatched-ceiling lobby with the tantalizing depth of a lion's yawn. Here, pupils swell as the eyes dart from the suspension bridge to the huge mud fireplace, from the gushing approximation of Victoria Falls to the blur of African masks and artifacts and

Mickey Rates the Resorts

Disney's ranking system for its resorts provides a convenient framework for considering WDW lodging options. Categories reflect not only price, but the style of the accommodation and the level of service. The hotels fall into Deluxe, Moderate, and Value classifications. Disney Vacation Club encompasses villa-type lodgings (and the Wilderness Cabins at Fort Wilderness), while Disney's Camping category is occupied by the Fort Wilderness campground.

For the sake of clarity and comparison, we have used these same categories in this chapter, with a few exceptions for Fort Wilderness and other properties with two types of accommodations. In general, here's what to expect in our categories:

- Deluxe properties (rates for double rooms range from about $205 to $805 per night) are defined by their larger, practically appointed rooms, several restaurants, and such amenities as 24-hour room service.

- Disney Vacation Club and Camping (rates from about $39 to $1,790) applies to villas, vacation homes, all-suite hotels, wilderness cabins, and campsites.

- Moderate properties (rates from about $134 to $199) feature comfortably sized rooms, full-service restaurants as well as food courts, and bellhop luggage service.

- Value properties (rates from about $79 to $127) offer fewer frills and smaller, yet adequate, quarters. Meals are provided at food courts. Recreation options at these resorts are usually limited.

the chandeliers made of Masai shields. Oh, yes, and the four-story welcome-to-the-savanna window, which is sure to make momentary bumper cars of slack-jawed new arrivals.

Romance and adventure cling to every richly appointed inch of the semicircular lodge, which serves as a five-story animal-observation platform, from its viewing parlors to its vibrant restaurants and its expansive swimming pool. Although with 1,293 rooms, the resort is bigger than its African counterparts, it hides the fact well: Built into the landscape, its front drive leads to the third-floor lobby. (Traditionally, such buildings protect against predators.) Nine out of ten guest-room balconies overlook the savanna.

BIG DRAWS: Luxury laced with an undeniable spirit of adventure and romance. Balconies serve as box seats for animal viewing.

Animal Kingdom Lodge Tips

- Although you can view animals from many vantage points, it is not possible to touch or feed them without participating in a special program. Visit Lobby Concierge for more information.

- Recreational activities are limited due to the presence of animals. For example, no bike rentals are available and there is no jogging path. Guests may indulge in these pursuits at neighboring Disney resorts.

- Willing to forego wildlife-watching from your balcony? Rooms *sans* animal views are significantly cheaper.

- This 33-acre tropical savanna is inhabited by 100 grazing animals and 130 birds—the safari begins as soon as you enter the resort.

43

WORTH NOTING: Accommodations at this resort are comparable to those at most deluxe hotels in the World; both the deluxe rooms and the smaller standard guestrooms typically include two queen-size beds. Deluxe rooms have a child's daybed. Ask and you may receive a king-size bed or the polar opposite: bunk beds. Within each room's sandy-colored walls is a unique amalgam of African art pieces, traditionally patterned textiles, and dark-wood furniture handcrafted in Zimbabwe and South Africa. All rooms have private balconies; animals and their habitats are visible from 90 percent of the rooms. Lest guests lose their sense of place while reading in bed, there are (purely decorative) mosquito nets in every room; some rooms even have a map of Africa on the wall. Amenities include hair dryers, irons (with boards), newspaper delivery, and 24-hour room service. Refrigerators may be requested at no extra charge. Club level rooms with views of the animal zones are available.

The primary form of recreation here is spying on the roving impalas, Thompson's gazelles, giraffes, and flamingos from every possible vantage point all

Seasonal Rates For 2006

Rates quoted in resort entries are subject to change.

- Value rates apply January 1 to February 15, August 27 to October 4, and November 26 to December 19 for all Value and Moderate resorts, Wilderness Lodge and Villas, Animal Kingdom Lodge, and the Fort Wilderness Cabins; January 1 to February 15 and August 6 to November 16 for the Fort Wilderness Campground; and January 1 to February 15, July 5 to October 4, and November 26 to December 19 for other Disney-owned-and-operated resorts.

- Regular rates apply April 23 to August 26 and October 4 to November 25 for all Value and Moderate resorts, Wilderness Lodge and Villas, Animal Kingdom Lodge, and Fort Wilderness Cabins; April 23 to August 5 for Fort Wilderness Campground; and April 23 to July 4 and October 5 to November 25 for other WDW properties (except Swan and Dolphin).

- Peak rates apply February 16 to April 22 for all but the Swan and Dolphin.

- Pre-holiday rates apply November 17 to December 19 at Fort Wilderness Campground.

- Holiday higher-than-peak rates apply December 20 to 31 for all WDW resorts except the Swan and Dolphin.

- For details on Swan and Dolphin seasonal rates, call 800-227-1500.

day and night. In addition to the floor-to-ceiling window in the lobby, a rock outcropping one story down from the lobby allows views of the animals, and indoor viewing areas line the halls of the U-shaped resort. The property's enormous pool, sun deck, and two whirlpools have great animal-viewing potential (due to a strategically placed watering hole). The pool area is surrounded by restaurants. Zahanati Health Club rounds out the resort's recreation options.

Where to eat: Boma—Flavors of Africa (buffet featuring items prepared on a wood-burning grill in an African market setting); Jiko—the Cooking Place (comfort food meets multicultural-influenced cuisine); and The Mara (on-the-go grazing).

Where to drink: Victoria Falls (mezzanine lounge with African drums as tables); Cape Town Lounge and Wine Bar (near Jiko); Uzima Springs Pool Bar.

VITAL STATISTICS: Animal Kingdom Lodge enjoys enviable proximity to the Animal Kingdom and Blizzard Beach; the Disney-MGM Studios is also nearby. Animal Kingdom Lodge; 2901 Osceola Parkway; Box 10000; Bay Lake, FL 32830-1000; 407-938-3000.

Rates: Standard rooms without savanna views run $205 in value season, $249 regular, and $299 peak; standard rooms with savanna views are $285 value, $330 regular, and $380 peak; club level rooms with savanna views begin at $435 in value season, $490 regular, and $555 peak. Suites start at $640. A $25 per diem charge applies for each extra adult (beyond two) in a room.

BoardWalk Inn & Villas

This fetching resort and entertainment complex recaptures an ephemeral period in eastern-seaboard history. It has all the charm of a shore village awash in sun-bleached pastels. The name comes from the 48-foot-wide boardwalk out back, where you will find a lively piano club, a

Resort Primer

- Reservationists cannot guarantee a room location or view, so arrive early to request the best selection.
- Rooms on the upper floors afford the most privacy.
- Connecting or adjoining rooms and king-size beds can usually be requested but are not assured.
- Club level rooms, in addition to extra service, generally include continental breakfast and afternoon snacks.

dance hall, and a major-league sports bar, not to mention a bakery and a brewpub. When hunger calls, you can have a seafood dinner or buy a slice of pizza. For dessert, try a caramel apple from the sweetshop. Located lakefront directly opposite the Yacht and Beach Club, BoardWalk completes this seaside community in romantic fashion.

The BoardWalk Inn (a 371-room hotel) and BoardWalk Villas (583 villas styled in the tradition of family vacation rooms) share a lobby. Filled with antique miniatures of early boardwalk amusement rides, the lobby fronts an inviting porch with rocking chairs. A sweeping staircase leads to the main recreation area as well as to the restaurants, shops, and clubs of the BoardWalk entertainment district.

BoardWalk Tips

- Take advantage of the resort's romantic assets—surrey rides and sunset cocktails on the waterfront.

- When checking in, request a room near the lobby—you'll get enough exercise walking in the parks.

- Big games attract a big crowd at the ESPN Club, so get there as early as possible.

- In the evening, catch a bus to the BoardWalk from the TTC.

BIG DRAWS: Intimate charm, an entertainment zone right out back, and a walkway to Epcot's International Gateway.

WORTH NOTING: Guestrooms at the BoardWalk Inn are comparable in size to those at Disney's other deluxe properties and offer two queen-size beds; some have a child's daybed. Decor includes curtains imprinted with images and inscriptions from old postcards, and French doors that open to private patios or balconies. Two-story suites feature a master-bedroom loft (with king-size bed and adjoining bath with whirlpool tub), a living room with a wet bar, and a private garden enclosed in a white picket fence. Single-story club level rooms are similarly appointed (no gardens, alas).

The BoardWalk Villas is a Disney Vacation Club resort (see page 58 for details); all of its accommodations have either a kitchenette or a full kitchen. Villas, decorated in the eclectic fashion of seaside cottages, feature balconies or patios and carousel-print curtains. Studios offer a queen-size bed and a double sleeper sofa, plus a wet bar with microwave, coffeemaker, and small refrigerator. Larger villas (with one, two, or three bed-rooms) have a dining room, kitchen, laundry facilities, whirlpool tub, and VCR. They also have a king-size bed in the master bedroom, a spacious living room with a queen sleeper sofa, and two queen-size beds or a queen-size bed and double sleeper sofa in any additional bedrooms.

Both properties have room service from 6 A.M. to midnight. Room amenities include hair dryers, irons (with boards), and—at the Inn—weekday news-paper delivery. A conference center offers business services (for a fee). Guests have exclusive use of the amusement park–themed pool, two other pools, and three whirlpools.

Other recreational options include fishing excursions, two clay tennis courts, a health club (massages by appointment), a jogging trail, and croquet. Bicycles, pedal-driven carts, fishing poles, and inner tubes may be rented; a poolside library rents books and videos.

Where to eat: Big River Grille & Brewing Works (microbrews, pub food); BoardWalk Bakery (baked goods, sandwiches); ESPN Club (all-American sports bar, ballpark menu); Flying Fish Cafe (creative American, steak,

and seafood); Seashore Sweets' (saltwater taffy and ice cream); and Spoodles (Mediterranean).

Where to drink: Atlantic Dance (a ballroom/nightclub with songs from the '40s and the '80s and '90s and, sometimes, a deejay or live entertainment); the Belle Vue Room (cocktails and cognac flights); Jellyrolls (dueling pianos); ESPN Club; and Leaping Horse Libations (pool-side refreshments).

A Closer Look

Read (yes, read) the curtains, which were created using imprints of vin-tage postcards. During construction, a carpenter noticed one from 1933, written by his uncle to his aunt before they were married. They still live at the address on the postcard.

VITAL STATISTICS: BoardWalk guests have enviable access to Epcot, Disney-MGM Studios, and Fantasia Gardens Miniature Golf complex. BoardWalk; 2101 N. Epcot Resorts Blvd.; Box 10000; Lake Buena Vista, FL 32830-1000; 407-939-5100; fax 407-939-5155.

Rates: At the Inn, standard rooms start at $305 in value season, $345 regular, and $415 peak; club level rooms begin at $435 value, $490 regular, and $565 peak; and suites begin at $575. A $25 per diem charge applies for each extra adult (beyond two) sharing a room. At the Villas, studios start at $305 value, $345 regular, and $415 peak; one-bedroom villas begin at $410 value, $465 regular, and $540 peak; two-bedroom villas start at $575 value, $745 regular, and $945 peak; and three-bedroom villas start at $1,395.

Contemporary

First impressions might suggest that the enormous A-frame tower of this legendary resort is simply a 15-story concrete tent that's been pitched here, a stone's throw from Space Mountain, for the benefit of the monorail trains regularly passing through it. And the Contemporary is certainly defined by a 1970s futuristic vision. But there's more to the resort—namely, the reverie that plays out in its bold decor and stunning views: from the sleek lobby to the newly revitalized guestroom decor; three eateries, including the acclaimed California Grill; and views of the Magic Kingdom or Bay Lake, especially from rooms in the resort's tower (the higher, the better).

NOTE: Pop music often blares from the pool area, so for optimum quiet pick the Magic Kingdom side of the resort.

BIG DRAWS: Location. Monorail service. Ideally suited for serious tennis players. And the California Grill never disappoints.

WORTH NOTING: Many guestrooms here, (some have undergone a well-deserved refurbishment— the rest will be finished some-time in 2007), are larger than at any other Disney World hotel; most feature two queen-size beds plus a daybed (a king-size bed may be requested). Amenities at the 1,030-room resort include

Contemporary Tips

- The view is lovely from either side of the Contemporary, but the Bay Lake side is noisier.

- Rooms in the resort's garden buildings generally do not yield notable views, which is why the rates are lower than in the tower.

- Tennis players will do well to stay in the north wing because of its proximity to the resort's six lighted courts. Be sure to inquire about the resort's tennis clinics.

- The marina is full of choices for sailors, from Sea Raycer boats to sailboats.

- Tower guests have convenient access to business services at the convention center. Guests staying in the south wing are close to the pool and marina areas.

- There is a convenient walking path to the Magic Kingdom.

24-hour room service. Club-level services are available to guests on the 12th and 14th floors.

Based on its tennis courts alone, the Contemporary could be a recreational hub, but it also boasts a large pool area (with a free-form pool, an unguarded pool, and two whirlpools), a boat-rental marina, a parasailing program, tennis instruction, basketball and sand volleyball courts, a jogging trail, and a health club (massages by appointment). Waterskiing and fishing excursions may be arranged. One bonus of note: a walking path to the Magic Kingdom. A true time-saver.

Where to eat: California Grill (West Coast cuisine and a 15th-floor Magic Kingdom vista; in fact, the view from the observation deck is open to restaurant guests only); Chef Mickey's (breakfast and dinner character buffets); Concourse Steakhouse (casual for its genre); and Food and Fun Center (24-hour snacks).

Where to drink: California Grill Lounge (emphasis on wine); Contemporary Grounds (coffee bar); Outer Rim (comfy alcove overlooking Bay Lake); and Sand Bar (poolside refreshments).

VITAL STATISTICS: The Contemporary, which has the Magic Kingdom virtually in its front yard and Bay Lake out back, is the only hotel with a walkway—and one of three on the monorail line—to that park. Monorail links extend the resort's neighborhood to the Polynesian and the Grand Floridian, and provide convenient commutes to Epcot. Contemporary; 4600 N. World Dr.; Box 10000; Lake Buena Vista, FL 32830-1000; 407-824-1000; fax 407-824-3539.

Rates: Standard guestrooms start at $249 in value season, $279 regular, and $329 peak; tower rooms begin at $355 value, $390 regular, and $460 peak; suites start at $320. A $25 daily charge applies for each extra adult (beyond two) sharing a room.

Grand Floridian Resort & Spa

This romantic slice of Victorian confectionery, near the Magic Kingdom, recalls the opulent hotels that beckoned high society at the turn of the 20th century.

The Grand Floridian's central building and five guest buildings—white structures laced with verandas and turrets and topped with gabled roofs of red shingle—sprawl over acres of Seven Seas Lagoon shorefront. Every glance embraces towering palms, stunning lake views, or rose gardens.

The resort's magnificent lobby—Victoriana *in excelsis*—features immense chandeliers, stained-glass skylights, and live piano and orchestra music that might inspire spontaneous dancing. Guestrooms have old-fashioned armoires, marble-topped sinks, and room service delivered atop lace cloths.

BIG DRAWS: The height of Disney luxury with a view of Cinderella Castle. Great for honeymoons or an escape to a kinder, gentler era. And the monorail stops here, too.

WORTH NOTING: Standard accommodations at this 867-room resort are a bit larger than those at most deluxe hotels in the World and include two queen-size beds plus a daybed; many rooms have terraces. Amenities include hair dryers, toiletries, robes, minibars, 24-hour room service, and nightly turndown. Club level rooms and suites are on the upper floors of the main building and in the Sugar Loaf building.

The resort offers some of the best restaurants on property. Afternoon tea is served in the Garden View lounge. The Electrical Water Pageant (ask at the resort's front desk for information) and the Magic Kingdom fireworks can be seen from many lagoon-view rooms.

Grand Floridian Tips

- For maximum quiet and a striking panorama, make sure to request a lagoon-view room.
- You can watch the fireworks over Cinderella Castle from the beach with little or no company.
- Consider a honeymoon room for your second honeymoon.
- Indulge in a treatment (or two) at the spa after a long day in the parks.
- Book a special dinner at Victoria & Albert's 180 days in advance.
- Note that the resort is surprisingly popular with families, despite its posh surroundings.
- For pre-dinner drinks, opt for Cítricos lounge, the lounge at Narcoossee's, or cocktail service in the lobby.
- Ask at Lobby Concierge about sailing the Seven Seas on a private yacht (see page 176).

A convention center offers access to business services (for a fee). Boats may be rented, and fishing excursions may be arranged. Two clay tennis courts and volleyball equipment are available at no charge. The Grand Floridian Spa & Health Club is among Walt Disney World's most complete fitness facilities. The two swimming pools and a whirlpool are open 24 hours, with quiet hours in effect at night.

Where to eat: Cítricos (Florida cuisine with Mediterranean flair; closed Monday and Tuesday); Gasparilla Grill & Games (24-hour snacks); Grand Floridian Cafe (breakfast and lunch); Narcoossee's (seafood served waterside); 1900 Park Fare (character buffets); and Victoria & Albert's (seven-course dinners).

Where to drink: Cítricos lounge (wines and citrus martinis); Garden View (cocktails and afternoon tea); Mizner's (classic cocktails); Narcoossee's (wines overlooking the lagoon); and the Grand Floridian Pool Bar (poolside refreshments).

VITAL STATISTICS: The Grand Floridian's prime Seven Seas Lagoon locale allows for fast access to the Magic Kingdom. Proximity to the Palm and

Magnolia links pleases golfers. The monorail stretches the hotel's neighborhood beyond the adjacent Polynesian resort to include the Contemporary resort and provides for easy commutes to Epcot. Grand Floridian; 4401 Floridian Way; Box 10000; Lake Buena Vista, FL 32830-1000; 407-824-3000; fax 407-824-3186.

Rates: Standard rooms start at $359 in value season, $405 regular, and $475 peak; club level rooms begin at $475 value, $550 regular, and $635 peak; and suites start at $940. A $25 per diem

Made-to-Order Surprises

Flowers, custom gift baskets, and champagne can be delivered to any WDW resort (and some off-property hotels) by calling 407-827-3505 before or during your visit.

For an additional fee, Disney personal shoppers will further scour the World to track down favorite character merchandise and other special-request items.

charge applies to each extra adult (beyond two) sharing a room.

Polynesian

This resort echoes the romance and beauty of the South Pacific with enchanting realism. Polynesian music is piped throughout the lushly landscaped grounds, which boast white-sand beaches with hammocks, torches that burn nightly, and sufficient flowers to perfume the air.

Sprawled amid tropical gardens are 11 two- and three-story village longhouses, all named for Pacific islands, where 847 newly refurbished guestrooms are located. But the Polynesian's centerpiece and primary mood setter is unquestionably the Great Ceremonial House, which (in addition to the usual front desk, shops, and restaurants) contains a three-story-high garden that all but consumes the atrium lobby.

BIG DRAWS: A breathtaking, you-are-there South Seas ambience makes the Polynesian exceptionally romantic and helps to explain the resort's busy wedding calendar. And the convenience of monorail service is a definite plus.

WORTH NOTING: Standard guestrooms, comparable in size to

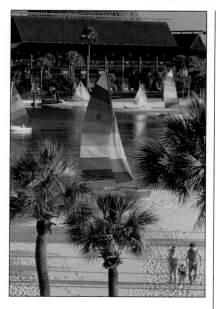

those at the Contemporary, are roomy and feature two queen-size beds plus a daybed. Those in Tokelau, Tahiti, and Rapa Nui are slightly larger. Room decor includes vibrant bedspreads, ti-leaf–shaped mirrors, bamboo accents, and woven reed canopies draped over and behind the beds.

All third-floor rooms (and second-floor rooms in the Tonga, Tokelau, Tahiti, and Rapa Nui buildings) have balconies. Room service is offered until midnight. A club-level lounge with a choice view of the Magic Kingdom is a comfy retreat for guests in Hawaii and all-suite Tonga, the resort's most luxurious digs.

In addition to the impressive volcano-themed pool, there is a second, more removed pool. Near Tokelau, a grassy knoll known as Sunset Point offers a hammock. The resort boasts great vantage points for Magic Kingdom fireworks and the Electrical Water Pageant. (For information, ask at the front desk.) Boats may be rented, fishing excursions may be arranged, and a 1¼-mile trail invites jogging around the tropical grounds.

Where to eat: Captain Cook's Snack Company (24-hour grazing—it's one of the better Disney snack bars); Kona Cafe (Asian-influenced casual fare and adjoining coffee bar); and

Polynesian Tips

- For a taste of tropical tradition, catch the Torch Lighting Ceremony, held on weekend nights at 6 P.M. in the main lobby.

- Tahiti is a good choice for its relative seclusion and Magic Kingdom views (request a lagoonside room).

- For a better view, hit the Seven Seas Lagoon on a private specialty cruise. See page 176 for details.

- Tucked down below Sunset Point, in front of Tahiti, is a beach that many guests don't realize is there.

- Couples can celebrate a special occasion with a moonlit dinner on the beach. Call Room Service for more information.

- The Grand Floridian Spa & Health Club is a short walk away.

'Ohana (character breakfast and family-style Pacific Rim dinners featuring grilled meats).

Where to drink: Barefoot Bar (poolside refreshments) and Tambu lounge (tropical drinks).

VITAL STATISTICS: The Polynesian is located on the shore of Seven Seas Lagoon, directly opposite the Magic Kingdom and offers fast access via monorail to the park. The monorail also links the resort with the Grand Floridian and Contemporary and provides for easy commutes to Epcot. Golfers appreciate having both the Palm and Magnolia courses nearby. Polynesian; 1600 South Seas Dr.; Box 10000; Lake Buena Vista, FL 32830-1000; 407-824-2000; fax 407-824-3174.

Rates: Standard rooms start at $315 in value season, $369 regular, and $435 peak; club level rooms begin at $440 value, $500 regular, and $570 peak; suites start at $550. A $25 per diem charge applies to each extra adult (beyond two) sharing a room.

Swan & Dolphin

While they occupy choice real estate within the borders of Disney property, these hotels are not owned or operated by Disney and attract a lot of business travelers. The motto for these resorts might be "expect the unexpected." Certainly, noted architect Michael Graves designed these postmodern bookends with entertainment in mind. At the Dolphin, a 27-story triangular tower is flanked by buildings that are topped by two 56-foot-tall dolphin statues and covered in a mural of banana leaves. It's more of the same playful luxury next door at the Swan, which carves its own distinctive silhouette with 47-foot namesake statues perched atop its 12-story central building, and facades accented with turquoise waves. The Swan has 758 rooms, about half as many as the Dolphin.

BIG DRAWS: Luxury in a light-hearted wrapper. Exceptional facilities. Top-notch service. And you can walk to Epcot, Board-Walk, and, if you're ambitious, the Disney-MGM Studios.

Special Room Requests

All WDW resorts offer rooms equipped for guests with disabilities, as well as nonsmoking rooms. For more detailed information, inquire with Central Reservations (407-934-7639). For more specifics related to travelers with disabilities, see the "Customized Tips" section of the *Planning Ahead* chapter.

WORTH NOTING: The Swan and the Dolphin (operated by Westin and Sheraton) are the only two WDW hotels whose value season extends through the summer months. Guests staying at either hotel have access to all recreational activities and may charge any meals and activities enjoyed at the sister hotel to their room tab. Such charging privileges do not extend beyond the two hotels. Disney's Magical Express program isn't extended to guests here, either.

Guestrooms at the Swan and Dolphin are comparable to those at Disney's other deluxe resorts. Whereas standard rooms at the Dolphin feature two double beds, queen-size beds are the rule at the Swan (king-size beds are available at both). Room amenities at both hotels include stocked mini-bars and 24-hour room service (the best at Walt Disney World), plus free high speed Internet service, coffeemakers, hair dryers, and irons with boards. Club level rooms at the Dolphin are in the tower; at the Swan they're on the top two floors of the hotel's main building.

Both hotels boast luxurious presidential suites. In addition to a beach with a volleyball net and boat rentals, the resorts have enviable lap pools, grotto pool with waterfalls, a small kiddie pool, several whirlpools, and a spa.

Where to eat: At the Swan: Garden Grove Cafe (greenhouse setting), and Palio (Italian bistro). At the Dolphin: Dolphin Fountain (ice cream parlor); Fresh (Mediterranean); Shula's Steakhouse (steak); Todd English's bluezoo (seafood); and Tubbi's (cafeteria with 24-hour convenience store).

Where to drink: At the Swan: Kimonos (lounge with sushi bar); Lobby Court (coffees); and

Swan & Dolphin Tips

- Request a corner room with a king-size bed at the Dolphin, and if it's available, you'll get two balconies for the price of one.

- Both hotels have large convention centers. If you're visiting for pleasure, ask if there will be major business action before you book.

- Swan and Dolphin guests pay a resort fee each day. It covers weekday newspaper delivery, in-room coffee, local calls, unlimited high-speed Internet access, and use of the health club.

- Four tennis courts at the Dolphin are kept lighted all night.

- Light sleepers should note that some Swan rooms are steps from BoardWalk's Jellyrolls and Atlantic Dance clubs.

- The Dolphin is home to a new pampering palace: the Mandarin Spa. Visit *www.swandolphin.com* for details.

Splash Grill (poolside). At the Dolphin: Cabana Bar & Grill (poolside); and Shula's Steakhouse Lounge (nook adjacent to dining area), and a lobby lounge.

VITAL STATISTICS: The Swan and Dolphin resorts offer easy access to Epcot, the Disney-MGM Studios, and BoardWalk. Located side by side on the shore of Crescent Lake, a short walk from Epcot's World Showcase, the hotels are flanked by BoardWalk on one side and the Yacht and Beach Club on the other. Walt Disney World Swan; 1200 Epcot Resorts Blvd.; Lake Buena Vista, FL 32830-1000; 407-934-3000; fax 407-934-4499. Walt Disney World Dolphin; 1500 Epcot Resorts Blvd.; Lake Buena Vista, FL 32830-1000; 407-934-4000; fax 407-934-4844.

Rates: At press time, rates at the Swan and Dolphin, standard rooms began at $339 in value season and $459peak, and club-level rooms are $435 value and $495 peak. For suite prices, call 800-227-1500. A $25 per diem charge applies for each extra adult (beyond two) sharing a room. Up to four people may stay in one room. Call 800-227-1500 to make reservations or visit *www.swandolphin.com*.

Wilderness Lodge & Villas

Rustic romance infuses every detail of this resort, patterned after the grand National Park Service lodges of the early 1900s. Hidden away on an isolated shore of Bay Lake, Wilderness Lodge is surrounded by pine forests that provide a drumroll of sorts along the winding road leading to the timbered hotel.

The soaring atrium lobby kindles the spirit of the American West with an imposing pair of totem poles, tepee chandeliers, a bubbling hot spring, and an 82-foot-tall fireplace whose layered stones actually replicate the

Wilderness Lodge Tips

- Tours offer a closer look at the resort's architecture or restaurants.
- Courtyard and lakeview rooms are most romantic, with waterfalls gushing and brooks babbling. Woods views provide maximum quiet.
- The Lodge's junior suites are a good value, given their spaciousness. Honeymooners should request room 7084 for its fireworks views and whirlpool tub.
- Some rooms at the lodge come with a queen-size bed and a bunk bed instead of two queens. Be sure to make your preference known.
- The bad news? The Wilderness Lodge is not on the monorail loop. The good? It's less expensive because of it!

Grand Canyon's strata. And the natural landscape is supplemented by a roaring waterfall, a swimming area surrounded by boulders, wildflowers, and even a gushing geyser. The guestrooms at the Lodge are located in two wings that extend back from the lobby to the lakefront, forming a U-shaped frame around an inner courtyard. The adjacent Villas at Wilderness Lodge are styled after the railroad hotels of the late 1800s. They extend the resort's neighborhood with 136 villas. The units are further distinguished by a red-shingled roof and a five-story central atrium. The Lodge and Villas share a lobby, and a covered walkway connects the resort buildings. There's also a club level floor at the Lodge.

BIG DRAWS: Luxury. Undeniable romance. The bottom line: a truly extraordinary setting at a considerable value to guests.

WORTH NOTING: While all 728 Wilderness Lodge guestrooms have balconies or patios, quarters here are slightly more compact than those at Disney's other deluxe resorts, and feature two queen-size beds. Quilted bedspreads, buffalo lamps, and armoires etched with mountain scenes maintain the theme.

The Villas at Wilderness Lodge is a Disney Vacation Club resort (see page 58 for details); accommodations are equipped with a wet bar or a full kitchen. Studios and larger villas with one or two rooms feature balconies (or patios). Guests staying at the

57

villas enjoy full access to the Lodge next door and vice versa.

At the Lodge and Villas, room service is available for breakfast and dinner. The four corridors ringing the lobby provide access to porches overlooking the courtyard and hold cozy nooks with sofas and tucked-away fireplaces. Fire Rock Geyser spouts off 180-foot water plumes at the top of every hour from 7 A.M. until 10 P.M. An unguarded pool, whirlpool spa, and Sturdy Branches health club are located in the villa section. Both resorts share a beach (sunbathing only) on the lake. Guided fishing excursions can be arranged. Boats and bikes may be rented, and there is a path for biking, jogging, and walking that leads to Fort Wilderness.

Where to eat: Artist Point (Pacific Northwest cuisine); Roaring Fork (snacks); and Whispering Canyon Cafe (high-spirited—and decibeled—family-style dining).

Where to drink: Territory Lounge (western motif) and Trout Pass (small poolside bar).

VITAL STATISTICS: Wilderness Lodge and Villas; 801 and 901 West Timberline Dr.; Box 10000; Lake Buena Vista, FL 32830-1000; 407-824-3200; fax 407-824-3232.

Rates: At the Lodge, standard guestrooms begin at $205 in value season, $249 regular, and $299 peak; suites start at $760. Honeymoon rooms (with whirlpool tub) start at $380. A $25 per diem charge applies for each extra adult (beyond two) sharing a room (at the Lodge only). At the Villas, studios start at $295 value, $335 regular, and $399 peak; one-bedroom villas begin at $400 value, $453 regular, and $550 peak; two-bedroom villas start at $570 value, $735 regular, and $890 peak.

Join the Club?

Frequent visitors who consider WDW a home away from home might want to join the Disney Vacation Club. For a one-time price and annual dues, members may stay at Old Key West, BoardWalk Villas, The Villas at Wilderness Lodge, Beach Club Villas, Saratoga Springs Resort & Spa, or choose from 450 resorts beyond WDW, including Disney's Hilton Head Island Resort, in South Carolina, and, just two hours from WDW, Disney's Vero Beach Resort (see page 78). They can also opt for the Disney Cruise Line or another Disney resort. For more details, visit www.disneyvacationclub.com or call 800-800-9100. (Non-members may also book Disney Vacation Club accommodations by the night—based, of course, on availability.)

Yacht & Beach Club and Beach Club Villas

This setting conjures such a heady vision of turn-of-the-century Nantucket and Martha's Vineyard, you'd swear you smelled salt in the air. Surely, architect Robert A. M. Stern's evocation of the grand old seaside hotels has the gulls fooled. The resort stretches along a picturesque shoreline complete with a swimming lagoon, lighthouse, and marina.

As the five-story gray clapboard structure of the Yacht Club gives way to the sky-blue Beach Club (they're connected), the interior motif shifts from seriously nautical to seashore whimsical. The Yacht Club has a rich, exclusive feel to it—there's a stunning globe anchoring the lobby, and polished brass abounds. Next door at the Beach Club, beach umbrellas act as pillars, and clambakes occur nightly. The Beach Club Villas are inspired by Cape May seaside homes designed in the early twentieth century.

BIG DRAWS: Compelling theming. Exceptional swimming area. Some of the World's best restaurants. Close access to Epcot and the Disney-MGM Studios.

WORTH NOTING: There are 630 guestrooms at the Yacht Club and 583 rooms at the Beach Club. Room size is comparable to those at Disney's other deluxe resorts. As a rule, they feature two queen-size beds and a daybed (king-size beds are

Yacht & Beach Club Tips

- The stunning views belong strictly to those with lakeside rooms.
- At both resorts, it's a long walk to the lobby from the outermost reaches of guest wings.
- At the Beach Club, all rooms have patios or balconies.
- Balconies at the Yacht Club are bigger than those at the Beach Club.
- Inquire at the Yacht Club's Lobby Concierge desk about the free weekly garden tours.
- Take a ride on the *Breathless* speedboat. See page 176 for more.
- The resorts are just a short walk from Epcot's back door, aka International Gateway.

available). At the Yacht Club, rooms maintain the nautical theme. Most rooms have good-size balconies. At the Beach Club, rooms keep the seashore motif.

Amenities at both resorts include minibars, an iron and board, a hair dryer, and 24-hour room service. Yacht and Beach Club both offer club level rooms. The five-story Beach Club Villas is a Disney Vacation Club resort. Accommodations have either a wet bar or a kitchen. The 208 units, which include both studios and one- and two-bedroom villas, feature wooden porches and pastel colors.

A three-acre mini water park called Stormalong Bay earns the Yacht and Beach Club bragging

rights to the World's best resort swimming area; the sprawling, sandy-bottomed pool, open only to hotel guests, includes sections with jets, swirling currents, and a slide (traditional whirlpools also stand by). Each resort also has a smaller pool and whirlpool, so removed you must seek them out.

The Ship Shape health club is among the most extensive fitness centers at a Walt Disney World property. Boat rentals and two tennis courts are offered, fishing excursions can be arranged, and volleyball and croquet equipment is available.

Where to eat: At the Beach Club: Cape May Cafe (character breakfasts and clambake buffet dinners). At the Yacht Club: Yacht Club Galley (buffet breakfast, lunch, and dinner) and Yachts-man Steakhouse (breakfast, lunch, and dinner). Shared by both hotels is the Beach Club Marketplace (a new combination eatery/retail shop).

Where to drink: At the Beach Club: Martha's Vineyard (cloud nine for wine lovers) and Rip Tide (lobby niche). At the Yacht Club: Ale and Compass (cozy lobby nook) and Crew's Cup (well-heeled beer emporium). For poolside refreshments and snacks, there's Hurricane Hanna's Grill.

VITAL STATISTICS: The Yacht and Beach Club enjoy close proximity to Epcot, Disney-MGM Studios, BoardWalk, and the Fantasia Gardens Miniature Golf complex. Located side by side on a shore of Crescent Lake that offers a footpath to Epcot's International Gateway entrance, these sister resorts are joined lakeside by the BoardWalk, Swan, and Dolphin. Yacht Club; 1700 Epcot Resorts Blvd.; Box 10000; Lake Buena Vista, FL 32830-1000; 407-934-7000; fax 407-934-3450. Beach Club; 1800 Epcot Resorts Blvd.; Box 10000; Lake Buena Vista, FL 32830-1000; 407-934-8000; fax 407-934-3850.

Rates: Standard rooms at the Yacht and Beach Club begin at $305 in value season, $345 regular, and $415 peak; club level rooms at the Yacht Club start at $435 value, $490 regular, and $565 peak; Yacht Club suites start at $555 and Beach Club suites start at $525. A $25 per diem charge applies to each extra adult (beyond two) sharing a room. At the Villas, studios start at $305 value, $345 regular, and $404 peak; one-bedroom villas begin at $410 value, $465 regular, and $540 peak; two-bedroom villas start at $575 value, $745 regular, and $945 peak.

Disney Vacation Club
Disney's Old Key West Resort

Pastel-hued clapboard guesthouses with tin roofs and white picket fences set the cheerful tone of this Key West-erly retreat. Here, Disney luxury dovetails with a laid-back atmosphere to create the look and feel of a friendly resort community.

A sprawling village, it is bounded by the wooded fairways of the Lake Buena Vista golf links, and anchored at its center by a lighthouse that overlooks the main pool area, which moonlights as a sauna. A waterway called the Trumbo Canal flows from the heart of the resort, eventually uniting with Lake Buena Vista. Accommodations equipped with kitchens may set this resort apart, but what gives the place charm is its warmth.

Old Key West Tips

- For a waterfront setting that's removed from the main recreation area, book a villa near the Turtle Shack. Buildings 43 and 44 are good, given their water views and proximity to the pool, snack bar, tennis court, and bus stop.

- All accommodations but the studios feature whirlpool bathtubs.

- One-bedroom villas yield more than twice the space of a studio for a relatively small jump in cost.

BIG DRAWS: Spacious accommodations, ideal for long stays. Homey environs. Value for groups. Convenience of kitchens. Well located for golfers.

WORTH NOTING: This resort was the first Disney Vacation Club property. It features studio accommodations and one-, two-, and three-bedroom villas. The villas have a distinctly Key West feel, and are decorated in light woods with ceiling fans and color schemes of sea-foam green and mauve.

Each studio has a large bedroom with two queen-size beds; a wet bar with a microwave, coffeemaker, and small refrigerator; and a spacious bathroom. Larger villas have a dining room, and kitchen, laundry facilities, whirlpool bathtub, and DVD. They also feature a king-size bed in the master bedroom, two queen-size beds in each additional bedroom, and a living room with queen-size sofa bed. All accommodations have balconies or porches.

Boats and bicycles are available for rent. Fishing excursions can be arranged. The three tennis courts tend to be relatively quiet and accessible. The main swimming area supplements three smaller pools. There is a fitness center. Conch Flats Community Hall has table tennis, board games, and DVD rentals.

Where to eat: Good's Food to Go (meals and snacks on the go) and Olivia's Cafe (casual all-day dining with Key West flourishes). Grills and picnic tables are available. Pizza delivery from Port Orleans Riverside is offered until midnight. Conch Flats General Store stocks some grocery items.

Where to drink: Gurgling Suitcase (tiny pub) and Turtle Shack (poolside drinks).

VITAL STATISTICS: This resort is well located for golfers. It also has easy access to Downtown Disney and good proximity to Epcot and Disney-MGM Studios. Disney's Old Key West Resort; 1510 N. Cove Rd.; Box 10000; Lake Buena Vista, FL 32830-1000; 407-827-7700; fax 407-827-7710.

Rates: Studios are $269 in value season, $299 regular, and $349 peak; one-bedroom villas are $360 value, $405 regular, and $470 peak; two-bedrooms are $500 value, $590 regular, and

$720 peak; and three-bedrooms start at $1,100 value, $1,225 regular, and $1,385 peak.

Campground

Fort Wilderness Resort & Campground

No fewer than 700 acres of woodland combine with WDW's largest lake to provide the foundation for Fort Wilderness, a retreat that relies on the outdoors for atmosphere.

Cabins and campsites are arranged on 28 loops, linked by thoroughfares. While some of the 784 sites are designated for tents, most are devoted to RV camping; hundreds of spots sport air-conditioned Wilderness Cabins, comfortable units that are comparable to well-equipped trailer homes.

BIG DRAWS: Natural setting. Value. And recreation galore.

WORTH NOTING: Most loops have at least one air-conditioned comfort station equipped with restrooms, phones, showers, laundry facilities, and an ice machine.

Campsite lengths range from 25 to 65 feet. All sites have a charcoal grill, picnic table, and a 30/50-amp electrical outlet. Most sites have sanitary-disposal connections; about half have cable TV hookups.

Wilderness Cabins are separated from other campsites and feature rustic decor and a deck with picnic table; amenities include a hair dryer and an iron and board. Each cabin is air-conditioned and offers daily housekeeping service, as well as an eat-in kitchen, living room with television and VCR, and full bathroom.

Pets are welcome at designated campsites ($5 per day). Pet loops are finally wired for cable television. Recreational options include swimming, boating, tennis, and biking. Guided fishing trips may be arranged (407-WDW-BASS).

Horse-drawn wagon rides ($8; no reservations necessary; 45 minutes long) and 30-minute, horse-drawn carriage rides ($30; call 407-939-7529) take guests on a scenic trip between Fort Wilderness and Disney's Wilderness Lodge. The Hoop-Dee-Doo Musical Revue dinner show is presented nightly.

Where to eat: Most guests cook their own meals (a small selection of foodstuffs is sold at Meadow Trading Post and Settlement Trading Post), but there's also Trail's End restaurant (buffet-style dining). Grocery stores are located just minutes from Walt Disney World. Ask for directions when you check in.

Where to drink: Crockett's Tavern (cocktail service).

VITAL STATISTICS: Fort Wilderness occupies Bay Lake's southern shore. Its nearest theme park neighbor is the Magic Kingdom, and it closely borders the Osprey Ridge and Eagle Pines golf courses. The area is served by the WDW bus transportation system. Bus stops are strategically located and plentiful. Fort Wilderness; 4510 N. Fort Wilderness Trail; Box 10000; Lake Buena Vista, FL 32830-1000; 407-824-2900; fax 407-824-3508.

Rates: Preferred sites with full hookups, including water, electricity, sewage, and cable TV, are $53 in value season, $72 regular, and $82 peak; sites with full hookups minus the cable TV are $44 value, $66 regular, and $76 peak; sites with electricity hookups only are $39 value, $55 regular, and $64 peak.

There is a limit of ten people per campsite, and a $2 per diem charge applies to each extra adult (beyond two) sharing a site. Rates for Wilderness Cabins are $239 value, $279 regular, and $319 peak. Maximum occupancy is six, and there is a $5 per diem charge that applies to each extra adult (beyond two) sharing a unit.

Fort Wilderness Tips

- Bikes and electric carts are, sudden rains aside, the preferred means for getting around.

- A car is the quickest way to get to other parts of the World from here.

- Views of Magic Kingdom fireworks and the Electrical Water Pageant are readily available.

- Tent campers should request loop 1500 or 2000 for quiet; RV campers will find greater privacy on loops 1600 through 1900 (pets welcome).

Saratoga Springs Resort & Spa

Long for the relaxation of a lakeside retreat—complete with fragrant gardens, bubbling springs, and a spectacular spa? Look no further. Disney's newest haven has all of the above, plus colorful Victorian architecture, rolling hills, and even a lakeside veranda. The resort aims to recapture the charm and rejuvenating ambience of Saratoga Springs, New York, circa the late 1800s.

Saratoga Springs Resort & Spa is a Disney Vacation Club resort. (See page 58 for details.) The phone number is 407-827-1100.

Rates: Studios are $269 in value season, $299 regular, and $349 peak; one-bedroom villas are $360 value, $405 regular, and $470 peak; two-bedrooms are $509 value, $590 regular, and $720 peak; and three-bedrooms start at $1,100 value, $1,225 regular, and $1,385 peak.

BIG DRAWS: Relaxing environs. Great spa. Golf nearby. Village Lake fishing excursions. A stone's throw from Downtown Disney.

WORTH NOTING: There is a total of 552 guest units—studios, one- and two-bedroom villas, and grand villas—spread over 12 buildings. Each studio has a queen-size bed and full-size sofa bed, plus a kitchenette with a microwave, coffeemaker, and fridge. Larger villas sleep four to twelve, and all have a dining area, kitchen, laundry room, master bath with whirlpool tub, and a DVD player. They include a king-size bed in the master bedroom, living room with queen-size sofa bed, and queen- and full-size beds in the extra room.

Guests enjoy a smorgasbord of recreational diversions, including a nearby golf course, swimming pools, whirlpool spas, trails for walking or jogging, tennis courts, bike rentals, and more.

Where to eat: The Artist's Palette is the one food source here, with snacks, sandwiches, and hearty entrées. There are some grocery items available, too.

Where to drink: Resort guests may imbibe at the Turf Club (next door to the Artist's Palette) and at On the Rocks (poolside bar), or at Downtown Disney (a scenic water launch or bus ride away).

Moderate
Caribbean Beach

In this colorful evocation of the Caribbean, the spirit of the islands is captured by a lake ringed by beaches and villages representing Barbados, Martinique, Trinidad, Jamaica, and Aruba.

Each village is marked by clusters of two-story guest buildings that transport you to the Caribbean with cool pastel facades, white railings, and vivid metallic roofs. Old Port Royale, which houses eateries and shops, takes cues from an island market.

BIG DRAWS: Excellent value. Cheery environs with a decidedly Caribbean feel.

Caribbean Beach Tips

- Aruba is a good choice for seclusion and for proximity to Old Port Royale (they're linked by a bridge).
- For honeymoon-style isolation, request a room in Trinidad South. Located just off the main loop, its buildings and beach are especially removed.
- Martinique tends to be the liveliest village.
- The 1.4-mile promenade circling Barefoot Bay is ideal for biking and jogging. Bikes and boats may be rented.
- Families flock here, so plan on encountering plenty of children.

WORTH NOTING: The resort has 2,112 rooms. Slightly larger than those at Disney's other moderately priced resorts, they feature two double beds (king-size beds are available) and soft-hued decor. A small fridge may be ordered for free. Amenities include an in-room coffeemaker (with coffee). Room service, which ventures a touch beyond pizza, is offered from 4 P.M. until midnight.

Villages are sprawled around the resort's Barefoot Bay in a way that can make travel between some guest areas cumbersome despite footbridges and "local" buses.

The resort's whirlpool is nestled into its bustling themed pool. Each village offers its own beach, pool, and courtyards.

Where to eat: Shutters at Old Port Royale (Caribbean-influenced American fare) and a food court with six counter-service options.

Where to drink: Banana Cabana (poolside refreshments) and the above-mentioned Shutters (beer, wine, and cocktails).

VITAL STATISTICS: Caribbean Beach is off on its own but well situated for pursuits other than the Magic Kingdom, with Epcot, the Disney-MGM Studios, and Blizzard Beach close at hand, on one side, and Typhoon Lagoon and Downtown Disney nearby, on the other. Caribbean Beach; 900 Cayman Way; Box 10000; Lake Buena Vista, FL 32830-1000; 407-934-3400; fax 407-934-1940.

Rates: Rooms begin at $139 in value season, $155 in regular season, and $175 during peak times. A $15 per diem charge applies for each extra adult (beyond two) sharing a room.

Coronado Springs

The architecture of this sprawling resort gives its nod to Mexico and the American Southwest, with brightly tinted buildings accented by tile roofs, soaring columns, and arched entryways. Three clusters of regionally themed guest buildings rim the 15-acre Lago Dorado lagoon. The terra-cotta Casitas occupy a citylike landscape that segues into rural surroundings. Here, pueblo-style Ranchos invite guests to dwell among cacti adjacent to a dry stream bed. In the resort's third section, the scenery shifts once more, with rocky beaches, hammocks, and Cabanas filling the horizon. Rooms in the three areas are similarly appointed, with yellow, scarlet, or deep-blue accents.

Walkways around the lagoon lead from guestroom areas to the main recreation zone (dominated by a five-story Mayan pyramid) and the central building that holds the resort's temporal treasures: an intricately tiled rotunda lobby, two eateries, a lounge, and a gift shop.

BIG DRAWS: A standout among the moderates for its health club, suites, and business hotel facilities.

WORTH NOTING: Guestrooms at this 1,921-room resort are smaller than those at Disney's deluxe hotels. Most of the 46 suites are in the Casitas area. Decor reveals Mexican and Southwestern influences, and reflects the style of each guest

Coronado Springs Tips

- There is a ten percent gratuity automatically added to all dine-in purchases made at the Pepper Market food court.

- January, May, September, and October are popular convention months. Most groups are housed in the Casitas area, near the convention facilities, and a separate check-in area is provided.

- The Ranchos are nearest the pool area; the Casitas are closer to the main building, convention center, and health club; and the Cabanas are convenient to both.

- There's a lot of ground to cover between the central building and some guestrooms. If you want a room near the hub, be sure to make your preference known when you make the reservation.

area. Standard rooms feature two double beds (some king-size beds are available). Amenities include a coffeemaker, hair dryer, iron and board, modem port, and limited room service. Small fridges are available, too.

In addition to a themed pool—which has a whirlpool and a sand volleyball court on the side—there is a pool in each guest area. La Vida health club and the Casa de Belleza salon are in the Casitas area. Bike and boat rentals are available. The nearly mile-long path around the lake, known as the Esplanade, is

excellent for biking and jogging. A convention center offers access to business services.

Where to eat: Maya Grill (steak and seafood) and the Pepper Market (food court).

Where to drink: Francisco's (lounge with Mexican snacks) and Siesta's (pool bar).

VITAL STATISTICS: Located near Animal Kingdom and Blizzard Beach. Coronado Springs; 1000 W. Buena Vista Dr.; Box 10000; Lake Buena Vista, FL 32830-1000; 407-939-1000; fax 407-939-3837.

Rates: Rooms begin at $139 in value season, $155 regular, and $175 peak; suites start at $300. A $15 per diem charge applies for each extra adult (beyond two) sharing a room.

Port Orleans Riverside

Southern hospitality takes two forms at this 2,048-room resort: pillared mansions with groomed lawns and *Gone With the Wind* elegance and, upriver, rustic homes with tin roofs and bayou charm. Rooms in the three-story Magnolia Bend mansions and the two-story Alligator Bayou lodges are similarly appointed.

The man-made Sassagoula River curls around the resort's main recreation area like a moat.

Bridges link guest lodgings with this area and the steamship-style building that houses eateries, a gift shop, and check-in facilities.

BIG DRAWS: Excellent value. An exceedingly lovely natural setting.

WORTH NOTING: Rooms here are smaller than those at Disney's deluxe hotels, but pleasantly inviting. Each features two double beds (some king-size beds and trundle beds are available). This is a large, sprawling resort with twice as many rooms as its French Quarter counterpart; some accommodations are a bit removed from the central building or the nearest bus stop. Room service delivers pizza and supplements from 4 P.M. to midnight. Bikes and boats may be rented. The resort's pathways are well suited for joggers, and a carriage path leads to Port Orleans French Quarter. Five additional pools (open 24 hours, provided they stay quiet) are sprinkled around the Bayou and Mansion guest areas. There is one whirlpool near the main pool.

Catch-and-release fishing excursions are offered, as is a stocked, secluded fishing hole (cane poles available). Guests may use the pool at Port Orleans

French Quarter in addition to the one here. New this year are 30-minute carriage rides ($30; call 407-WDW-PLAY for reservations) through the resort area.

Where to eat: Boatwright's Dining Hall (casual restaurant specializing in southern cuisine) and Riverside Mill (food court).

Where to drink: River Roost (fireplace and occasional entertainment) and Muddy Rivers (poolside refreshments).

VITAL STATISTICS: Port Orleans Riverside, located on a bank of the Sassagoula River, is within walking distance of Port Orleans French Quarter. Epcot and the

Port Orleans Riverside Tips

- The Sassagoula River Cruise is a pleasant outing and a convenient means of transportation to Downtown Disney.
- For optimal atmosphere and minimal walking, request a room in Magnolia Bend's Oak Manor, or lodge number 18 or 27 in the resort's Alligator Bayou section.
- Mansion rooms exude honeymoon-style elegance and seclusion.
- Elevators are available in the resort's Magnolia Bend section only.
- Try River Roost's southern snacks (consider the spicy Cajun Hot Nuts).
- The resort offers horse-drawn carriage rides.

Studios are close by, as are three of WDW's 18-hole golf courses. Port Orleans Riverside; 1251 Riverside Dr.; Box 10000; Lake Buena Vista, FL 32830-1000; 407-934-6000; fax 407-934-5777.

Rates: Rooms begin at $139 in value season, $155regular, and $175 peak. A $15 per diem charge applies for each extra adult (beyond two) sharing a room.

Port Orleans French Quarter

New Orleans's historic French Quarter is evoked in this resort's prim row house–style buildings, which are wrapped in ornate wrought-iron railings and set amid romantic gardens and tree-lined blocks. Old-fashioned lampposts add to the ambience, as do street signs such as *Rue D'Baga* and *Café Au Lait Way*.

The resort is entered via Port Orleans Square, an atrium with adjoining buildings that house the front desk, gift shop, and arcade

Port Orleans French Quarter Tips

- A convenient, though tiny, water shuttle ferries resort guests to and from Port Orleans Riverside and Downtown Disney.

- This is too pretty a place to wake up to a view of the parking lot, so consider reserving a room overlooking the gardens or splurge on riverscape digs. Note that pool views can spoil the ambience.

- Of the buildings with riverfront rooms, number 1 is nicely isolated. Buildings 2 and 5 are close to the pool area.

- Experience the area's romantic atmosphere via a bike ride along the river.

- Don't miss the fresh beignets (a true taste of the Big Easy), whose aroma regularly wafts through the festive food court.

- The main whirlpool is set off in a courtyard by vine-covered arches.

on one side, and a lounge and food court on the other.

Guestrooms are located in seven three-story buildings, which are set on either side of the central thoroughfare that begins just beyond Port Orleans Square. The whole enclave is set alongside a stand-in Mississippi known as the Sassagoula River. The Sassagoula River Cruise, which transports guests to Port Orleans French Riverside and Downtown Disney, is a pleasant and convenient way to travel.

BIG DRAWS: A good bang for the buck. The charming environs rank among Disney World's most memorable. It's the least sprawling of the moderate resorts.

WORTH NOTING: The pretty, homey rooms are a bit smaller than those at Disney's more expensive hotels but are perfectly comfortable. Each of the 1,008 rooms features two double beds; some king-size beds are available. A Dixieland band occasionally entertains in the main courtyard; a street artist may be available for portraits. A carriage path—ideal for jogging, strolling, and biking—wends alongside the river to Port Orleans Riverside, less than a mile upriver.

Bikes and boats may be rented. In addition to the swimming pool and whirlpool here, Port Orleans French Quarter guests are permitted use of Port Orleans Riverside's pool; they can also take advantage of its fishing hole (catch-and-release only). Guided fishing trips depart from the resort daily (reservations are required; 407-WDW-BASS).

Where to eat: Boatwright's Dining Hall (at Port Orleans Riverside) and Sassagoula Floatworks & Food Factory (food court with Mardi Gras ambience and inexpensive fare).

Where to drink: Mardi Grogs (pool bar) and Scat Cat's Club (for specialty drinks).

VITAL STATISTICS: Port Orleans French Quarter enjoys special access to Downtown Disney Marketplace via water taxi, which also links it with Port Orleans Riverside. It's close to Epcot, the Disney-MGM Studios, and three 18-hole golf courses as well. Port Orleans French Quarter; 2201 Orleans Dr.; Box 10000; Lake Buena Vista, FL 32830-1000; 407-934-5000; fax 407-934-5353.

Rates: Rooms begin at $139 in value season, $155 regular, and $175 peak. A $15 per diem charge applies for each extra adult (beyond two) sharing a room.

Value
All-Star Movies,
All-Star Music &
All-Star Sports Resorts

Bright in a manner normally reserved for toy packaging, these fun-loving resorts exist at the intersection of entertainment architecture and pop art. Picture a landscape in which three-story football helmets, cowboy boots, and Dalmatians are the norm, and you have an idea of the oversize sense of whimsy that governs the All-Star Movies, Music, and Sports resorts.

Each All-Star property has its own central check-in building, complete with food court, and its own pair of signature swimming pools. Each features ten guest buildings that are divided into five distinct (movies, music, or sports) themes and 1,920 themat-ically correct rooms.

Sports fans enjoy All-Star Sports resort's homages to basket-ball, baseball, football, tennis, and surfing. The All-Star Music resort makes exaggerated overtures to

calypso, jazz, Broadway, rock, and country music. All-Star Movies reprises *101 Dalmatians*, *The Mighty Ducks*, *Fantasia*, *The Love Bug*, and *Toy Story*.

BIG DRAW: All the advantages of staying on WDW turf at a fraction of the cost of its other resorts.

WORTH NOTING: Requests for specific motifs cannot be guaran-teed, but are likely to be met, considering the resorts' large capacity (384 rooms per theme, five themes per resort).

The rooms, which are the smallest of those at any WDW resort, are perfectly adequate, if a tad lack-ing in drawer space. Rooms with king-size beds are available on request, as are amenities such as down pillows and hair dryers.

On-site recreation is limited to two whimsically designed pools at each resort. Pizza delivery is available until midnight.

Where to eat: Each hotel has a vast, themed food court: All-Star Sports (End Zone); All-Star Music (Intermission); All-Star Movies (World Premiere).

Where to drink: At All-Star Sports: Team Spirits pool bar. At All-Star Music: Singing Spirits pool bar. At All-Star Movies: Silver Screen Spirits pool bar.

All-Star Resorts Tips

- These resorts attract families with small children in droves. All-Star Music tends to host large groups of young guests (think school bands, cheerleaders, etc.).

- For more quiet, request a third-floor room in a building far from the food court or main pool (at All-Star Music, it's Broadway or coun-try; at All-Star Sports, tennis or basketball; at All-Star Movies, *The Love Bug* or *The Mighty Ducks*).

- Reservations are required for lug-gage assistance upon check-out; call the night before.

- All-Star guests can rent boats at any of the other WDW resorts.

- Unless you plan to drive every-where, request a room near the lobby (i.e., bus stop).

VITAL STATISTICS: The All-Star resorts are close to Animal Kingdom and Blizzard Beach; Epcot and the Studios are also nearby. All-Star Movies; 1991 W. Buena Vista Dr.; Box 10000; Lake Buena Vista, FL 32830-1000; 407-939-7000; fax 407-939-7111. All-Star Music; 1801 W. Buena Vista Dr.; Box 10000; Lake Buena Vista, FL 32830-1000; 407-939-6000; fax 407-939-7222. All-Star Sports; 1701 W. Buena Vista Dr.; Box 10000; Lake Buena Vista, FL 32830-1000; 407-939-5000; fax 407-939-7333.

Rates: Rooms begin at $79 in value season, $99 regular, and $115 peak. A $10 per diem charge applies to each extra adult (beyond two) sharing a room.

Pop Century Resort

Open up a 20th-century time capsule and throw in a yo-yo, bowling pin, Rubik's Cube, cell phone, and other icons of the century's toys, fads, dance crazes, and classic and kooky catchphrases, and then turn it into a place for travelers to stay. That's Pop Century, one of the newest additions to Disney's family of value-priced resorts. Pop Century is made distinctive by an intentionally kitschy decorative style and

Pop Century Resort Tips

- Pop Century resort boasts a whopping 2,880 guestrooms, which could make reserving a room at the last minute a bit easier than at smaller resorts.

- Want to be near a pool? Request a room in the 1950s, 1960s, or 1980s lodge buildings; they're adjacent to the Bowling Pin, Hippy Dippy Pool, and Computer pools, respectively. Keep in mind that all three pools are equally bustling.

- This colorful resort is very popular with families. Buildings and areas by the computer pool have a slightly less frantic atmosphere.

larger-than-life icons found throughout the landscape.

BIG DRAW: Like the All-Star resorts, Pop Century provides a Disney resort experience at a fraction of the cost of other resorts.

WORTH NOTING: The five buildings in the 2,880-room Classic Years—each with a theme based on a different decade from the 1950s through the 1990s—began hosting guests in 2003. Rooms (which are smaller than those at other Disney resorts) are available with two double- or one king-size bed, and hair dryers, and other amenities can be requested.

For amusement, there are three pools to choose from, as well as an arcade for the young at heart. Pizza delivery is available.

Where to eat: Everything Pop is a food court in Classic Hall. It has four counter-service stations, a lounge area, plus a "grab and go" market.

Where to drink: Hippy Dippy pool bar. It also serves a wide variety of fast food.

VITAL STATISTICS: The resort is located near Disney's Wide World of Sports complex. Pop Century; 1050 Century Dr.; Box 10000; Lake Buena Vista, FL 32830-1000; 407-938-4000; fax 407-938-4039.

Rates: Rooms begin at $79 in value season, $99 regular, and $115 peak. A $10 per diem charge applies to each extra adult (beyond two) sharing a room.

Disney Cruise Line

The Disney Cruise Line fleet features two 2,700-passenger ships, each casually elegant and designed to recapture the majesty of early ocean liners. They're equipped to satisfy even the most savvy of cruisers, with a mix of traditional seafaring diversions and classic Disney touches. Recreation areas are designed to lure families and adults sans kids to different parts of the ship. Each ship has a pool, restaurant, and nighttime entertainment "district" earmarked for adults only.

Lest anyone forget who owns these vessels, Disney characters crop up from stem to stern. A statue of Mickey as helmsman greets arriving guests on the *Disney Magic*, Goofy hangs over the stern. Characters are also on hand to mix, mingle, and otherwise assist the captain.

By day, fun in the sun alternates with lunch, indoor distractions, and catnaps. When the sun goes down, the focus shifts to dining and party spots.

Cruise Line land-sea vacations begin with a stay at WDW and finish with a voyage on the *Disney Wonder*. At Port Canaveral, guests embark on a three- or four-night cruise to the Bahamas. (Seven-night Caribbean cruises with Eastern and Western itineraries take place aboard the *Disney Magic*.) En route to Castaway Cay, Disney's private isle, the *Wonder* makes a stop at Nassau.

BIG DRAWS: The ultimate surf-and-turf experience, Disney-style. Private island rendezvous.

WORTH NOTING: Each room has a safe, TV, hair dryer, small refrigerator, and telephone with "land line" (check rates before dialing). Facilities include three pools, a sports deck, and the Vista Spa & Salon. The ship boasts adult-oriented enrichment programs, deck parties, and two theaters (showing first-run films and musical stage shows).

Where to eat: On the *Disney Magic*, Animator's Palate (room undergoes a spectral metamorphosis), Parrot Cay (casual Caribbean), Lumière's (continental, casually elegant), and Palo (Italian fare, reserved for adults). Topsider Buffet is a casual daytime spot. On the *Disney Wonder*, Triton's replaces Lumière's, and Beach Blanket Buffet replaces Topsider. Should you wish to avoid the inevitable crush of wee ones, request the second dinner seating.

Where to drink: Both ships are home to the Promenade Lounge (a quiet, elegant bar), Diversions (sports bar), and Cove Cafe (adults-only coffee/cocktail lounge). Exclusive to the *Disney Magic* are Rockin' Bar D (band and deejay) and Sessions (an

Disney Cruise Line Tips

- Room keys can be used to charge drinks, merchandise, and salon services, as well as gratuities for servers and cabin crew.
- Palo, the adults-only dining room, is the only restaurant that requires reservations. Book it as soon as you're onboard.
- Unlike a visit to World Showcase, you really do leave the country on a Disney Cruise Line vacation. Pack a passport (or birth certificate with a raised seal).
- Surf the 'Net (for $.75 a minute, or, for a flat fee, enjoy unlimited use) as well as the waves, at the ships' Internet cafes. Wireless Internet service is available, too.

Land Ho!

Each voyage on the Disney Cruise Line includes at least one daylong stop at Castaway Cay, Disney's charted yet private isle. With all the perks of a tropical paradise, an afternoon at Castaway Cay is sure to cure even the most severe cases of Gilligan envy. Disney has maintained the island's natural beauty while accommodating a variety of activities, including volleyball, snorkeling, biking, and boating. The 1,000-acre Bahamian island features a mile-long stretch of secluded sand reserved for adult sun worshippers, as well as those seeking private open-air massages in cabanas overlooking the ocean. There's also a lunch buffet, bar, and more for Bahama mamas and papas to explore.

intimate piano bar). The *Disney Wonder* has Barrel of Laughs, Wave-Bands, and The Cadillac Lounge. Both ships have poolside bars.

VITAL STATISTICS: Shipboard accommodations are about 25 percent roomier than cabins on most other ships. Most have a queen-size bed or two twin-size beds and a convertible sofa or pull-down bed. A majority are outside staterooms with a bath and a half; almost half have verandas.

Rates: Twelve stateroom categories correspond to comparable rooms at Disney resorts. Inside and ocean-view staterooms yield Moderate resorts; veranda staterooms net Deluxe resorts. Value rates for a seven-night, land-sea vacation begin at $799 per person, based on double occupancy.

Price includes stateroom and Walt Disney World resort accommodations, park admission, and shipboard meals and recreation.

(Seven-night cruise-only packages also start at $799.)

Packages including airfare and ground transfers are available. Call 800-910-3659, or visit *www.disneycruise.com* for additional information.

Resorts on Hotel Plaza Boulevard

These resorts occupy a unique position among non-Disney resorts because they, along with four other hotels (Best Western Lake Buena Vista, Holiday Inn, DoubleTree Guest Suites, and Grosvenor), are within the boundaries of WDW.

Guests have easy access to Disney golf courses, reservations at select restaurants and dinner shows, and the opportunity to buy tickets for "E-Ride" nights at the Magic Kingdom.

All the hotels have Disney gift shops, as well as ESPN, and a WDW information channel. They also sell park (and other) tickets, and provide free bus service to the Magic Kingdom, Epcot, the Disney-MGM Studios, Animal Kingdom, Typhoon Lagoon, Blizzard Beach, and Downtown Disney (allow extra time for bus travel). *Note that the Hilton is the only resort on Hotel Plaza Blvd. that participates in the theme park "Extra Magic Hours" program (for details, see page 15).*

Rooms can be booked through the individual hotels or through WDW Central Reservations (407-934-7639).

Hilton

Set on 23 well-groomed acres, the 814-room Hilton has an air of laid-back gentility.

BIG DRAWS: Located across the road from the Downtown Disney Marketplace. Pool areas with adult appeal. Free transportation to all Disney golf courses.

WORTH NOTING: All guestrooms have minibars; corner rooms

Hilton Tips

- Rooms with the best views overlook the pools or the fountain at the hotel's entrance.
- For easy access to the pool, request a ground-floor room.

have balconies. There's a health club, two swimming pools, and two whirlpools, along with 24-hour room service. This is the only property on Hotel Plaza Boulevard to offer guests the "Extra Magic Hours" perk (see page 15).

Where to eat: Finn's Grill (Key West with steak and seafood dinners); Benihana Japanese steak house and sushi bar; Covington Mill (all-day dining in a cheery, New England setting); and Mainstreet Market (deli, ice cream counter, and well-stocked country store).

Where to drink: Rum Largo Pool Bar & Cafe (tropical drinks); John T's Sports Bar; and Mugs (wine and coffee).

VITAL STATISTICS: Conveniently located just across the road from the Downtown Disney Marketplace. Hilton; 1751 Hotel Plaza Blvd.; Lake Buena Vista, FL 32830; 407-827-4000 or 800-782-4414; fax 407-827-3890; *www.hilton-wdwv.com.*

Rates: Rooms are $160 to $345, and suites are $359 to $1,500, depending on the season.

Royal Plaza

As accommodating as its pineapple motif intimates, the Royal

Plaza is a cozy hotel with big adult appeal (the pineapple is a symbol of hospitality). Besides an outstanding pool area, there are four lighted tennis courts on the grounds of the resort.

BIG DRAWS: Nice pool area with large outdoor whirlpool and live music; adult ambience.

WORTH NOTING: The 394 rooms, including 22 suites, are divided between a 17-story tower and two-story wings. Each room has a sitting area, bath, safe, and mini-bar. Other amenities include a hair dryer, coffeemaker, and iron.
   Where to eat: Giraffe Grill; Marketessen (for snacks).
   Where to drink: Giraffe Grill and Sips (poolside bar).

VITAL STATISTICS: Located about a half mile from the Downtown Disney Marketplace. Royal

Royal Plaza Tips

- There are separate gamerooms for adults and for kids, and no one under 16 is allowed in the large fitness room.
- The enormous king rooms feature baths with separate glass-enclosed showers.
- The Burt Reynolds, Barbara Mandrell, and Bermuda suites are accessorized with pertinent memorabilia.

Plaza; Box 22203; 1905 Hotel Plaza Blvd.; Lake Buena Vista, FL 32830; 407-828-2828 or 800-248-7890; fax 407-827-3977; *www.royalplaza.com*.
   Rates: Guestrooms are $89 to $179 for up to five guests; suites range from $209 to $699.

Wyndham Palace Resort & Spa

The largest of the resorts along Hotel Plaza Blvd., the Wyndham Palace is a cluster of towers. The

A Great Beach Add-on

A stay at Disney's Vero Beach Resort—an oceanfront Disney Vacation Club property just two hours away by car—combines nicely with a WDW vacation. The resort's homey comforts are similar to those at Disney's Old Key West Resort (see page 61).

Among its assets are pristine beaches and proximity to manatee retreats and sunken ships fit for dive trips (this is called the Treasure Coast, after all). A tropical tangle separates the resort and beach. Packages combining a Vero Beach trip with a WDW visit are available. For more information, call 800-828-8101.

grounds are lushly landscaped, with shaded walkways. Inside, the decor is elegant. The reception area offers several cozy sitting nooks that invite lingering, and the Island Suite building has secluded courtyards. Many of the 1,014 rooms and suites have a private patio or balcony with a view of Spaceship Earth.

BIG DRAWS: A European-style spa (see page 180); popular nightspots; and many recreational options. Close proximity to the Downtown Disney Marketplace.

WORTH NOTING: All guestrooms have ceiling fans, two phones (one bedside, one on the desk), voice mail, and 24-hour room service. Four rooms feature whirlpool tubs. One- and two-bedroom suites are available. There's a fitness center, a luxurious spa, a sand volleyball court, three pools, three lighted tennis courts, and two lakeside gazebos.

Where to eat: Arthur's 27 (rooftop spot with a continental menu); the Outback restaurant (specializing in fresh seafood and Black Angus beef; not part of the chain bearing the same name); Watercress Cafe and Pastry Shop (24-hour counter service, baked goods, and deli

Wyndham Palace Tips

- The Top of the Palace lounge provides a good view of Epcot's fireworks, serves desserts and many wines by the glass, and offers a free glass of champagne at sunset.
- For the allergy-prone, 65 rooms feature filtered air and water.

items); and the Courtyard Mini-Market (for snacks and smoothies in a quiet outdoor setting).

Where to drink: The Laughing Kookaburra Good Time Bar (spirited spot known for live music); and Top of the Palace (quiet lounge with a stunning view and live entertainment Wednesday through Saturday).

VITAL STATISTICS: The resort is across from the Downtown Disney Marketplace. Wyndham Palace Resort & Spa; 1900 Buena Vista Dr.; Lake Buena Vista, FL 32830; 407-827-2727 or 800-327-2990; fax 407-827-6034; *www.wyndhampalace.com*.

Rates: Room rates range from $129 to $269; rates for suites are $229 to $529.

Spectacular fireworks come with the territory at Walt Disney World.

Theme Parks: The Big Four

To experience Walt Disney World's quartet of major theme parks without children is tantamount to celebrating a major holiday without the complication of traffic or in-laws. It's positively liberating.

Let the theme parks runneth over with strollers and too-tired toddlers. As adults free to roam the Magic Kingdom, Epcot, Disney-MGM Studios, and Animal Kingdom on our own terms, we need not be concerned with such things. We are a minority (read: non-school-age individuals under no obligation whatsoever to facilitate the entertainment of any maturity-challenged person within 47 square miles) in one of those rare settings in which the minority holds all the advantages.

If we sometimes feel a bit conspicuous touring the parks as unaccompanied adults, it's because we're flaunting the inherent freedom. We're taking advantage of the fact that we're among friends who readily agree that a shaded bench, a nap in a hammock, or a soak in the whirlpool back at the resort would really hit the spot right now. We are free to buzz through the Magic Kingdom at a clip no character-conscious family could maintain, or meander through Epcot's World Showcase pavilions at what might be called an escargot pace. All the while we're taking advantage of time-saving techniques like Disney's Fastpass, which allows walk-on access to several popular attractions in all four theme parks.

With a dizzying array of attractions to choose from, the task of mapping out an itinerary is a critical one. Fight the urge to see and do everything and craft a manageable list of must-sees. You're on vacation. It's a time to relax and have fun.

You may want to devote day one to the Magic Kingdom to get that long-anticipated dose of classic Disney magic. Then, with Cinderella's castle a delightful memory, you'll appreciate a day at Epcot on its own merits. Follow Epcot with a day at the Disney-MGM Studios. (Enchantment is a great chaser for enlightenment.)

If you're raring to go on safari or be chased by a dinosaur, spend your fourth day exploring Animal Kingdom. (This also happens to be the order in which the parks opened: Magic Kingdom, 1971; Epcot, 1982; Disney-MGM Studios, 1989; and Animal Kingdom, 1998.)

MAGIC KINGDOM

As once-upon-a-timish and happily-ever-afteresque a place as exists, the Magic Kingdom is proof that you can judge a park by its largest icon (in this case, Cinderella Castle). While it is the most character-intensive and certainly the strongest kid magnet of all the parks, flying elephants couldn't keep us away.

What puts the Magic Kingdom on the adult map? For starters, it's manageable. Most of the essentials here are easily traversed in a day. High on the list of imperatives is Disney's own mountain range—Space Mountain, Splash Mountain, and

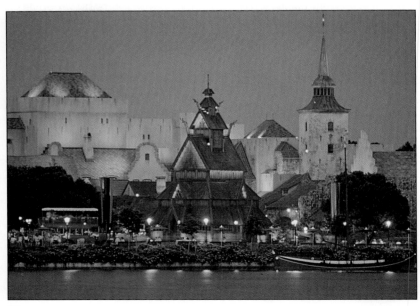

Big Thunder Mountain Railroad—an undeniably thrilling threesome of rides.

What it lacks in fine cuisine and opportunities to imbibe, it more than makes up for in magic. Disney has made a real art of coaxing folks into a state of wonderment that seldom occurs in adulthood, and this park represents that art taken to its highest level. It's a rare adult who doesn't fall under the spell of the Magic Kingdom's ball-room of waltzing apparitions, or its convincing den of leering pirates. For nostalgic whimsy, there are kiddie rides such as Peter Pan's Flight that don't aspire to recapture the magic of childhood so much as to momen-tarily revive it.

The nighttime parade is also bound to reacquaint you with your inner child. This spectacle of fiber-optic delight showcases 600,000 miniature bulbs that light in wildly changing patterns, and move in perfect concert with sound effects and a musical score. The parade is absolutely illuminating.

Of course, wall-to-wall kids can get on anyone's nerves after a while, so some strategies are in order. First, master the art of noticing little ones only when they are being cute. To keep the "magic barometer" from falling, take advantage of less crowded evening hours, and weave in and out of major traffic zones (Fantasyland and Mickey's Toontown Fair are generally the most congested areas; Liberty Square, the least).

Seek refuge in the quiet nooks described in the margins of this chapter and in such havens as The Hall of Presidents; for a bigger break, indulge in a leisurely lunch at one of the resorts that are easily accessible via monorail.

Save Time in Line

DISNEP's
FASTPASS

Want to waltz onto an attraction without waiting in line? By using Disney's Fastpass system—complimentary (at press time, but that may change) to guests holding all valid ticket media—at selected attractions in all four theme parks, you can do just that. How does it work? Slip your admis-sion ticket into the machine. It will spit out your ticket along with a timed voucher. Come back at any point within the voucher's time frame and you'll bypass the long wait (aka "the stand-by line"). Consult the Touring Priorities in the margins of this chapter for a roster of Fastpass attractions, and check each park's guidemap for a current list of attractions that feature this service.

GETTING ORIENTED: Go through the turnstiles, pass an area with rental lockers, and you're in Town Square, the cul-de-sac at the foot of Main Street. From here look straight out to the park's most recognizable landmark, Cinderella Castle. It's at the opposite end of Main Street, behind an area known as the Hub, or Central Plaza. On the left before the Hub is the main **Tip Board**, an information board listing current waiting times for the park's most popular attractions. It's helpful to think of the layout of the Magic Kingdom as a tree. Main Street, U.S.A., is the trunk; the other six themed areas—Adventureland, Fantasyland, Frontierland, Liberty Square, Mickey's Toontown Fair, and Tomorrowland—dangle at the ends of the tree's gnarled boughs (actually bridges). The

---

Magic Kingdom Hours

The Magic Kingdom is usually open from 9 A.M. to 7 P.M.; park hours are extended during holiday periods and summer months, abbreviated during slower times.

Call 407-824-4321 or log onto *www.disneyworld.com* for details. One-day park admission is $59.75, plus tax, for adults. Prices are subject to change.

first bridge on your left leads to Adventureland; the second bridge to Liberty Square and Frontierland; the pathway straight ahead passes through Cinderella Castle on its way to the heart of Fantasyland; another bridge passes to the right of the castle to enter Fantasyland nearest Mickey's Toontown Fair and Tomorrowland; and the bridge on your immediate right leads directly to Tomorrowland. The lands are also linked via a broad footpath that winds its way behind the castle.

A Walking Tour

Let's begin our tour in **Town Square**, which is important as the location of **City Hall**, where a person can make all manner of inquiries and arrangements (no, you can't get married here). Even if you don't need to pick up a guidemap, make reservations for a restaurant, exchange foreign currency, or check the lost and found, stop by to play Q&A with the informed folks behind the counter. Note that the local ATMs are under the train station, near the lockers.

The archway we walked under to get here is the foundation of the **Walt Disney World Railroad** depot. A 1928 steam engine that once carted sugarcane across the Yucatán now hauls freight (largely first-time visitors, train buffs, and homesick commuters) on a 20-minute loop around the Magic Kingdom. It's a fine way to get to Frontierland and Mickey's Toontown Fair if you don't want to walk. Onward.

Main Street, U.S.A.

Main Street is notable as the tidy strip of storefronts where adults gawk at, then feel compelled to photograph, Cinderella Castle. This year, the beloved castle is especially photogenic—as it's decked out in festive finery in honor of Disneyland's golden anniversary. There's no shame in it; but don't be so distracted that you overlook the street's early 1900s charm. Amusements here are decidedly low-key. For grooming as entertainment, there's the Harmony Barber Shop (tucked in between the Emporium and the Horse Barn), where the Dapper Dans sometimes accompany a haircut. Definitely check out their sweet four-part harmonies. Main Street stays open a half hour after the rest of the park has closed, although the shops (see "Shopping" in the *Diversions* chapter) tend to be less crowded in early afternoon.

Tomorrowland

Futuristic in a way that would likely go right over Buck Rogers's head, Tomorrowland is a city of the future that never was. Because it's home base for one of the park's most popular attractions—Space Mountain—Tomorrowland is best visited first thing after the gates open.

Space Mountain, a must-do for all but those who categorically avoid the fast stuff, is one to head for straightaway, as Fastpasses may run out before day's end. Once the stand-by line reaches outside this white structure at the far side of Tomorrowland, it doesn't generally ease up until evening. To gauge whether Space Mountain is for you, consider how you feel about roller coasters. This one rockets through a space-age sheath of darkness, shooting stars, and flashing lights. It's a fast and furious ride with special effects—an absolute must for the adventurous, and an unforgettable adventure for the suddenly courageous. Space Mountain is also a turbulent ride, so passengers must be in good health and free from heart conditions, back and neck problems, and other physical limitations (such as pregnancy), as the posted signs warn. If you've just eaten, wait awhile. If you decide you would rather observe the rockets' red glare going only seven miles per hour, the **Tomorrowland Transit Authority** offers a preview to Space Mountain and other attractions on a track that's strictly horizontal. The train is boarded in the heart of Tomorrowland

near **Astro Orbiter** (an elevated ride with rockets that's for kids but good fun for adults; it seems to go faster the lower you fly in your Buck Rogers–mobile).

Next door, in the spot that used to house an attraction featuring a fearsome alien, is **Stitch's Great Escape!** Like its predecessor, this attraction also involves an AWOL alien—but this time, he's really more of a menace than a threat and merely impolite, as opposed to angry. The alien in question is none other than Experiment 626, aka Stitch, from the Disney animated film *Lilo and Stitch*.

One need not be familiar with the film to get a kick out of Stitch's antics (though it helps!). In this "prequel" to the movie, the rambunctious critter is being transported to the Prisoner Processing Center at Galactic Federation Headquarters. Audience members are enlisted to guard him while he awaits his sentence. No offense, but theme park guests make lousy guards, as Experiment 626 escapes several dozen times a day. During his little bouts of giddy freedom, he is known to wreak havoc on audience members. Don't be surprised if he messes your meticulously coiffed do or hocks an alien loogie on your head. And to think, you *paid* for this. . . .

Across the street is the Day-Glo adventure-zone known as **Buzz Lightyear's Space Ranger Spin** (yes, grown-ups love it). Here *Toy Story*'s Mr. Infinity and Beyond solicits your assistance in cuffing the universe's most insidious battery hoarder. The 4½-minute journey is part video game, part shooting gallery, thanks to your spaceship's spin-control joystick and laser guns (how else to combat the likes of Rock'em Sock'em Robot?).

Heading north toward Fantasyland, you pass Space Mountain and come upon the rather low-octane **Tomorrowland Indy Speedway**.

Mickey's Toontown Fair

This tiny blip between Tomorrowland and Fantasyland is a land geared toward the very young. When you visit the area, you'll find an old-fashioned county fair in progress.

The cuteness is in the details (Mickey's ear-bearing crops, Minnie as the local craft queen). Don't miss your chance to tour

Touring Priorities

DON'T MISS	DON'T OVERLOOK	DON'T KNOCK YOURSELF OUT
Splash Mountain*	Walt Disney World Railroad	The Barnstormer
Space Mountain*	Liberty Belle Riverboat	The Enchanted Tiki Room— Under New Management
Big Thunder Mountain Railroad*	Mickey's Toontown Fair	Swiss Family Treehouse
The Haunted Mansion	Mad Tea Party	Snow White's Scary Adventures
Pirates of the Caribbean	Tomorrowland Transit Authority	Dumbo the Flying Elephant
Buzz Lightyear's Space Ranger Spin*	The Hall of Presidents	Stitch's Great Escape!
It's a Small World	Tomorrowland Indy Speedway	Tom Sawyer Island
Peter Pan's Flight*	Country Bear Jamboree	The Magic Carpets of Aladdin
The Many Adventures of Winnie the Pooh*	Astro Orbiter	*Fastpass attraction as of press time. Consult your guidemap for new additions.
Mickey's PhilharMagic*	Cinderella's Golden Carrousel	
Jungle Cruise		

the homes of Mickey and Minnie. At **Mickey's Country House**, take a peek in the kitchen but watch out—he's in the process of remodeling. Attractions are primarily for kids, but it's still fun to wander. For a one-stop character meeting, the **Toontown Hall of Fame** can't be beat. Wanna meet the big cheese himself? Mickey greets guests in the barn behind his cottage. And if you're looking to take some baby steps before venturing onto Space Mountain, **The Barnstormer at Goofy's Wiseacre Farm** may be just your speed.

Fantasyland

The optimum way to take in this cheery land is to visit just before and during the daily 3 P.M. parade or in the evening when the parks are open late. Because there is nothing adult about Fantasyland—whimsy is the name of the game.

That said, certain attractions are so artfully executed that they transcend the kiddie genre. Of these, the recently spruced up **It's a Small World**—a ten-minute boat ride through the happiest, busiest, and most diversely populated dollhouse on the planet—is surely the most elaborate. Much more subtle is

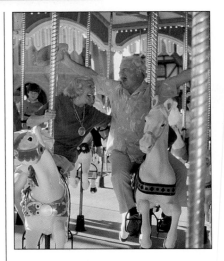

Peter Pan's Flight, an alluring sprinkle of pixie dust in which you can—and do—fly for three minutes above absolutely delightful scenes of Captain Hook and nighttime London in a pirate ship built for two.

Fantasyland's newest attraction, **Mickey's PhilharMagic**, brings many of your favorite characters to in-your-face life in a 3-D musical show starring Mickey and Donald, plus such other Disney favorites as Ariel (of *Little Mermaid* fame), Aladdin and Jasmine (from *Aladdin*), and Simba (direct from *The Lion King*)—all coming your way from a towering 150-foot-wide screen.

Then there are the purely nostalgic attractions, worth your time only if you're hankering to relive a certain story or amusement ride from your past. Have a thing for carousels in general or **Cinderella's Golden Carrousel** in particular? Go for it. Think you'd get a huge kick out of squeezing your group into an oversize teacup and spinning yourselves silly? Get to the **Mad Tea Party**. Don't skip **Dumbo the Flying Elephant** if you'll regret it later, but at the same time, don't expect to be wowed by a straightforward kiddie attraction such as **Snow White's Scary Adventures**. Although it has more happy moments than it did in the old days, the twisting journey still feels like a trip through a witch-filled fun house. **The Many Adventures of Winnie the Pooh** is a sweetly tempting honey jar of a journey through the Hundred Acre Wood.

Whatever you do, don't miss the mosaic murals beneath the open archway of **Cinderella Castle**. No less than a million well-placed pieces of Italian glass tell the tale, ugly stepsisters, glass slipper, and all.

Liberty Square

Tucked between Fantasyland and Frontierland, this small area tends to be relatively peaceful. Brick and clapboard buildings carry the theme—Colonial America—as does the Liberty Tree, a 130-something oak tree hung with 13 lanterns to recall the original Colonies.

Though Liberty Square has just a few attractions, it still takes more than an hour to see them all. **The Hall of Presidents** merits attention not just as a well-delivered 20-minute dose of patriotism in which Abraham Lincoln speaks, but as a chance to observe all chief executives of our country in action. The shifting, swaying, and nodding (and snoozing) begins the moment the curtain rises on the impeccably dressed group of Audio-Animatronic figures. The pace is slow, but just right for an air-conditioned theater with comfy seats. Don't be intimidated if there is a big line—this is one *big* theater.

The Liberty Belle Riverboat —a large, romantic, paddle wheel-driven steamboat that makes 17-minute loops around Tom Sawyer Island — is a pleasant distraction, especially on a steamy afternoon. Don't ask what **The Haunted Mansion** is doing in Liberty Square. Just note that it's a not-to-be-missed experience overrun with clever special effects and ghoulish delights (your typical ballroom of waltzing ghosts, door knockers that knock by themselves, and spirited grave-yards). On your way in, be sure to stop and read the epitaphs. They're killer funny.

Frontierland

This land conjures something of the Old West, with a little country charm thrown in for good measure. Although there's more to Frontierland than mountains, it is most notable as the home to two of the Magic Kingdom's most addictive thrills—Splash Mountain and Big Thunder Mountain Railroad.

The first thing to know about **Splash Mountain** is that it's okay to feel anxious just watch-

---

Quiet Escapes

- Rose garden on the right as you face Cinderella Castle
- Cinderella Wishing Well, near the castle
- Walt Disney World Railroad
- Harmony Barber Shop
- Shaded tables behind the shops in Liberty Square
- *Liberty Belle* Riverboat
- Rocking chairs on the front porches of Frontierland and Liberty Square shops
- Tomorrowland Transit Authority
- Anywhere but Fantasyland and Toontown

---

ing the log boats plunge down this ride's big drop—you're looking at one of the steepest flumes in the world (although it appears to be a straight drop, it's actually 52 feet down at a 45-degree angle). Even so, this water-bound ride themed to Disney's *Song of the South* is tamer than it looks from the ground. Steep plunge aside, there are just three smaller dips during the 11-minute trip.

If you're like us, the first time around you'll be way too nervous about when "it" is going to happen to fully appreciate the delightful humor, enormously appealing characters, and uplifting "Zip-A-Dee-Doo-Dah" ambience. But coax yourself into riding once and you'll be hooked. If you prefer to get splashed, not drenched, sit in the back and on the left of the log. Onlookers should note that a water cannon takes aim at the observation bridge without warning. A note on timing: Both Splash Mountain and Big Thunder Mountain Railroad tend to draw big crowds all day; your best bet is to shoot for early morning or evening.

Think of **Big Thunder Mountain Railroad** as a thrilling ride on the mild side. As roller coasters go, this one's exciting as much for the

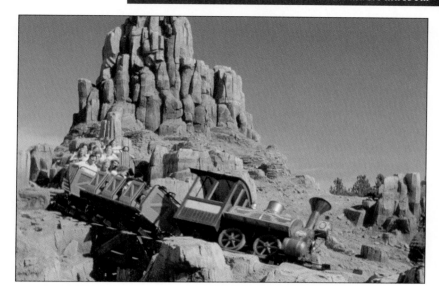

surrounding scenery your runaway mine train races past—bats, goats, a flooded mining town—as for the ride itself. Big Thunder Mountain Railroad is not nearly so fast or turbulent as Space Mountain, and nothing in its four-minute series of reverberating swoops and jerky turns comes close to Splash Mountain's intimidating plunge. For a bigger thrill, ride it after dark, when you can't clearly see what lies ahead, even from the first car. For the wildest of rides, request a seat near the back.

But Frontierland's appeal extends beyond its two high-profile attractions. The **Country Bear Jamboree**, a 16-minute musical variety show put on by 20 or so hopelessly corny Audio-Animatronic bears, is the perfect attraction to hit when you're feeling a little punchy. **Tom Sawyer Island**, just a raft ride away, provides a nice break from the more structured parts of the park.

Adventureland

Adventureland has been transformed into the marketplace of *Aladdin*'s Agrabah. One part is **The Magic Carpets of Aladdin**, a Dumbo-style ride on which riders pilot mystical flying carpets. Among this land's other attractions are the immensely popular Pirates of the Caribbean and Jungle Cruise, best visited during the early morning and evening.

The Enchanted Tiki Room— Under New Management is worthy of a traffic-stopping whistle. The nine-minute affair still showcases Disney's earliest Audio-Animatronic figures but adds plucky company to the chirping, chattering birds of yore. *Aladdin*'s Iago and *The Lion King*'s Zazu push the limits of caged-bird choreography. Remember **Pirates of the Caribbean** as an elaborate, engaging boat ride in which you watch pirates raid a Caribbean village. A classic attraction, it provides plenty of leering, jeering examples of how wonderfully, almost frighteningly realistic Disney's Audio-Animatronics can be. Note that the ten-minute Pirates of the Caribbean ride includes a small dip and some loud cannon blasts.

The **Jungle Cruise**, another classic, transports passengers on a steamy ten-minute boat trip through the Nile Valley and the Amazon rain forest. Although the flora is quite beautiful, the lines for this ride can be prohibitively long—use Fastpass if it's offered. Finally, if you feel up to climbing some serious stairs, **Swiss Family Treehouse** is a replica of the Swiss Family Robinsons' ingenious perch that's worth the effort, even though the tree itself is a product of the prop department's imagination.

Entertainment

The character-laden floats in Disney's Share a Dream Come True parade take over Main Street daily at 3 P.M. The Dapper Dans often pop onto Main Street to serenade guests with four-part harmonies.

When the park is open late, the spectacular fireworks show, Wishes, is presented on selected nights. The dazzling SpectroMagic light parade, which replaced The Main Street Electrical Parade, wends its luminous way down Main Street on select nights too.

If there are two performances of the parade, the later one is often less crowded. Note that the evening parade is subject to change.

Check a park guidemap and times guide for the parade route and show schedules.

EPCOT

Think of Epcot as an extraordinary balancing act. This park is huge—about three times the size of the Magic Kingdom—and it performs two rather ambitious feats simultaneously. While the part of Epcot known as Future World offers a multifaceted look at what lies ahead for humankind, its alter ego, World Showcase, transports guests (at least in spirit) to many different countries. This division of labor works well, and it certainly keeps things interesting here. While the more serious-minded Future World is striving to spark the

imagination, illuminate the technological future, and heighten environmental awareness, lively World Showcase is serving forth Oktoberfest, traditional English pub grub, and panoramic views of France, China, and Canada.

As Future World is ushering visitors into an ultramodern hydroponic greenhouse, World Showcase is escorting others along a calm river deep in the heart of Mexico and over a stormy Norwegian sea. Together, the two entities stimulate guests to discover new things about people, places, and, indeed, their own curiosity.

If Epcot boasts a tremendous following among legal voters, it's because it has more of the things adults appreciate: live entertainment; quiet gardens; beer, wine, and frozen drinks; tasteful shops and galleries; international cuisine; sophisticated restaurants;

and specialty coffees—and that's just the supplementary stuff. Epcot also woos the older crowd by making Mickey a little more scarce and by splicing enrichment of one form or another into the greater part of its amusements. It appeals to adults on a purely aesthetic level as well: World Showcase, wrapped around a vast lagoon, has a commanding natural and architectural beauty that changes with each border crossing. And Future World more than holds its own with the massive, gleaming silver geosphere of Spaceship Earth. Not surprisingly, we've met a number of Walt Disney World regulars who spend their entire vacations here at Epcot.

Epcot has its die-hard Future World fans and its World Showcase fanatics, but most visitors list favorite pavilions on both sides of the lagoon. Ongoing renovations and additions to Epcot make this especially true today. Disney Imagineers have made smart changes in

Entertainment

Epcot's entertainment slate is ever-changing. So pick up a times guide at Guest Relations (or elsewhere in the park) and check it often.

In Future World, acrobats and a trash-can percussive unit dressed in custodial wear are popular head-turners.

The Innoventions Fountain erupts into a computer-choreographed water ballet every 15 minutes.

In addition, each World Showcase pavilion has performers, any of whom could be appearing at some point during your visit. Among the possibilities: a rock 'n' roll band in Canada, a mop-top band paying tribute to the British Invasion in the United Kingdom, belly dancers in Morocco, drummers in Japan, oompah musicians in Germany, and acrobats in China.

The American Adventure features the Voices of Liberty and American Vybe a cappella groups and stage shows at America Gardens Theatre.

Epcot's IllumiNations: Reflections of Earth all but sets fire to the senses in its dramatic, hypnotic simulation of our planet's evolution. This nightly finale starts off with a bang and ends on an even more explosive note. Stand anywhere along the promenade and prepare to be moved.

Keep in mind that the lineup of entertainment is ever-changing and may be altogether different when you visit Epcot.

Epcot's entertainment mix that have lightened up Future World, livened up World Showcase, and in the process, earned the theme park a fresh crop of admirers—both young and old.

We'll describe the attractions later so that we can first present "The Official Six Things We Bet You Didn't Know You Could Do at Epcot" list: (1) You can get some terrific gardening tips. (2) You can simultaneously break a sweat and split the 100th annual Rose Bowl Parade right down the middle. (Pedaling against the tide, and seemingly catching floats, bands, horses, and majorettes quite by surprise, we got a Wonder Cycle up to 15 miles per hour.) (3) You can experience the British Invasion. Or at least think you did, when you hear this band playing Beatles tunes. (4) You can watch a butterfly open its wings for the first time. If you want, you can nibble on a freshly picked spearmint sprig while that beautiful orange-barred sulphur butterfly decides when to flee the hatching box. (5) You can send a picture postcard of yourself anywhere in the world via e-mail. (6) You can get an impromptu lesson in belly dancing from an obliging Moroccan dancer.

Hot Tips

- Not a morning person? Head to crowd-free World Showcase (opening around 11 A.M.) while everyone else is in Future World.
- Fight the urge to start at Spaceship Earth. The line thins out as the day wears on.
- Epcot is bigger than it seems, so allow yourself plenty of time to get from place to place—especially if you've already got reservations for a meal at a World Showcase restaurant.

The most important thing to know about Epcot is that it is no small undertaking. Even the choosiest visitor will need two full days to cover the park effectively at a comfortable pace. Since Future World and World Showcase keep different hours, strategically minded guests will do well to follow our lead. In the name of efficiency, here's what we say: Take in a few key Future World pavilions during the hours before World Showcase opens. Explore World Showcase during the early afternoon, when Future World is most congested. Return to Future World to explore a few more pavilions during the relatively uncongested hours of late afternoon and early evening. Finally, revisit World Showcase during pleasant evening hours to experience the beauty of the park at twilight, as well as IllumiNations.

95

GETTING ORIENTED: It's helpful to think of Epcot as the park with the hourglass figure. In this conception, the gleaming silver ball of Spaceship Earth is the head and northernmost point; the other Future World pavilions, arranged on either side of Spaceship Earth in southward arches, form the outline of Epcot's "upper body"; and the promenade of World Showcase pavilions connects to Future World at Epcot's "waist" and, tracing the lines of a long, full skirt, wraps around World Showcase Lagoon. The American Adventure pavilion, located due south of Spaceship Earth along the bottom hem of the World Showcase skirt, effectively serves as the foot of Epcot.

Visitors should come prepared to do a great deal of walking, as the World Showcase Promenade itself is 1.2 miles around. Avid walkers and the health-conscious will be interested to know that a person typically covers more than two miles in one full day of touring Epcot. Don't be dismayed, though; Epcot is equipped with plenty of resting spots (see the margins of this section for tips to the whereabouts of said nooks), as well as a key foot-saving alternative. Water taxis link Showcase Plaza at the foot of Future World with Germany and Morocco, located at the farthest corners of World Showcase. Many seniors who choose to tour the smaller theme parks on foot rent a wheelchair or a self-driven Electric Convenience Vehicle (ECV) here at Epcot.

A Walking Tour

Our tour begins at the main entrance. This is where you take care of logistics while the gleaming ball of Spaceship Earth offers a 16-million-pound hint as to the precise direction of Future World. Epcot's monorail station is right outside the gates here, as is an ATM (located on the far left just before you enter the park). On the far right side of the entranceway, also outside the gates, you can exchange currency, make a phone call, and pick up any cumbersome purchases you arranged to have forwarded here during your visit.

Note: If you need to use any of these services mid-visit, have your hand stamped upon exiting so that you may re-enter the park. Lost and Found is in the Guest Relations lobby at Innoventions East. As you close in on the big ball, remember that there are still more services in its shadows. If you need a storage locker, pass around Spaceship Earth's right side. Otherwise, keep left. This course will lead you past the stroller and wheelchair rentals.

If you haven't made dining plans, stop by Guest Relations by Spaceship Earth to make restaurant reservations or hold your horses until you get to the eatery of your choice. Otherwise, focus on Innoventions Plaza, where you'll find the **Tip Board**, listing wait times for popular attractions.

Future World

You know you're in Future World when you see a thunderous fountain that acts like it owns the place, something resembling a remarkably oversize golf ball that would require a club bigger than the Empire State Building, kaleidoscopic fiber-optic patterns in the walkway, gardens that could pass for modern art, and freewheeling water fountains that do swan dives and geyser imitations.

This land is awash in the sort of grand music that might trumpet the credits of an Academy Award–winning film. And it wears its sleek architecture and futuristic landscaping like a power suit.

The nine themed pavilions that make up Future World document humanity's progress in this world

Touring Priorities

DON'T MISS	DON'T OVERLOOK	DON'T KNOCK YOURSELF OUT
Soarin'*	Spaceship Earth	El Rio del Tiempo boat ride in Mexico
Test Track*	China**	Innoventions
Universe of Energy	Italy	Journey Into Imagination with Figment
The Living Seas	Living with the Land*	
Honey, I Shrunk the Audience*	Mexico	
France**	Morocco	* Fastpass attraction as of press time.
The American Adventure**	Germany	
Canada**	United Kingdom	** Pay close attention to performance schedules.
Maelstrom*	Circle of Life	
Mission: SPACE*	Norway	
(but ONLY if motion sickness is a non-issue and you have no health issues whatsoever)	Wonders of Life	

and offer visions of our technological fate. Such major concerns as communications, health, and the environment serve as springboards for the attractions, which make stimulating experiences of topics that commonly make boring conversation.

If you haven't paid a visit here lately, you'll notice that an ongoing tweaking spree has invigorated Future World. In fact, Test Track, Mission: SPACE, and the popular new Soarin'attraction put Epcot in a novel spot—atop the thrill seeker's list.

A reminder: This park tour is designed to provide a sense of place, not an itinerary.

Spaceship Earth

This 180-foot-tall "geosphere" sticks out like a wayward planet come to roost. You may be interested to learn that the silver exterior comes from layers of anodized aluminum and polyethylene, and is composed of 11,324 triangular panels, not all of equal size or shape (although it takes a keen eye to discern any differences). Or maybe you would rather hear the story of how the gleaming exterior funnels every raindrop that hits it into World Showcase Lagoon.

The **Spaceship Earth** ride inside the geosphere winds past exquisitely detailed three-dimensional scenes, tracing the evolution of human communication using Audio-Animatronic figures that here, in their element, seem more natural than many sitcom actors. In about 14 minutes you've gone from Cro-Magnon grunts all the way to the fabled information superhighway. Narration by Jeremy Irons adds an element of drama.

The finale provides a forward-looking finish for Spaceship Earth. Take away the lasers and it would still be the ride's biggest head-turner. This popular attraction—your worst bet first thing in the morning—is least crowded during the hours just prior to park closing.

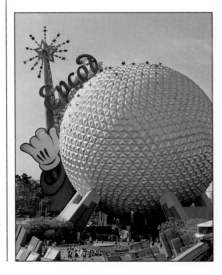

Innoventions

Think of the latest incarnation of Innoventions as a trip down future lane. Disney recast this showcase of technological goodies as entertaining rest stops and scenery along a very important piece of pavement: The Road to Tomorrow. When it comes to the traffic on this freeway, pedestrians —and the occasional electric car—rule the road.

If The Road to Tomorrow is frequently congested, it's because Innoventions is a bright labyrinth of activity that hot rods and Sunday drivers alike find difficult to pass through quickly. Well-marked exits ensure that you won't miss a single turnoff (hands-on exhibit), even if you're looking at your handy, dandy road map upside down. That's right, there's a road map.

The Living Seas

The Caribbean is not as far away as you think. If you want to catch a wave, some mammoth lettuce-munching manatees, and a richly stocked coral reef environment (pop.: 2,000) that even a scuba diver would find extraordinary, look no further. This pavilion, dedicated to the study of oceanography and ocean ecology, ranks among Epcot's most inspired areas. During the toasty summer months, it's particularly refreshing to ogle The Living Seas' *pièce de résistance*, a 5.7-million-gallon tank in which a simulated Caribbean Sea and man-made reef support a glorious array of life, including sharks, dolphins, and sea turtles.

To immerse yourself thoroughly without getting wet, take a make-believe voyage to the bottom of the sea at the **Caribbean Coral Reef**. This journey features a waterlogged film that takes you on a simulated descent to the ocean floor, and, finally, to the **Sea Base Alpha**. Here, you can linger all you like in front of enormous eight-inch-thick windows to the undersea world. Exhibits offer insight into marine research methods and—unless you encounter those endangered, impossibly animated sea barges known as manatees frequently in your travels—compelling reasons to stick around awhile. In addition to colorful sea life (including real-life versions of *Finding Nemo* characters) you can actually interact with Crush, that wacky, animated turtle. The short-but-enormously-popular "Turtle Talk with Crush" has to be seen to be believed.

99

Of course, no seafaring adventure is complete without the opportunity to shout "Land ho!" so it's only right that The Land is the next pavilion.

The Land

This popular six-acre plot explores themes related to food and farming while planting seeds of environmental consciousness. Underneath this pavilion's dramatic skylighted roof, you'll find a well-balanced slate of attractions, a bountiful food court, and a lazy Susan of a restaurant, the Garden Grill, which rotates very slowly past several of the ecosystems featured in the pavilion's boat ride. All things considered, The Land merits two green thumbs up as the purveyor of one of Future World's strongest lineups.

The **Living with the Land** boat ride is an informative 13½-minute journey that escorts you through a stormy prairie, a

windswept desert, and a South American rain forest en route to experimental greenhouses and an area given over to fish farming. The dripping, squawking rain forest is so realistic, you'd need to chomp on a faux fern to convince yourself it's all plastic. The narration is an interesting commentary on the history and future of agriculture. The greenhouses show futuristic technology at work on real crops (many of which are served right here at Epcot), with NASA experiments and cucumbers in

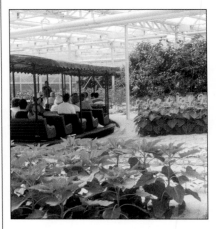

desert training among the highlights. This popular attraction is best visited in the morning or during the hours just prior to park closing. ***The Circle of Life*** is an ecological fable featuring Timon and Pumbaa, the wisenheimer meerkat-warthog duo from

The Lion King, as developers, and Simba as the environmentally sensitive lion. The 20-minute film includes stunning nature footage.

If you, like many humans, have ever had that happy dream in which you can fly—this is your chance to live it while actually *awake*. **Soarin'**, one of the most popular attractions at Disney's California Adventure park (in Anaheim, California) comes east and invites guests to swoop and soar above the clouds, while taking in various scenes of the California countryside. To achieve the effect, guests sit in special seat-belts-mandatory, hang-glider-type vehicles and are suspended 45 feet in the air, above a giant IMAX projection dome. We love it.

If heights aren't your thing, sit this one out. Other than that, it's exceptionally smooth sailing, er, flying—unless you're highly susceptible to motion sickness.

A Healthy Crop

If you're eating your vegetables (and fruits) at the Garden Grill, Coral Reef, or Sunshine Season Food Fair, odds are good that you're sharing in The Land pavilion's bounty. Some 30 tons of produce are harvested each year from The Land's greenhouses. Talk about fresh local ingredients!

Imagination!

While you'd think that glass buildings would leave very little to the imagination, the glass pyramids that house the Imagination! pavilion have quite the opposite effect. If necessity is truly the mother of invention, then this is where she resides, playing with minds as if they were Play-Doh. Fronted by fountains that seem to have agendas of their own, this pavilion is one of Epcot's more whimsical.

Ever-curious about what it feels like to be an inventor with those little lightbulbs always appearing above your head, you enter the **Journey Into Imagination with Figment** attraction and discover that you have stumbled upon an open house hosted by the Imagination Institute.

This attraction features the antics of a character named Figment. The little purple dragon is here to teach you a few secrets about capturing the imagination.

Before you can fasten your

thinking cap, you've become a test subject for a project called the Imagination Scanner. During your visit, you're put through a series of illusory experiments designed to spark your imagination. Afterward, stop by **Image-Works**, an interactive area meant to stimulate sensory skills.

But the attraction at the Imagination! pavilion that earns the most exuberant high five is **Honey, I Shrunk the Audience**. If you have time to visit only a few

Future World Unplugged

For a close-up look at Future World, check out:

- **Epcot Seas Aqua Tour:** Non-scuba divers can use snorkel equipment at The Living Seas in this 2½-hour tour (about $100) of the Disney version of the deep. Call 407-WDW-TOUR (939-8687).

- **DiveQuest:** This 3-hour program (about $140) invites certified scuba divers to a dive in The Living Seas aquarium. For information call 407-WDW-TOUR (939-8687).

- **Dolphins in Depth:** A bit more (about $150) buys you a 3-hour introduction to dolphin research and conservation, 30 minutes in the water with the dolphins at The Living Seas, and a videotape to prove it. Call 407-WDW-TOUR (939-8687) for details and reservations.

attractions at Epcot, this spectacle of a 3-D movie should be high on your list. The 25-minute film is so riddled with effects that the audience is consistently reduced to a squirming, giggling mass. The experience is not rough, but the effects are heightened with a bit of suspense, so we'll say no more. Crowds are smallest early in the morning and late in the evening.

Test Track

Behind this pavilion's steely doors lies the fastest ride at Walt Disney World. In this supercharged introduction to the world of automobile testing, the ride's computer-controlled vehicles barrel up steep hills, zip down straightaways, squeak around heavily banked hairpin turns, and slam on the brakes. Test Track is much more than a thrilling ride: It's a realistic runthrough of tests performed on real cars at real facilities, known as proving grounds.

As you walk through the plant you see everything from the all-important seat-squirming test to the crucial trials endured by air bags, tires, and the human interface clan (our courageous crash-prone counterparts) to ensure our safety. Then you hop into a six-person vehicle, fasten your seat belt, and—making note that you've got a video display, but no steering wheel or brake pedal—prepare for an exciting five-minute road trip. As the sporty open-top cars traverse the nearly one-mile track, you experience a rough-and-tumble suspension workout, become seriously indebted to antilock brakes, narrowly avoid a crash, and whiz outside and around the pavilion at speeds up to 65 miles per hour. Incredible insight into cars is a given; you'll also gain respect for the complex systems contained therein. On the way out, be sure to stop and check out the smarty-pants car demo and the "Inside Track," which features gear for car buffs.

Test Track is an altogether different experience by day and by night (you can guess which is more intense). If it's raining, we suggest you turn your face to the sky and ask yourself this question: Would I enjoy zooming down a highway in a convertible with the top down right about now?

For the least intimidating crowds, grab a Fastpass or try to visit in the evening while everyone else is viewing IllumiNations.

Note: Since this is something of a rough attraction, riders must be free from heart conditions, back and neck problems, and other physical limitations.

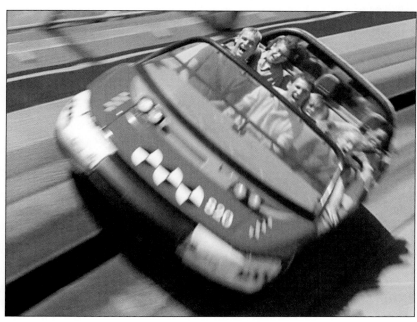

Mission: SPACE

Three . . . two . . . one . . . liftoff! Words you only expect to hear from flight control at Cape Canaveral are now part of the ever-expanding lexicon at Walt Disney World. Mission: SPACE is one of Epcot's most popular and engaging attractions. Its bold mission? To train guests to be astronauts.

The training process begins with guests strapping themselves into 4-person simulator pods. In lieu of an actual blastoff, guests are shot into orbit via a motion simulator—not unlike the ones real astronauts use. Former NASA advisers and astronauts worked with Disney Imagineers to lend more than a bit of authenticity to this thrill ride.

Think you have the right stuff to enjoy this simulated trip into outer space? Ask yourself: Do I have a heart condition? Have I *ever* experienced motion sickness? Does moving in a circle make me queasy? Am I pregnant? Claustrophobic? Do I have *any* health issues whatsoever? If the answer to any of the above is yes or maybe, sit this one out. And consider this: Mission: SPACE is the first theme park attraction in history to be equipped with motion-sickness bags. Still, most who don't get sick absolutely love it.

Wonders of Life

The Wonders of Life pavilion operates seasonally, which is Walt Disney World-speak for during peak or very busy times. That generally includes summer and holiday periods. Keep in mind that the entire pavilion or sections within it may not be open during your visit.

The major attraction is **Body Wars**—a frenetic five-minute trip through the human body in a flight simulator. It's similar to the Disney-MGM Studios' Star Tours, but is a few months a few notches rougher than its Studios counterpart. Plus, there's the whole blood factor to consider.

Hidden Mickey

If you look very, very closely, you can spot Mickey in the mural above the entrance to Body Wars at the Wonders of Life pavilion.

The premise of Body Wars is that you are along for the ride on a routine medical probe to remove a splinter (from the inside) when things get out of hand. Before you know it, you're barreling through regions such as the human lungs, heart, and brain. Body Wars is an exciting journey, both visually and physically, that rates among Epcot's bigger thrills, but it is also a turbulent ride with a lot of herky-jerky movements.

If you're especially squeamish, you may find the visual content to be too much in this context. In addition, you should not venture onto this ride if you are pregnant. You should also bypass Body Wars if you've eaten recently, have a back problem or heart condition, are prone to motion sickness, or have any other physical limitations.

Another Wonders of Life attraction that merits not-to-be-missed status is **Cranium Command**, an utterly tame, utterly delightful 19-minute journey into the mind of a 12-year-old boy. This is an attraction so good, Billy Crystal would have a tough time making it funnier. Here's the setup: The commander of a specialized corps of brain pilots is issuing assignments, and our pal Buzzy must pilot an adolescent boy. The show follows a day in this boy's life, with Buzzy calling the shots. Celebrity cameos include George Wendt (from *Cheers*) manning the stomach, Dana Carvey and Kevin Nealon (playing Hans and Franz of *Saturday Night Live* fame) as the heart, and Bobcat Goldthwait as the adrenal gland.

For some more mind-bending fun, explore the Sensory Funhouse, located just outside Cranium Command. And don't neglect the Wonder Cycles, computerized stationary bicycles that let you pedal through the Rose Bowl Parade and Disneyland. Hey, when will that opportunity present itself again?

Universe of Energy

Behind this mirrored facade lies a pavilion on a serious power trip (it draws some of its electricity from photovoltaic cells mounted on the roof). Universe of Energy has always been notable for its lifelike dinosaurs, some of Walt Disney World's largest Audio-Animatronic animals. But the show here also boasts some familiar faces and fetches a few nominations for Best Comedy in an Epcot Pavilion.

The pavilion is given over entirely to a 45-minute presentation that explores the origins of fossil fuels and muses about alternative energy sources. **Ellen's Energy Adventure** is powered by Ellen Degeneres's sudden yen for knowledge about such things—largely so that she can beat her know-it-all former college roommate Judy (a face you'll likely recognize) when they land on a game show together.

Bill Nye, the Science Guy, offers to educate a befuddled Ellen, and just happens to have some rather extensive visual aids handy. As Bill lectures Ellen, arresting visuals are shown on a series of huge screens. (Keep your eyes peeled for a cameo by a caveman you'd swear was a famous sitcom actor.)

When Bill insists they travel back 220 million years to seek greater knowledge, the seating area rotates and splits into six vehicles that then move into the clammy air of the primeval world. Here, you encounter erupting volcanoes, an eerie fog, and prehistoric creatures locked in combat, rearing up suddenly from a tide pool, and gazing down at you like vultures. You also come upon an Audio-Animatronic Ellen, desperately attempting to reason with a creepy, snakelike dinosaur. She makes it out of the forest in one piece, and happily hits the big time on her game show, if only in her dreams.

This pavilion is best visited in the late afternoon. A large group is let into the theater every 17 minutes, so don't let a crowd scare you. If the line extends beyond the marquee, try again later.

Leave Future World by walking through Innoventions Plaza. As you head to World Showcase, be sure to look to each side. On the right, you'll pass an ATM near a spontaneously erupting fountain delivering a merciless soaking (mostly to children). Down on the left, you'll spot what appears to be an ancient pyramid. Welcome to the flip side of Future World!

World Showcase

Think of World Showcase as a handful of gourmet jelly beans, the sort so flavorful, they make your taste buds believe you're actually putting away strawberry cheesecake, champagne punch, and chocolate pudding. You know they're just jelly beans, of course, but you pretend, fully savoring the essence of that piña colada.

In the same way, World Showcase cajoles your senses into accepting its international pavilions at face value, enveloping you in such delectable representations of Germany, Japan, Mexico, and more, that you are content to play along.

This parade of nations, a cultural thoroughfare wrapped around a lagoon the size of 85 football fields, is marked by dramatic mood swings. The atmosphere changes markedly with each border crossing, going from positively romantic to utterly serene, toe-tappingly upbeat, patriotic, festive, wistfully Old World, or cheerfully relaxed in a matter of yards.

Of course, the World Showcase pavilions are not simply outstanding mood pieces but occasions to get uniquely acquainted with the people, history, and beauty of the world's nations. Each pavilion has a strong, unmistakable sense of place that announces itself with painstakingly re-created landmarks and faithful landscaping that ensures bougainvillea in Mexico and lotus blossoms in China. Each contributes culinary specialties from the apple-tart-to-ice-cream smorgasbord that makes World Showcase one of the hottest meal tickets in Walt Disney World.

To transport yourself totally, try to supplement the smattering of attractions—panoramic films,

Quiet Escapes

Parts of Epcot boast an energy that interrupt the calm you might crave; here are some of our favorite quiet spots.

- Fountain View Espresso and Bakery in Future World
- Plaza de los Amigos inside Mexico's pyramid
- Stave Church Gallery in Norway
- Benches near the reflecting pools in China
- Lagoonside benches near the gondola in Italy
- Garden alongside The American Adventure
- Bijutsu-kan Gallery, hillside gardens, and Matsu No Ma in Japan
- Tucked-away garden with benches in France
- Gardens at rear of United Kingdom pavilion and Rose & Crown Pub
- Waterfall and mountain setting in Canada

theater and dinner shows, boat rides, and the nightly not-to-be-missed fireworks extravaganza—with the legions of less structured pursuits.

Start by trying to catch at least one street performance per country. So frequent it's practically ongoing (check your guidemap for exact times), this feast of live entertainment encompasses everything from mariachi bands to acrobats and belly dancing, and it makes a great accompaniment to a mobile wine tasting. Take time, too, to chitchat with the "locals" in each village (nearly all of whom claim the represented country as their homeland).

To personalize your journey even more, make a mission of snacking, drinking, shopping, gallery-hopping, or even bench-warming your way around the World. For adults, these relaxing activities are the very essence of a visit to World Showcase.

Structurally, World Showcase is perhaps the most user-friendly area of Walt Disney World's theme parks. You may get tired walking along the 1.2-mile promenade that leads past all pavilions as it encircles the lagoon, but you won't lose your sense of direction. While locations of countries here don't correspond at all to their placement on the planet, the landscape offers a wealth of Eiffel Tower–like clues that *almost* preclude the use of a map. Because World Showcase focuses less on attractions (6 of the 11 pavilions have no attractions, per se), it requires less strategic maneuvering.

If World Showcase came with instructions, the handy booklet might say:

- Touring is a clockwise or counterclockwise proposition best begun on an empty stomach.

- Shops are optimally saved for the afternoon, when the throngs from Future World have descended, lengthening lines for movies, rides, and shows.

- The movies at Canada, France, and China are often better appreciated when spaced out over two days.

- IllumiNations is the biggest entertainment draw in all of Epcot. The nightly spectacle of fireworks, lasers, and music is visible from most any point around World Showcase.

Moving along, this Epcot tour describes pavilions in the order they're encountered when entering World Showcase from Future World and walking counterclockwise around the lagoon.

Canada

In a marked departure from the real world, a refreshment stand poised a good 50 yards before the border makes it possible to arrive in Canada with a cup of Moosehead in hand. This pavilion is the site of an outstanding panoramic film, an "underground" steak house, interesting shops, and the coolest spot in World Showcase. It covers an impressive amount of territory in its bid to capture the distinctive beauty and cultural diversity of

International Gateway

Think of this second entrance as Epcot's back door. The turnstiles here provide a direct "in" to World Showcase, depositing guests between the France and United Kingdom pavilions. Because the International Gateway is connected via walkway to the Yacht and Beach Club, BoardWalk, Swan, and Dolphin resorts, guests at these lodgings have exceptional access to Epcot. (Water launches also make the trip.) Note that:

- Wheelchairs are available for rent at this entrance.

- Nothing in World Showcase opens until about 11 A.M., so guests arriving earlier must walk to Future World at the far end of the park.

- You can make a quick exit from here after IllumiNations.

the Western Hemisphere's largest nation. An artful ode to the Indians of Canada's Northwest (towering totem poles and a trading post) leads to an architectural tribute to French Canada (the Hôtel du Canada here is a hybrid of Ottawa's Château Laurier and Quebec's Château Frontenac).

From here, follow the sounds of rushing water to find the cooling sprays of a miniaturized Niagara Falls that's tucked neatly into the face of a Canadian Rocky and may be blessed with a rainbow. A feature film, a visual anthem of sorts appropriately called **O Canada!**, is shown in all its Circle-Vision 360 glory within the mountain itself.

The 18-minute standing-room-only movie places you in the middle of most things Canadian, including a hockey game, enormous reindeer herds, and the Royal Canadian Mounted Police.

As you leave, check out the bountiful greenery inspired by the famous Butchart Gardens, in Victoria, British Columbia—while not as cool as the falls, they're still a great place to claim a bench, especially when the Pipes of Nova Scotia or the Off Kilter troupe of Celtic rock musicians is performing.

United Kingdom

This cheery neighborhood, which reveals its cultural identity via the bright-red phone booths dotting its cobblestoned streets, is a fine place for a bit of shopping or a pint of ale. What's less obvious: the herb garden tucked behind the thatched-roof cottage (note the spearmint plants); the butterfly hatchery on the hill; and the courtyard at the rear of the pavilion, where you'll find a traditional English hedge maze. You may even catch a decidedly Beatlesque rock group that

Tired of Walking?

The *FriendShip* water taxis link Showcase Plaza at the foot of Future World with Germany and Morocco, across the lagoon at the farthest corners of World Showcase. It's convenient—but keep in mind that it may be quicker to walk.

performs in the garden. A table at the Rose & Crown Pub is the best perspective from which to view this pavilion, because the Tudor, Georgian, and Victorian structures seem all the more real from the window of a friendly pub.

Architectural enlightenment is a great excuse to dally in the fine shops. You can cover 300 years of building styles just by walking from the slate floor of The Tea Caddy straight through to the carpeted room with the Waterford crystal chandelier, which signals your arrival at the Neoclassical period and the shop known as The Queen's Table.

France

A footbridge from the United Kingdom leads across a picturesque canal to one of the most romantic areas of World Showcase. Petite streets and Eiffel Tower aside, you're looking at Paris during the *Belle Epoque* ("beautiful age") of the late nineteenth century.

The one-time Parisian institution Les Halles is re-created here, as is a one-tenth-scale Eiffel Tower that would be infinitely more evocative were it not so obviously perched atop a building. Luxurious boutiques, sidewalk cafes, and, of course,

> ## For the Lovebirds...
>
> Epcot's World Showcase has some great romantic spots, namely:
> - El Río del Tiempo boat ride and the San Angel Inn in Mexico
> - The lovely courtyard at the rear of the United Kingdom
> - Italy's piazza and gondola landing
> - Every inch of France

pastries that announce their presence *par avion* are among the big draws here, as is the wine-tasting counter at the nicely stocked La Maison du Vin. Beckoning, too, is one of the most peaceful spots in all of Epcot—a quiet park on the canal side of the pavilion that might have leapt off the canvas of Georges Seurat's *Sunday Afternoon on the Island of La Grande Jatte.*

But the biggest lure here is the 18-minute film **Impressions de France,** which puts its five 21-by 27-foot screens to terrific use in a *tour de France* that ranges from Alpine skiing to foothills of buttery pastries. If you know France, you'll love it; if you aren't familiar with the country, you'll want to be. The superb score, featuring French classical composers, could stand on its own. *Impressions de France* is least congested during the morning and early-evening hours.

Morocco

This enchanting area—arguably the most meticulously crafted of all the represented nations—also happens to be the loudest World Showcase pavilion. The authenticity has something to do with the fact that nine tons of tile were handmade, hand-cut, and hand-laid by Moroccan artisans into the mosaics seen here. The prayer tower at the entrance takes after the famous Koutoubia Minaret, in Marrakesh. The Bab Boujouloud gate, patterned after one in the city of Fez, leads to the Medina (old part of the city), a tangled array of narrow passageways where baskets, leather goods, and brass items are among the wares for sale.

The Medina also brings you to the entrance of the Marrakesh restaurant, notable for its North African menu, its belly dancers, and the fact that it's one of the only full-service restaurants in World Showcase where you can often get a table without advance reservations. You can also savor Mediterranean-style chicken, beef, and lamb sandwiches, salads, and desserts at the more casual Tangierine Cafe.

Stop at Mo' Rockin' for Arabic rhythms with a contemporary flair. Make a point of checking out the extraordinary tile work and costumes displayed at the Gallery of Arts and History, and be on the lookout for visiting artisans demonstrating their crafts.

It's interesting to note that the gardens are irrigated by an ancient working waterwheel located on the promenade. Morocco is easily toured any time of day. If you'd like a more structured look at the pavilion, sign up for a guided tour at the Morocco National Tourist Office inside. The complimentary tours last from 20 to 40 minutes and are available at 1, 3, and 5 P.M.

Where the Art Is

Exhibits change periodically, but here's an indication of what you can expect to see:

- Mexico's "Reign of Glory" exhibit features pre-Columbian pieces (some are on loan from the Smithsonian).
- Norway's tiny Stave Church Gallery holds exhibits documenting the once-common churches.
- Japan's Bijutsu-kan Gallery becomes a toy museum with "The Kitahara Collection of Tin Toys."
- Morocco's Gallery of Arts and History showcases intricate tile work and costumes.
- China's House of Whispering Willows displays ancient Chinese art and artifacts.

Japan

As quietly inviting as Morocco is vibrantly enticing, Japan is a pavilion of considerable beauty and serenity. Its most prominent landmarks are the red torii gate (a good-luck symbol), which stands close to the lagoon, and the five-tiered pagoda, created in the mold of an eighth-century shrine located in Nara. Each level of the pagoda represents one of the elements that, according to Buddhist teachings, produced everything in the universe (from bottom to top: earth, water, fire, wind, and sky).

The most compelling features of this pavilion are the entertainment (Matsuriza drummers), the elaborate detail of its manicured gardens, and an art exhibit called "The Kitahara Collection of Tin Toys" at the Bijutsu-kan Gallery.

Japan also claims one of the largest shops in Epcot. Housed

inside a structure reminiscent of a section of the Gosho Imperial Palace, which was originally constructed in Kyoto in 794 A.D., the Mitsukoshi Department Store counts bonsai trees, kimonos, dolls, tea sets, incense, jewelry, and decorative ceremonial swords among its offerings.

All that shopping may spark your appetite. At Teppanyaki Dining Rooms, a feast consisting of vegetables, steak, chicken, and seafood is prepared tableside by authentic Japanese chefs. This pavilion is easily toured any time of day.

The American Adventure

The centerpiece pavilion of World Showcase is so devoted to Americana, it can bring out the Norman Rockwell in you even when you're cranky. Housed in a Colonial-style manse that combines elements of Independence Hall, the Old State House in Boston, Monticello, and various structures in Colonial Williamsburg, it's dressed for the part.

The 28-minute show inside— an evocative multimedia presentation about American history— is among Disney's best, both for its astonishingly detailed sets and sophisticated Audio-Animatronic figures and for its ability to rouse goose bumps from unsuspecting patriots. Ben Franklin and Mark Twain lead what's been called "a hundred-yard dash capturing the spirit of the country at specific moments in time."

Two superb a cappella vocal groups, the Voices of Liberty and Epcot Vybe, sometimes entertain in the lobby before the show begins.

The wait for The American Adventure attraction can be long because the show itself is lengthy, so check a times guide or stop by for curtain times and plan accordingly. It's definitely worth the effort.

This patriotic pavilion also features an All-American fast-food restaurant and the lagoonside **America Gardens Theatre**, where you just may find some rousing entertainment. An interesting aside: The garden alongside The American Adventure pavilion acknowledges the days before red, white, and blue by showcasing different plants used traditionally by Native Americans for food and medicinal purposes.

Italy

This little Italy is defined by an abiding you-are-there ambience and meticulous authenticity that extends from the gondolas tied to striped moorings at the pavilion's very own Venetian island to the homemade (before your very eyes) fettuccine and spaghetti at its popular L'Originale Alfredo di Roma Ristorante.

Look to the very top of the scaled-down Venetian campanile dominating the romantic piazza here, and you'll see an angel covered in gold leaf that was molded into a spitting image of the one atop the bell tower in the real St. Mark's Square, in Venice.

The Doge's Palace here is so faithfully rendered that its facade resembles the marbled pattern of the original. Adding to the effect are tall, slender stands of Italian cypress, replicas of Venetian statues, an abundance of potted flowers, and fragrant olive and citrus trees.

This Italy pavilion has no major attractions per se, but between its memorable street performers and the strolling musicians who play during dinner at Alfredo's, it has all the entertainment it needs.

Among the various shopping options is a gem of a gourmet food purveyor, called La Bottega Italiana, that also stocks fine Italian wines.

Germany

In a word: *oompah*. Arguably the most festive country in all of World Showcase, Germany is immediately recognizable by its fairy tale architecture. To the rear of the central cobblestoned square (which is named for Saint George), you'll see an enormous cuckoo clock, complete with Hummel figurines that emerge on the hour. Immediately past this clock lies the Biergarten, the vast restaurant and entertainment hall that—thanks to spirited dinner shows primed with German beer, sausages, and yodelers— serves as the pinnacle of this festive pavilion's entertainment.

Germany also scores with tempting shops, and the Weinkeller, which offers wine-tasting opportunities. In Glas und Porzellan, it's usually possible to watch a Goebel artist demonstrating the elaborate process by which Hummel figurines are created. Outside, note the miniature 1930s German village, complete with castle, farmhouse, monastery, and even a wee commuter railroad. Germany is easily toured at any time of day.

China

This pavilion is marked by a dramatic half-scale replica of Beijing's Temple of Heaven set behind stands of whistling bamboo and quiet reflecting pools. Traditional Chinese music wafts over the sound system. In addition to its gardens, the pavilion features the House of Whispering Willows, an exhibit of ancient art and artifacts from well-known collections that's always worth a look. Live entertainment here is invariably stirring, especially when it's a demonstration by the local acrobats.

But the main reason to visit China is the Circle-Vision 360 film shown in the Temple of Heaven. Basically, you stand, and *Reflections of China* whisks you on a 12-minute, blink-and-you've-missed-the-Great Wall journey that reflects the ways in which China has changed over the past 20 years—with the addition of Hong Kong and Macau. From ancient Mongolia and Beijing's Forbidden City to ultramodern Shanghai, the film provides the most fascinating glimpses of China and its people. Pay special attention to the fleeting mist-enshrouded Huangshan Mountain, if you can; the filming of this amazing view of China was no small endeavor: the film crew and 40 laborers had to haul the 600-pound camera nearly a mile uphill for those three seconds of footage.

Norway

This 11th addition to the World Showcase landscape is immediately intriguing. A curious array of buildings rings the pavilion's cobblestoned square, including a reproduction of a wooden stave church (an endangered species of sorts, with just 28 remaining in Norway) and a replica of the 14th-century Akershus Castle that still stands in Oslo's harbor. Beside a grassy-roofed, thick-logged structure, there's a statue of a Norwegian running champion, living legend Grete Waitz. This Land of the Midnight Sun has added some twists to the World Showcase lineup—among them, the promise of troll encounters and Norwegian handicrafts of the hand-knit-sweater variety.

The stave church houses a gallery of artifacts recalling the history of these charming benchmarks of Norwegian culture (don't skip it, if only to see the inside of this teensy church). But Norway scores with **Maelstrom**, a trip in dragon-headed boats through Viking territory that is enjoyable, if not thrilling. An inspired voyage that surprises you with a troll here, a backward plunge there, a

---

World Showcase Unplugged

These walking tours offer great insight into one of Disney's more enlightened creations.

- **Hidden Treasures of World Showcase:** The instructor stops short of turning pavilions inside out to display their scrupulous detailing and eye-fooling design.

- **Gardens of the World:** A horticulturist leads guests through the distinctive gardens. Discover the lengths to which Disney goes to create authentic-looking landscapes, and find out how to apply clever techniques at home.

Tours last three hours and cost about $59 (and require Epcot admission). Schedules vary; reservations are necessary but may be made the morning of the tour. Call 407-WDW-TOUR (939-8687).

sudden waterfall here, a storm there, Maelstrom doesn't throw many big punches; it just keeps you guessing.

The five-minute trip lets you out at a Norwegian village, then finishes up with a brief film on the essence of Norway. This attraction is least crowded in the evening. If you'd like to take a more in-depth look at this pavilion or learn more about the architecture of Norway, stop at the Tourism information desk at the end of the ride. Free tours are given twice daily.

Mexico

There's no mistaking this pavilion's identity. A wild thicket of tropical foliage leads to a great pyramid. Inside, you wend your way through a brief but consistently engaging cultural exhibit to the main event. What you see

next—a thoroughly romantic vision of a quaint Mexican village at dusk—is among the most wondrously escapist visions in World Showcase. True to form, there are stands selling colorful sombreros, baskets, pottery, and piñatas (the shop off to the left sells higher-quality Mexican handicrafts). In the rear of the plaza, note the dimly lit San Angel Inn and, behind it, the river and smoking volcano.

Here, too, you'll find the embarkation point for El Río del Tiempo, a six-minute boat trip through Mexican history that might be described as a south-of-the-border It's a Small World knock-off. If you encounter long lines early in the day, skip it, and check back later. Note, too, that the mariachi band that performs inside and outside this imposing pavilion is quite good.

Drinks Around the World

There's Samuel Adams lager at The American Adventure and at least one good imported excuse to bend the ol' elbow in each World Showcase country. Namely: Moosehead and more from carts in Canada; shandies, Guinness, black and tans, Tennent's, and beyond from the Rose & Crown Pub in the United Kingdom; a bottle of Kronenbourg from the Boulangerie Pâtisserie or a glass of wine from La Maison du Vin in France; Kirin beer or sake specialty drinks at Matsu No Ma, in Japan; vino from Italy can be sampled (with a pastry, of course) at La Bottega Italiana in Italy; Beck's beer and H. Schmitt Söhne wine at Germany's Sommerfest; Chinese wine and beer at the Lotus Blossom Cafe; Ringnes drafts from Kringla Bakeri og Kafe, in Norway; and what else but margaritas in Mexico's Cantina de San Angel.

DISNEY-MGM STUDIOS

Like an actress just right for the part, the Disney-MGM Studios is perfectly cast as the vivacious, showbiz-obsessed theme park that is seemingly incapable of keeping a secret. Since its debut, this park has worked to make the transition from sidekick to leading lady, and it has succeeded.

Think of the Studios as the adults' Magic Kingdom: magical, but in a more sophisticated way; marked by a whimsicality far more ageless than that which pervades the Magic Kingdom. Sure, it has a Beauty and the Beast stage show, and

there's a funny 3-D Muppet movie, but these hardly constitute a satellite Fantasyland. At times the Studios even seems to have been scripted for a mature crowd, crafted with a wink of the eye by (and for) grown-ups to elicit knowing laughs and no-holds-barred nostalgia.

GETTING ORIENTED: The Disney-MGM Studios is smaller than Epcot, but somewhat difficult to navigate since it has no distinctive shape or main artery. You enter the park—and 1940s Tinseltown—via Hollywood Boulevard, a bustling shopping venue. The first major intersection you come to is Sunset Boulevard, an equally starry-eyed venue that branches off to the right of Hollywood Boulevard; this shopping and entertainment strip ends in a cul-de-sac right at the foot of the park's tallest (and spookiest) landmark, the 199-foot Tower of Terror.

Hollywood Boulevard ends where The Great Movie Ride begins—at a replica of Mann's (formerly Grauman's) Chinese Theatre. This ornate building is tucked behind the 12-story Sorcerer Mickey hat, the most centrally located landmark at the Studios; the plaza fronting it is

Disney-MGM Studios Hours

The park is usually open from 9 A.M. to an hour after sunset; hours are extended during holiday weekends and summer months and abbreviated during slower periods. Some shows don't open until late morning, depending on the season. Call 407-824-4321 for schedules. One-day admission is $59.75 (plus tax) for adults. Prices are subject to change.

called Hollywood Plaza. If you stand in Hollywood Plaza facing Disney's Chinese Theater, you'll see an archway off to your right; this leads to Mickey Avenue, an area with more of a backstage feel, where a tours of working studios are among the attractions. If you make a left off Hollywood Boulevard and proceed past Echo Lake, you are on course for such attractions as Sounds Dangerous starring Drew Carey, Indiana Jones Epic Stunt Spectacular, and Star Tours. Just past Star Tours lies one more entertainment pocket. Muppet*Vision 3-D theater is the main draw here, together with realistic reproductions of city streets. Walk left past the skyscraper end of street and you're on a track back to Hollywood Plaza and the Chinese Theater.

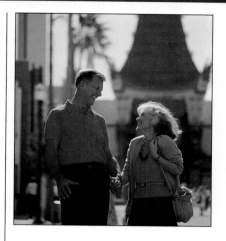

A Walking Tour

Just inside the gates, you may be too distracted by the bright Art Deco looks of Hollywood Boulevard to notice a building on your left. This is Guest Relations, where you can go for information as well as first aid. Stop here or at Crossroads of the World (the gift stand in the center of the entrance plaza) to pick up a guidemap if you need

one. To your immediate right, check out Oscar's Super Service, which has a 1949 Chevrolet tow truck parked out front. This is one of several striking and utterly unscratched classic autos you'll notice along the streets. (We're not sure how they got through the turnstiles.) Oscar's is the spot for lockers and wheelchair rentals; the Lost and Found, along with package pickup, is right next door. There is an ATM just outside the turnstiles here.

Hollywood Boulevard

One look at this main drag and you have a hunch you're not in Central Florida anymore. The strip oozes star quality with a Mae West sort of subtlety. Movie tunes from Hollywood's Golden Age waft through the air. Palm trees make like Fred and Ginger in the tropical breeze. Streamlined

Hot Tips

- Many guests adore Fantasmic!, a look into the dream world of Mickey Mouse, highlighted by fireworks, lasers, and special effects. This lavish musical is very popular, so plan ahead: If there are two shows, opt for the second, and allow 90 minutes before showtime for good seating (we recommend sitting toward the back for the best view—and the easiest exit).
- There is a path that leads you from the BoardWalk resort area on to Epcot. (It takes about 20 minutes.)

storefronts with neon and chrome Art Deco flourishes line the boulevard like would-be movie sets hoping to get noticed.

Note that the shops along Hollywood Boulevard typically stay open about a half hour after the rest of the park has closed. (Consult the "Shopping" section in the *Diversions* chapter for specifics on our favorite shops; wares generally include a sampling of movie memorabilia and plenty of Disney character merchandise.)

However you get there, it's important to stop at the corner of Hollywood and Sunset boulevards to check the **Tip Board** (it lists current wait times for popular studios' attractions). Until 1 P.M., this is also the place to make advance reservations for full-service restaurants.

Sunset Boulevard

This Studios block is a broad, colorful avenue every bit as glamorous as Hollywood Boulevard. It has the same high-cheekbone style and its own stock of towering palms, evocative facades, and tempting shops. It also has stage presence, in the form of the 1,500-seat Theater of the Stars amphitheater, where you can see live performances of *Beauty and the Beast* on Sunset Boulevard begins innocently enough, with a friendly farmers' market, and a shop called Once Upon A Time that's in a replica of the Carthay Circle Theatre where *Snow White and the Seven Dwarfs* premiered. But don't let your guard down: the white-knuckle Tower of Terror looms at the end of the road.

Somehow, **Beauty and the Beast—Live on Stage**, a production that was the *raison d'être* behind the Broadway musical, manages to remain oblivious to its eerie neighbor. The show is 30 minutes of rich music, costuming and choreography, and uplifting entertainment. While a canopy keeps the sun's heat at bay, we still aim for an evening performance during the summer. For early birds, note that this show generally opens soon after the park does.

Then there's **The Twilight Zone Tower of Terror**, a hair-raising experience. Because few of us have a natural yen to drop several stories (more than once, we might add) down a dark elevator shaft, this one requires some bravery. It helps to know what to expect. And, if you're brave enough to ride more than once, you may experience a whole new sequence of ups and downs!

Basically, "guests" enter the mysteriously abandoned Hollywood Tower Hotel and are invited into a library, where even the cobwebs seem to be circa 1939. Here, Rod Serling appears on a black-and-white television set to brief you (dark, stormy night, Halloween 1939, lightning strikes, guests disappear from hotel elevator) and welcome you to tonight's episode of *The Twilight Zone*:

When you reach a boarding area—last call for chickening out—and file into an elevator (look at the diagram above the doors and pray you haven't been assigned to the front row). Once you are seated and restraints are secured, the doors shut and the elevator ascends. You're soon so entranced by astonishing special effects—apparitions that appear in a corridor that vaporizes into a dark, star-filled sky and a gigantic eye straight from the fifth dimension—that dread becomes (almost) secondary. When the elevator moves over into a second, pitch-black shaft, anything can happen, since Disney's Imagineers deviously transformed this ride from a two-screamer into a five-screamer. The bottom falls out more than once, and not subtly: Multiple plummets are scripted. One thing's for sure: Your cue to strike a great casual pose is when you're at the top of the shaft. You want to look good in the group picture, which is taken as a panorama of the park

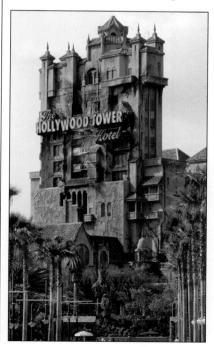

suddenly gives way to a drop. The plunges are incredibly fast downward pulls with surprisingly smooth landings. It may be a small comfort, perhaps, but the really hairy part is over faster than many vocal cords are able to respond.

A few notes: The jitters tend to stay with you a bit after the 12-minute drama has ended. If you have back or neck problems, a heart condition, or are pregnant, we suggest you pass on this one.

If you've been on the ride before, you're no doubt familiar with the "scary seat." That used to be the lone seat that had a simple lap belt as opposed to a sturdy steel bar as restraint. Well, the good news is: every seat is now a scary seat! Yep, the lap bars are history.

If you're willing (and able) to continue the thrill-fest after your tumultuous stay in The Hollywood Tower Hotel, get ready to shake, rattle, and roll on the **Rock 'n' Roller Coaster**. As the first WDW roller coaster to flip you upside down, this dark, indoor, steel construction goes from zero to 60 miles per hour in just under three seconds.

The premise: You've just scored backstage passes and VIP transport to a sold-out Aerosmith concert at the Hollywood Bowl. During your drive through Southern California, you twist

Touring Priorities

DON'T MISS	DON'T OVERLOOK	DON'T KNOCK YOURSELF OUT
Tower of Terror*	Voyage of The Little Mermaid*	Honey, I Shrunk the Kids Movie Set Adventure
Star Tours*	Indiana Jones Epic Stunt Spectacular*/**	Playhouse Disney—Live on Stage
Muppet*Vision 3-D	Disney-MGM Studios Backlot Tour	
The Great Movie Ride		* Fastpass attraction as of press time. Consult a guidemap for new additions.
Beauty and the Beast —Live on Stage**	Sounds Dangerous starring Drew Carey	
Rock 'n' Roller Coaster*	Walt Disney: One Man's Dream	**Pay close attention to performance schedules.
Lights, Motors, Action! Extreme Stunt Show	The Magic of Disney Animation	
Stars and Motor Cars parade	Who Wants to Be a Millionaire—Play It!	
Fantasmic!		

sion production studios. Passing under an archway located off Hollywood Plaza, you see Animation Courtyard immediately in front of you, with Mickey Avenue to your left.

Disney recently shut down the working Animation studio, so this attraction has dropped a notch in appeal. Consider **The Magic of Disney Animation** a worthwhile detour, if no longer a must-see.

The **Disney-MGM Studios Backlot Tour** is a two-pronged gig that begins with an entertaining six-minute demo of how a realistic sea storm or naval battle

and turn to a rockin' sound track—and feel like you may have stepped inside a runaway music video.

Pay attention to the warning signs posted as you enter the ride. If you have back or neck problems, a heart condition, or if you're pregnant, sit this one out. Finally, we urge you *not* to try it on a full stomach. (We made that mistake once. It wasn't pretty.)

Animation Courtyard & Mickey Avenue
Adjacent to Sunset Boulevard and Hollywood Boulevard is the section of the park that takes you under the sea with a diminutive mermaid and into working televi-

Quiet Escapes

- Starring Rolls Cafe
- Tune-In Lounge
- Far corners of the Sunset Ranch Market
- Benches on Sunset Boulevard near Theater of the Stars
- Shaded benches around Echo Lake
- Brownstone stoops in the Streets of America area

might be filmed. The second segment, a 29-minute tram ride, starts calmly enough, but sit on the right side to stay dry. You visit the wardrobe area and the lights, camera, and props departments. (The backlot neighborhood of facades, which used to be part of the tour, is but a memory.) All of a sudden, there you are smack-dab in the middle of a special-effects zone called Catastrophe Canyon, which specializes in nature's wrath: violent downpours, fiery explosions, flash floods, and the like. Things calm down with a visit to a realistic-looking city street. (It's a neighborhood of facades made mostly of fiberglass and Styrofoam.) Lines here tend to be shorter in the late afternoon (ask the attendant for an E.T.A., and if it's more than 30 minutes, check back later). The tour exits through the **American Film Institute Showcase**, a revolving display of costumes, props, and partial sets that features interactive elements related to film lore and legends.

Whether or not you're lucky enough to glimpse a hot set, you'll want to park yourself in TV's most famous "hot seat" at **Who Wants to Be a Millionaire —Play It!** The attraction is

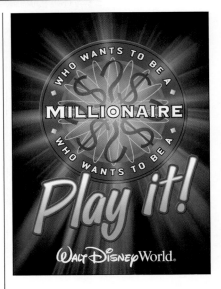

a surprisingly faithful re-creation of the classic game show, right down to the high-tech set and lighting, distinctive music, and 50/50, Ask the Audience, and Phone-a-Friend (or in this case, a randomly chosen park guest) lifelines. Players are chosen from the 600-member audience based on scores from a fastest-finger round, and answer trivia questions to win points that can be redeemed for fabulous prizes. The half-hour presentation runs continuously.

At the Lights! Camera! Action! theater, you won't want to miss **Walt Disney: One Man's Dream**, a tribute to the man who really did start it all. A combination artifact-filled walk-through exhibit and retrospective film, the attraction looks at the life and times of Walter Elias Disney as both imagineer and innovator.

If you can get near **Voyage of The Little Mermaid**—and at this 15-minute musical adapted from the movie, that's no easy task—give it a go. What makes the show so compelling is the upbeat music, amusing puppetry, the occasion to watch children ogle this real, live mermaid *whose tail is moving*, and the mist-infused feeling that you are underwater. Check the times guide for schedule. Seats in the middle to back rows afford the best views.

Only if you're eager to return to your *Romper Room* roots, follow the trail of giddy toddlers to **Playhouse Disney—Live On Stage!** (keeping in mind that there are no seats in the theater, though you are welcome to sit on

The Mouse Is Spoken For

Walt Disney himself supplied the voice for Mickey Mouse from 1928 to 1946.

the floor). If this isn't your speed, it's time to move on to bigger and better things.

Echo Lake Area

Heading back through the archway into Hollywood Plaza, you come upon **The Great Movie Ride**. This drive-through theater

of sorts is a classic in its own right and the best ticket we know to a quick video rental decision your next time out. Housed in an artful replica of Mann's Chinese Theatre, this not-to-be-missed 22-minute attraction is bursting with Audio-Animatronic figures that bring motion-picture legends and moments from almost every genre to life. It's "Chim Chim Cher-ee" meets "Here's looking at you, kid," cigarette-puffing Clint Eastwood meets broom-brandishing Wicked Witch of the

125

West, *Alien* meets *Singin' in the Rain,* and then some—be prepared for surprises.

The ride has meticulous detailing and astounding realism. However, with queues that wind past some *Wizard of Oz* props and a screening of famous movie scenes, it provides one of the most entertaining waits in Walt Disney World (or anywhere for that matter).

Heading through Hollywood Plaza toward Echo Lake, the next major landmark you encounter is the ABC Sound Studio, home of **Sounds Dangerous—Starring Drew Carey**. But you'd better arrive all ears. Expect 12 of the most interesting minutes you have ever spent wearing headphones (in the dark!). Easy-listening this is not.

Here's the deal: You're attending a sneak preview of a live-action TV show that stars Drew Carey as an undercover detective. Thanks to a camera discreetly tucked into Carey's tie tack, you see everything his tie tack wishes it could see. And, of course, no one whispers, crashes, or so much as whimpers during the

determined detective's madcap pursuit of diamond smugglers without word—or major vibrations—getting back to your headphones.

When a bad move by a panic-stricken Carey (open mouth, insert camera) zaps the television picture, you have no choice but to follow the action in the dark. Those clean ears you toted into the theater strain and contort with every twist in the furious plot. Fully enveloped in the audacious realism of 3-D audio, you attempt to sit calmly while your ears carry you into a swarm of 5,000 restless bees.

Listen carefully and you'll doubtless marvel at the palpable snip, snip, snip of the barber's scissors. Your head will spin with the wildly screeching tires of Carey's speeding car. And as attuned as you become, you'll likely still be unprepared for the finale (think close encounters with a circus elephant).

If you are a fan of the action-movie genre, it's worth risking life and limb to catch a performance of the **Indiana Jones Epic Stunt Spectacular!** Arrive a good 45 minutes before showtime to snare a

A Striking Resemblance

- Chinese Theater—Mann's Chinese Theatre in Hollywood
- Once Upon A Time storefront—Carthay Circle Theatre in Hollywood, where Disney's *Snow White* premiered
- Mickey's of Hollywood storefront—Frederick's of Hollywood
- Muppet*Vision 3-D theater—the theater from *The Muppet Show*
- Hollywood Brown Derby—Brown Derby of Hollywood's heyday

seat toward the front of the 2,000-seat amphitheater. The half-hour performance steals its thunder from *Raiders of the Lost Ark* and begins with the selection of a few fearless "extras" (they're put to use during a scene involving a sword fight in Cairo).

Nimble stuntpeople perform one death-defying caper after another, leaping between buildings, dodging snipers and boulders, and eluding fiery explosions. You feel the heat of the flames, you fear for the Harrison Ford look-alike. Tricks of the trade are revealed and you're *still* impressed. The Indiana Jones Epic Stunt Spectacular nearly always plays to capacity audiences, so your best bet for getting a great seat is the first or last show of the day. Seating begins 30 minutes prior to each performance.

Keep in mind that a Fastpass does not guarantee a seat.

As exciting as the Indiana Jones Epic Stunt Spectacular is, the attraction just around the corner packs even more punch. At **Star Tours**, you don't sit in an amphitheater; you strap yourself into a flight simulator.

You don't live vicariously through professional stuntpeople; you experience the sensation of barreling through space at the speed of light for yourself. The premise: Enterprising droids R2-D2 and C-3PO are working for an intergalactic travel agency whose fleet of spacecraft makes regular trips to the Moon of Endor. As luck would have it, you draw a rookie pilot who gives new meaning to "reckless abandon." Soon you're

VIP Tour Allure

You may have seen them in the theme parks—those perky people in the plaid vests. They are VIP guides, happily leading guests on customized trips through Walt Disney World.

The VIP program minimizes the hassle factor while maximizing the overall magic component. In addition to the aforementioned guide, tours entitle guests to special seating for many stage shows and parades. VIP transportation is also an option. For pricing information or to make a reservation, call 407-560-4033.

spiraling through space, dodging lasers and giant ice crystals. Be prepared for an intense five-minute ride that encompasses a lot of bucking, tilting, and a few disorienting movements.

Star Tours is one of those don't-miss-unless-you-have-a-very-good-reason attractions. (Among the very good reasons: just ate, heart condition, pregnancy, susceptible to motion sickness.) The lines are generally shortest in the morning, with waits of about 30 minutes the rest of the day.

Streets of America

Moving along, you arrive at the Studios' back corner. This is a glimpse at several American cityscapes—with a few alter-

ations, including the Empire State Building's dimensions and the size of the puppet population (correction: *Muppet* population).

You're here for *one* thing: the fabulously entertaining, special effects–laden presentation of **Muppet*Vision 3-D**. Miss it and you've deprived your sense of humor. So head straight for the Muppet theater and fill up on a 25-minute stream of amusing Muppet antics that push the creative envelope of 3-D movies with such effects as a cannon blast through the screen, some bubble magic, and a floating banana cream pie. (Yes, Muppet fans, the curmudgeons from *The Muppet Show* are in attendance, in their familiar balcony spot, cynical and crotchety as ever.)

After bonding with the Muppets, walk straight toward Big City Street, where you can take in the skyline or sit down on a stoop. A sign in the window of our favorite brownstone cautions NO SOLICITING, but it says nothing about stoop trespassing. So we take a seat, do some people-watching, and simply gaze at the Empire State Building. Disney used a technique called forced perspective to make the four-story version here appear to have 102 floors. If passersby ask for directions, it's good to know that the **Honey, I Shrunk the Kids Movie Set Adventure** playground is behind one of the facades here. It's worth a peek if you've got time to kill. And if they want to know where to find the Toy Story Pizza Planet Arcade (and its resident ATM), tell them it's across from the Muppet theater.

The newest kid on the Disney-MGM Studios block is **Lights, Motors, Action! Extreme Stunt Show.** Ever wonder how Hollywood pulls off high-speed car chases, ominous motorcycle leaps, and other seemingly death-defying displays? Some of your questions should be answered by the "insiders" hosting this show. It offers a behind-the-scenes peek at the techniques used to pull off some of the most astounding stunts. Inspired by the popular Stunt Show Spectacular in Disneyland Paris, the high-octane show stars specially designed cars, motorcycles, and jet skis.

Lights, Motors, Action! is presented in an area of the park that used to house Residential Street

(it was part of the Disney-MGM Studios Backlot tour). There is ample seating in the stadium, but it's always wise to arrive 20 or more minutes before showtime.

Entertainment

Disney's Tinseltown sticks close to its Hollywood heritage in its live entertainment. Because the marquee is ever changing, it's essential to check a times guide. You might run into budding starlets and gossip columnists along Hollywood Boulevard, or there may be a visiting celebrity about.

Disney Stars and Motor Cars Parade is an honest-to-goodness "stars in cars" Hollywood motorcade—only this lineup includes Ariel, Mary Poppins, Mulan, and other stars of Disney-MGM Studios, all riding in classic cars that have been customized to fit their unique personalities.

Last, but hardly least: Fantasmic!— a 26-minute pyrotechnic dazzler— cranes necks nightly in a lagoon-endowed amphitheater behind Tower of Terror. Shown just after dusk, this expression of Mickey's dreams (and nightmares) is filled with dancing fountains, characters galore, and special effects synchronized to classic Disney tunes. Note that the best seats are actually toward the back of the theater.

DISNEY'S ANIMAL KINGDOM

So strong is this park's sense of purpose that it's as if the animals of the world put their antlers and antennae together and created it themselves—to celebrate their aardvark-to-zebra diversity, remind us of their prehistoric heritage, and rally support for wildlife conservation efforts. Not that Disney's creative hand isn't greatly evident in this park.

Endangered-species breeding programs coexist with blockbuster attractions. Sophisticated Audio-Animatronic dinosaurs share the marquee with more than 1,700 animals (some 250 species), whose habitat needs dictate much of the landscape. Dinosaur fossils are abundant; plastic straws and Styrofoam cups, conspicuously absent. (One glimpse at the park and it's no surprise that Animal Kingdom is accredited by the

American Zoo and Aquarium Association, an organization that supports conservation, education, science, and recreation.)

GETTING ORIENTED: Although greenery reigns in these parts, relegating concrete, and indeed most architecture, to garnish status, successful penetration of this particular jungle requires no compasses, scythes, or snakebite kits. The park is set up as a set of themed lands decidedly unlike any you've encountered in your neighborhood.

To see the forest through the trees, look up: Like the icons of its Worldly siblings, Animal Kingdom's Tree of Life serves as an instant beacon for the momentarily disoriented. This massive spectacle also anchors the park's most central land, Discovery Island.

The layout of this park might be compared to the silhouette of a simple daisy. Acting as the stem is the lush expanse of the Oasis. Discovery Island (the land that serves as the park's hub), encircled by a river, is the flower's center. And extending from the center like petals are bridges leading sharply southeast to the primeval area known as DinoLand U.S.A.; northeast to Asia; northwest to Africa, the park's largest land; and southwest to Camp Minnie-Mickey, a character vacationland.

It's true that Disney's Animal Kingdom is more than double Epcot's size, but thanks to the considerable roaming room designated for animal residents only, it takes no more legwork to circumnavigate this park than to explore Epcot. As anyone who's been to Epcot can attest, this is

still a good amount of walking—so follow our efficient touring plan and take advantage of the park's many pleasant resting spots. Seniors who opt to tour the smaller parks on foot may choose to rent a wheelchair at Animal Kingdom—or better yet, given the steep inclines throughout the park, a self-driven Electric Convenience Vehicle (ECV).

A Walking Tour

Our tour begins much like any other intrepid adventure, assuming that intrepid adventurers have inexplicably omitted mention of turnstiles that must be traversed en route from urbane Central Florida to the Great Unknown. No matter. You're about to be enveloped by **The Oasis**, a canopy of nature that serves as

Touring Priorities

DON'T MISS	DON'T OVERLOOK	DON'T KNOCK YOURSELF OUT
Kilimanjaro Safaris*	Rafiki's Planet Watch	The Boneyard
Dinosaur*	Discovery Island Trails	TriceraTop Spin
Maharajah Jungle Trek	The Oasis	Primeval Whirl*
It's Tough to be a Bug!*	Flights of Wonder	
Festival of the Lion King**		
Kali River Rapids*		
Pangani Forest Exploration Trail		
Expedition Everest*		

* Fastpass attraction as of press time. Consult a guidemap for new additions.

** Pay close attention to performance schedules.

Animal Kingdom's inviting foyer. Two paths lead north to Discovery Island and the looming Tree of Life. As you proceed farther into the fragrant tangle of tropical trees and flowers, allow yourself to be distracted by waterfall-laden streams and glimpses of macaws, iguanas, and giant anteaters. Then tell yourself it's all a mirage and move on.

Emerging from the northern reaches of the Oasis entry-zone, you arrive at a bridge to Discovery Island and receive your cue to gasp—a panoramic view of Animal Kingdom's central land, the moatlike river, the soaring Tree of Life, and the balance of the park before you.

Discovery Island

Exotic in a neither-here-nor-there-but-certainly-not-North America sense, Discovery Island is awash in the sort of vivid color paintbrushes dream about imparting. Meticulously carved and painted building facades and smatterings of African and Caribbean folk art add to the eye-catching allure of environs intended to replicate a village in the tropics. Notable as the land that serves as the gateway to all other Animal Kingdom lands, it's

Hot Tips

- This park's layout can be confusing, especially for first-time visitors. Pick up a guidemap as soon as you enter the park. Use it to help plan your day, allowing enough time to travel from one area to the next for a show with a set start time.
- The animals are out and about all day—so any time's a good time to experience the safari ride.
- Weekends tend to be the most crowded days at Disney's Animal Kingdom.

also the park's core dining and shopping zone.

Take a minute to glance at the **Tip Board**, listing showtimes and current waiting times for popular attractions. This board is on the right as you enter Discovery Island. Checking the board to align your schedule with certain showtimes (listed in a park times guide) will help you structure your day.

The big draw here is the **Tree of Life**. The man-made tree looms 145 feet over the park as its main icon. Even dung beetles have their place on this arboreal masterpiece, whose 50-foot-wide trunk and windblown limbs contain nose-to-nose carvings of every animal Disney artists could fit. Certainly, Mickey's lineage is represented. The carvings are a tribute to the richness and diversity of animal life on our planet.

Don't neglect to check out the cockatoos, flamingos, deer, and other wildlife living among the tree's roots along **Discovery Island Trails**.

Before you leave the Tree of Life vicinity, consider the possible advantages of starting small. If you can bear eight minutes of animated insects creeping and crawling into your personal space, see **It's Tough to be a Bug!**, a 3-D special-effects show shown—where else?—inside the tree. It's a decidedly Off-Broadway show, starring Flik (from the film *A Bug's Life*) and a cast of a million bugs whose previous credits include such

shows as *Beauty and the Bees* and *My Fair Ladybug*.

You become an honorary bug in an effort to understand their world, but things go awry when several of Flik's buddies don't appreciate a visit from you.

After a demonstration of their talents, you may suddenly cease to be fazed by any creature with fewer than six legs.

Note: Anyone leery of spiders, roaches, and the like is advised to skip the performance, or risk being seriously bugged.

DinoLand U.S.A.

Once you stroll beneath the big brachiosaurus skeleton, you'll enter what appears to be a kitschy park created around a remote paleontological dig site.

This zone features intimate rendezvous with winners (crocodiles) as well as sore losers of the Cretaceous period's Survival of the Meteorproof. The big attraction here is **Dinosaur**, a time-travel trip fraught with asteroids and frightening run-ins with Disney's largest and most realistic Audio-Animatronic figures yet.

A 3½-minute thrill attraction that has earned raves, Dinosaur is inside the Dino Institute, a museum-like building that reveals nothing of the fast, jarring ride ahead. Of course, there's a larger mission that has nothing to do with the desire for an adrenaline rush and everything to do with selfless intentions to save an iguanodon. (Don't worry, we'll explain.) Basically, you have it on good authority that if you shoot 65 million years back in time, there's a chance you can bring back an iguanodon for paleontologists to study. The catch: You must do this seconds before the meteor blast thought to have sealed the dinosaurs' fate and ended the Cretaceous period. So you strap yourself into the vehicle and contemplate what to say to the 16-foot-tall creatures.

And so it is that you find yourself in a race against time, ducking meteors and attempting to blink away encroaching non-vegetarian dinosaurs as your vehicle rages out of control. Just when you think you're in the clear, you'll notice the nostril-flaring carnotaurus hot on your tail. What happens next is for us to know and for you to find out. Dinosaur is not to be missed (unless, of course, you have dinophobia, are pregnant, suffer from back or neck problems, or have a heart condition).

There's the potential for one last stop in these parts: a detour to the Theater in the Wild to take in the new stage show (Tarzan Rocks! closed up shop in 2005). You may have an encounter with Lucky, the audioanimatronic dinosaur, on the way!

Asia

A footbridge that wouldn't look out of place in the Himalayas, were it not filled with strolling theme park guests, leads from Discovery Island to this chip off Earth's largest continent. Your gateway to Asia is the village of Anandapur, where a musical welcome is provided by tiny brass bells that dangle from the eaves of pagodas, dancing in the wind. Speckling the landscape are temples overtaken by gibbons, ruins frequented by tigers, a pavilion leased to fruit bats, and the like.

That mountain ahead is a replica or the world's tallest peak—Mount Everest itself. Housed inside this not-so-natural wonder is a thrilling new ride known as **Expedition Everest** (scheduled to open by summer of 2006). Feeling brave? Climb aboard the train and brace yourself for a high-speed roller coaster–like experience. Expect the train to chug through bamboo forests, past waterfalls, and along

glacier fields as it climbs up snowcapped peaks. When it hits a bump in the road, hang on! You'll soon be hurtling through caverns and canyons—and visiting one mighty angry Yeti (aka Abominable Snowman).

If you survive the Yeti-encounter and are up for more adventure (and a quick shower) head to **Kali River Rapids.** You'll know you're in the right queue if you see a stream of soggy people filing by.

Once your raft shoves off from the boathouse, it parts the waters beneath a fog-shrouded steeple of greenery. Don't be lulled into security, no matter how sweetly the birds chirp. Soon you'll be trading this calm for a smoldering obstacle course lined with freshly shish-kebobbed forest. Yes, just ahead lies a precarious game of limbo under an abandoned logging truck and a burning tree. The sum total is a jostling five-minute ride that is best left to nonpregnant people *sans* heart conditions and neck or back problems.

Note that cameras and other non-waterproof valuables should not be taken on Kali River Rapids. While there is a storage space in the middle of the raft, we suggest entrusting them to a nice, dry locker or non-riding member of your party.

Did You Know . . .

- The carvings on the Tree of Life represent about 325 of the 1.4 million existing species.

- Many of the plastic benches in Animal Kingdom were made from recycled material.

- The Disney Wildlife Conservation Fund helps nonprofit organizations protect endangered animals. You can donate by adding a dollar for conservation projects to your shop purchase.

- Most of the animals here were born in other zoological parks. Many are registered in special management and breeding programs called SSPs (Species Survival Plans).

- WDW has eliminated most of its insecticide use, replacing chemicals with millions of predatory insects—many of which are bred at The Land in Epcot.

Quiet Escapes

Who says you can't find peace in a jungle? Consider these relatively relaxing spots and seek out others.

- The Oasis in the afternoon
- Discovery Island Trails (especially near the back of the Tree of Life)
- Pangani Forest Exploration Trail
- Tables along the river at Flame Tree Barbecue in Discovery Island (except at lunchtime)
- Cretaceous Trail
- Rafiki's Planet Watch
- Anywhere but Camp Minnie-Mickey

Continue your Far East itinerary with the **Maharajah Jungle Trek**, a tour through the nearest Southeast Asian rain forest in the most primitive of tour vehicles (your own two feet). Led by an unobtrusive, insightful guide (yourself), you do what great explorers in the wilds can't: parade unharmed past roving tigers and Komodo dragons.

Don't be afraid to linger. Even Olympians of these species can't breach Disney's security systems. Chicken out on passing through the darkened bat chamber, and you may never see a *Pteropus vampirus*—the closest thing to a Chihuahua with a six-foot wingspan—eating pineapple chunks. But you'll still spot Malaysian tapir, birds, and

acrobatic gibbons galore.

Speaking of chickens, here's another feather for your explorer's cap. The Caravan Stage, which struts out performances of **Flights of Wonder** several times daily, can accommodate 1,000 people and all manner of flappers. Check a guidemap for times.

Note: This show is actually much more enjoyable than one might expect. It's also a nice opportunity to rest your feet and escape the blazing sun.

Africa

If imitation is the sincerest form of flattery, then Africa has got to be blushing. In creating this largest section of the park, Disney seems to have stopped just shy of moving mountains (Kilimanjaro is conspicuously missing). The artfully reconstructed African savanna and woodland aren't merely stunning to behold. They're designed to satisfy the habitat specifications of each meerkat, zebra, and elephant. Countless trips to the continent, exhaustive planning, and some slick adaptations have enabled Disney to mesh the intimacy of a zoo with the aura of a safari.

Disney's Africa is truly a land of opportunities, among them: treading just a few yards from cavorting gorillas; observing rhinos, gazelles, and hippos en masse; exchanging glances with a passing giraffe; getting up to speed on wildlife protection and conservation efforts; and chasing renegade ivory poachers.

Of course, you wander over and find yourself suddenly surrounded by hippos and elephants. You acclimate to the continent in the atmospheric village of Harambe, patterned after modern coastal communities in East Africa. Harambe is important as the spot for food, drink, and shopping during your stay in Africa. It is also the gateway to some exceptional attractions.

Kilimanjaro Safaris, Disney's variation on the classic African travel adventure is one to beat a path to. The 20-minute guided trip through a simulated savanna escorts you within boasting distance of many of the world's most beloved animals—so close you'll begin to wonder which of the 32 people in your open-air gawkmobile (as we've loosely dubbed the roofed, rugged transportation of choice) has irrepressible animal magnetism. As the vehicle bumps along the dust-caked road, you'll observe animals on the move and watch for elephants, gazelles, rhinos, baboons, and lions. Such animals as giraffes and zebras may draw quite near.

Your guide will fill you in on less familiar species; for a preview, steal quick glances at the species identification cheat sheet above the seat in front of you. These animals have room to roam and thus better things to do than stare back at you. Of course, as on a real safari, you might not see certain animals on a given trip; they could be sleeping, hiding, or otherwise engaged. So consider riding more than once during your visit.

A good follow-up to the safari is a walking tour that invites lingering and offers a closer look at gorillas and other animals. Also accessible from Harambe, **Pangani Forest Exploration Trail** segues from a research lab to the enchanting environs of a free-flight aviary and an aquarium. Beyond that, you'll come upon a stream dammed with

Animal Kingdom Snacks

For a healthy treat, try the juice blends at the Safari Bar next to Rainforest Cafe or fruit from a stand in Africa. If you need a sweet treat, head for the fresh-baked cookies or ice cream at DinoBites in DinoLand, or the pastries at Kusafari Coffee Shop & Bakery, in Africa. For a cool pick-me-up, try chocolate-covered frozen bananas or Simba's Paw Print ice cream bars from a vendor, or the ice cream or fresh fruit smoothies from Tamu Tamu Refreshments, in Africa. Or try chicken-fried rice and other Asian specialties at Chakranadi Chicken Shop or the ever-popular smoked turkey legs on Discovery Island.

Entertainment

Entertaining distractions include African musicians and super-knowledgeable wildlife experts who wander the park with interesting animals. And don't miss Mickey's Jammin' Jungle Parade, featuring off-road-style floats like Rafiki's Adventure Rover and Goofy's Safari Jeep. Check a park times guide for current entertainment schedules.

glass—the site of a synchronized swimming demonstration by hippos. Okay, so maybe it's not synchronized. But the buoyant beasts don't have to wear nose plugs to be amusing in their underwater glory. Even so, we know what you're thinking: "Are we there yet? Where are the gorillas?" Rest assured, the chest thumpers are close at hand.

There's a bit more to see before you reach the gorilla sanctuary, however, namely, a scenic savanna overlook and an ensemble of Timon's meerkat cousins. (FYI: Don't expect to see any Pumbaas. Meerkats and warthogs don't pal around in the real world.)

After you peer into their habitat at close range through floor-to-ceiling glass, walk over a suspension bridge to the gorilla valley, and begin turning your head U.S. Open–style to take in the antics of the family brood and the bachelor brood now flanking you (provided that they're in the mood be seen). Back in Harambe, you'll find the train depot for the **Wildlife Express to Rafiki's Planet Watch**, a narrated 5½-minute train trip that chugs quietly behind the scenes of Africa, providing a reverse perspective of Kilimanjaro Safaris along with insights into the park's inner workings. For those wanting a rest, it offers a leisurely lift (and the only mode of transportation) to and from **Rafiki's Planet Watch**, the attraction that serves as Animal Kingdom's ideological cornerstone. As a center for wildlife preservation efforts and veterinary care, it crystallizes the park's environmental themes and encourages active support of wildlife programs while the safari's still fresh in your mind.

Camp Minnie-Mickey

If you want to commune with animals more accustomed to standing still for pictures, take a trip to Camp Minnie-Mickey.

The not-to-be-missed attraction here is **Festival of the Lion King**, an entertaining 30-minute spectacle of dance, song, and acrobatics by a troupe of talented tribal performers. The theater is huge (and air-conditioned!)—but the show is popular. Arrive 30 to 45 minutes before showtime. For a sweet morality tale (with live forest creatures!), follow the stream of very young guests and take in **Pocahontas and Her Forest Friends**.

Animal Kingdom Unplugged

If Rafiki's Planet Watch doesn't sate your curiosity, there are two three-hour behind-the-scenes tours that will. Backstage Safari, basically Animal Care 101, takes you through such creature facilities as the elephant barn and the veterinary hospital. The tour is offered on Monday, Wednesday, Thursday, and Friday, and costs $65, plus park admission.

Another tour, Wild by Design, shows how Disney's Animal Kingdom came to be—from architecture to artifacts and a whole lot more. It's offered on Tuesday, Thursday, and Friday. The cost is $58, plus park admission. Call 407-WDW-TOUR (939-8687) for reservations.

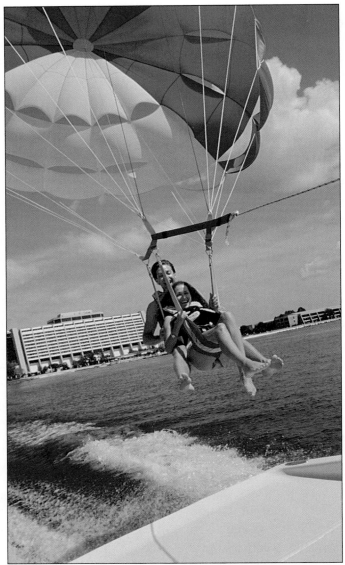

The sky's the limit for recreational activities beyond the theme parks.

Diversions: Sports, Shopping, and Other Pursuits

You've flown with Peter Pan in the Magic Kingdom, blasted into outer space at Epcot, got a backstage peek at Tinseltown at the Disney-MGM Studios, and bonded with bugs and dinosaurs at Animal Kingdom. Now what?

The World beyond the major theme parks offers a slew of terrific diversions that, interspersed between park visits, help establish perfect symmetry in a well-rounded Walt Disney World vacation. Once you get over the shock of finding such activities here in the first place, you're still pinching yourself because the quality of the experiences is so good. You'll find that even more world-class adventures for adults (thoroughly described on the following pages) exist within the playground that is Walt Disney World.

We're just hinting at the possibilities when we mention golf courses, widely considered among the country's best; tennis facilities, health clubs, and the Disney's Wide World of Sports complex—all perfect examples of Disney's ability to dazzle in the most unexpected arenas. On the shopping front, tantalizing stores (including a collection of character-defying options at Downtown Disney) are popping up property-wide. Add the last word in water parks, including a sky-scraping water slide and a humongous wave pool, and the list is still incomplete. For a full inventory of distractions (the categories: sports, shopping, and other pursuits) so compelling you might wonder why anyone bothers with those theme parks, read on.

SPORTS
Golf

Walt Disney World's 99 holes of golf—second only to the Mouse in drawing power—is renowned for the challenge, variety, and fairness of its courses. Disney World has become a familiar name on *Golf Magazine*'s biennial list of the best golf resorts in the country. *Golf Digest* has tabbed four of the World's five par-72 courses as outstanding ("plan your next vacation around it") or very good ("worth getting off the interstate to play"). And noted golf writer Glen Waggoner is hardly alone in giving Mickey Mouse's backyard the nod as America's greatest golfing haven. In Waggoner's own words, "Some other places have an individual course that is superior to any in Walt Disney World's line-up, but no other resort in the entire country has five courses this good." Solidi-fying this reputation is the Funai Classic at Walt Disney World Resort (October), a PGA Tour event with over a quarter century of prestige behind it.

KNOW BEFORE YOU GO: WDW's peak golfing season extends from January through April. During this period it is especially important to secure reservations well in advance for play in the morning and early afternoon (though starting times after 2 P.M. are usually available at the last minute). Tee times are particularly difficult to get during the third and fourth weeks of January, when some 30,000 truly serious golfers descend on the area for the PGA of America's Merchandise Show, and during the Funai Classic at Walt Disney Resort (October). The Capital One Bowl (January) and Daytona 500 (February) have also proven capable of filling the courses quickly. During such busy periods, the advance reservations and guaranteed tee time can be absolutely indispensable. Further, guests who opt for the Magic Your Way premium package may choose golf as an activity and book tee times 120 days in advance. (That's a full month before anyone else can.)

Rates: Greens fees for the 18-hole courses vary according to when you visit (peak versus non-peak seasons), which course you play (Osprey Ridge is more expensive), and your guest status (WDW resort guests get a break). Basically, though, you can count on paying about $60 to $175 per round (depending on the day or the week and your tee time), including the required cart. Throughout the year, golfers can save some money by teeing off in the late afternoon, when twilight rates may afford savings of more than 50 percent. The biggest savings can be had from May through late September, when rates for all courses drop to about $60 after 10 A.M. At Oak Trail, a 9-hole walking course, play starts at about $38 (half price on the second round), depending on the time of day. Annual Golf Memberships ($53), available to Florida residents only, can provide big savings (depending on the season) for play after 10 A.M., and also include use of a cart and a 20 percent discount on golf lessons given by the PGA teaching staff. The annual golf pass also permits members to bring up to 3 guests to use the discount.

Reservations: Golfers who book lodging at any on-property resort may secure tee times up to 90 days in advance (with the exception of those on the Magic Your Way premium package, who may book 120 days ahead). For everyone else, the window of opportunity is 60 days out. (It's often difficult for guests staying outside WDW to get prime tee times during busy weeks.) Note that four golfers are assigned to each starting time, so parties may be matched up. To book tee times, call 407-WDW-GOLF

Golf Rates

The following greens fees were in
effect at press time for the WDW
golf courses. Prices do not include
tax and are likely to go up in
2006. Prices fluctuate between
Peak and Nonpeak seasons. Walt
Disney World resort guests get
$10 off the Day Visitor Rate.

Day Visitor Rates
(subject to change)

- Osprey Ridge: from $109* to $169
- Eagle Pines: from $99* to $154
- Magnolia: from $84* to $139
- Palm and Lake Buena Vista:
  from $79* to $119
- Oak Trail: starts at about $38

* Summer discounts (late April through late
September) lower rates for all courses to
about $45 to $60 as of 10 A.M.

* Twilight rates begin at 3 P.M. during much of
the year, starting an hour earlier in certain
seasons. Rates range from $50 to $80,
depending on tee time and course chosen.

(939-4653). Reservations must
be made with a credit card.
Cancellations must be made 48
hours in advance or you'll be
charged in full.

Transportation: Transportation
is provided via taxi to the Palm,
Magnolia, Osprey Ridge, Eagle
Pines, and Lake Buena Vista
courses and is available from
select Walt Disney World resorts.
Call the Lobby Concierge; the
taxis work on a voucher system.

Dress: Proper golf attire is
required on all courses. Shirts
144

must have collars, and if shorts
are worn, they must be Bermuda
length. Soft spikes only.

Equipment rental: Gear,
including Footjoy shoes ($7) and
range balls ($6 a bucket), is
available for rent at all WDW pro
shops. Golf-club rentals run $45
to $55 per set for men, $45 for
women, depending on the style,
plus a refundable $500 credit
card deposit; photo ID required.
Prices are subject to change.

INSTRUCTION: Players looking to
improve their games have several
options: one-on-one instruction,
swing analysis sessions, and
playing lessons. At the Walt
Disney World Golf Studio, based
at the Palm and Magnolia, PGA
professionals offer 45-minute
sessions that concentrate on
improving players' swings
through video analysis; cost is
$75, plus tax.

Playing lessons, in which a
PGA pro provides on-course
instruction, delving into strategy,
club selection, and short game
skills, as well as the psychological
side of golf, are $150, plus tax.
Private lessons are available for
$63.60 per half hour.

Reservations are required for all
lessons; call 407-WDW-GOLF
(939-4653) up to one year ahead.

TOURNAMENTS: The Funai Classic at Walt Disney World Resort, which draws top PGA Tour players every fall, is among the most celebrated events on Disney's sports calendar. Because the Classic is one of the last regular PGA Tour stops of the year (usually in October), exciting competition is a given; pros are looking to vault themselves into the Tour Championship or secure spots on the top 125 money list.

Venues for the tournament are the Palm and Magnolia courses. During the first two days of the competition, the pros play each course once with an amateur player. After 36 holes, the field narrows to the low 70 pros, who compete for a percentage of the tourney's multimillion-dollar purse in the final two rounds, played on the Magnolia. Tickets are available on-site each day of the tournament. At press time, a one-day price for each round was $30. The weekly badge, good for admission throughout the tournament, costs $50. Practice rounds (held several days before the tournament) are open to spectators at no cost. Pricing and ticket structures are subject to change. For information and updates about the Funai Classic, call 407-835-2525.

Those who are willing to pay big dues may play the Classic alongside the pros. Card-carrying members of the Classic Club play with a different competing

Mickey and Mini Golf

Leave it to Disney to create 18-hole miniature-golf courses that eschew the typical tackiness for clever designs, both fanciful and devious. The first round is about $10; it's half price for the second. Hours are 10 A.M. to 11 P.M. Call 407-WDW-PLAY (939-7529) for more on these locations.

- Disney's Fantasia Fairways, one of the two courses at the Fantasia Gardens Miniature Golf complex near the BoardWalk, is ruled by daunting doglegs, sand traps, water traps, par 3s, and par 4s. Astute players may notice shrunken signature holes from famous links. (Play time: about 1½ hours.)

- At Fantasia Gardens, the second course near the BoardWalk, whimsical tees offer odes to *Fantasia*. En route, balls hit chimes and xylophone stairs, and spur water spouts and fife playing. (Play time: about an hour.)

- Disney's Winter Summerland, vacation spot to Santa and Christmas elves, offers the best of both seasons. Near Blizzard Beach, surfboards and sand castles speckle the summer-themed course, while igloos and ice sculptures give the wintry course the freeze. (Play time: about an hour per course.)

pro each day for the first two rounds of the tournament. Some memberships include lodging, reduced greens fees on Disney courses for a year, and admission to the theme parks for a week. For details, call 407-824-2250.

The Courses

PALM: This prickly yet picturesque course (located just west of the Polynesian resort) is marked by tight wooded fairways, a wealth of water hazards, and elevated greens and tees, which bear Joe Lee's unmistakable signature and make for challenging club selections. The par-72 Palm plays shorter and tighter than its mate, the Magnolia, and measures 5,311 yards from the front tees, 6,461 from the middle, and 7,010 from the back. The palm-dotted venue hosts the Funai Classic at Walt Disney World Resort, along with a fellow Lee design, the Magnolia course. Of the holes garnering the most locker-room curses (numbers 6, 10, and 18), the sixth, a 412-yard par 4, is the

most notorious. There's a lake on the left, woods and swamp on the right, and more water between you and the two-tier green. Although Palm number 6 is the number one handicap hole, number 18 (the number 2 handicap hole) has consistently baffled the pros more than any other Disney hole. The course—whose greens were resurfaced and tee boxes laser-leveled and rebuilt in 2004—opened in 1971 with the Magnolia and the Magic Kingdom itself. Facilities shared by the Palm and the Magnolia include two driving ranges, a putting green, and a pro shop. Walt Disney World Golf Instruction is also based here. Course record: 61 (Mark Lye, 1984).

Slope Scope

The slope ratings for the five par-72 Disney courses from the back tees are: Osprey Ridge, 131; Magnolia, 136; Palm, 138; Eagle Pines, 135; Lake Buena Vista, 133. By way of comparison, an average slope rating is around 115. The famously challenging links at Pebble Beach check in at 139; the formidable TPC Stadium course at Ponte Vedra, at 135.

MAGNOLIA: Like the Palm, the Magnolia opened with the Magic Kingdom in 1971. Its greens were resurfaced and several of its holes were tweaked in 2005. Course designer Joe Lee realigned teeing areas, recontoured greens, and replaced the original playing surface with a "faster" grass, among other things. The Magnolia features abundant water and sand, but what sets it apart—aside from the 1,500 magnolia trees and a mouse-eared bunker beside the sixth green—is exceptional length, vast greens, and a flaw-exposing layout that requires precision and careful course management. Meandering over 175 acres of wetlands and rolling terrain, the par-72 course measures 5,232 yards from the front tees, 6,642 from the middle set, and 7,201 from the back markers. Among the signature holes is number 17, a long par-4 dogleg left that dares long hitters to bite off the edge of a lake, then avoid water to the right of the green.

It is the Magnolia that has final say in the outcome of the Funai Classic at Walt Disney World Resort, and it takes full advantage with a final hole that rates among the tournament's testiest. Facilities shared by the Magnolia and the Palm are two driving ranges, two putting greens, and a pro shop. Course record: 61 (Payne Stewart, 1990).

OAK TRAIL: This nine-hole par-36 walking course in a 45-acre corner of the Magnolia is a good venue for beginners, yet it's no cream puff for better players. The 2,913-yard layout unleashes plenty of challenges—including two fine par 5s—and boasts well-maintained greens.

OSPREY RIDGE: Tom Fazio has taken his signature mounding along fairways and around greens to monumental heights here—most dramatically with a namesake ridge that meanders through the property and elevates some greens as high as 25 feet above the basic grade. The

Tee Time

Want to increase your chances of getting a WDW course tee time? Heed this advice:

- Play on Monday or Tuesday.
- Tee off in late afternoon.
- Come in the summer (when special rates are available).

147

In the Rough

"There's a lot of wildlife around the Palm course's property," says a former Disney pro. "People have seen deer, otters, turkeys, bobcats, and even panthers. One day, someone said he saw a couple of bald eagles."

designer counts Osprey Ridge among his best efforts, and the sentiment is echoed in the course's considerable popularity among experienced golfers. The long par-72 layout winds through a beautifully remote and thickly forested part of the property near Fort Wilderness; it has a deceptively gentle start, then raises the stakes en route to its three great finishing holes. Along the way, players will confront the signature par-3 third hole, with its elevated tee, and the fierce 14th, a long par 4 with a carry over water. Osprey Ridge plays to 5,402 yards from the front tees, 6,680 from the middle, and 7,101 from the back. Facilities shared by Osprey Ridge and Eagle Pines include a driving range, a putting green, pro shop, restaurant, and lounge. Course record: 65 (Daniel Young, 1992).

EAGLE PINES: The subtle contours of this low-lying link provide a decided contrast to the dramatic landscaping of its companion

course, Osprey Ridge, which also plays from the same clubhouse. Designed by Pete Dye on a (successful) mission to create a unique challenge for players of all levels, Eagle Pines features target fairways, expansive waste areas, and roughs lined with pine needles. True to its rustic environs (it's on the outskirts of Fort Wilderness), the course is sufficiently nestled in foliage and marshlands to summon comparisons to a nature preserve. Although water comes into play on 16 holes, the overall impression is one of great variety, from short par 4s to far sterner challenges—this is one course that lives up to the cliché of making you use every club in the bag. The course measures 4,838 yards from the front tees, 6,309 from the middle, and 6,772 yards from the back

Course for Celebration

The nearby town of Celebration, Florida, is home to the Celebration Golf Club, a joint venture of father-and-son designers Robert Trent Jones, Sr., and Robert Trent Jones, Jr. Fees for the par-72 course range from about $65 to $129, depending on the time of day and season; call 407-566-4653.

The Ten Most Humbling Holes

Cumulative toughest-playing Classic holes since 1983:

1. Palm No. 18
2. Palm No. 6
3. Palm No. 10
4. Palm No. 4
5. Magnolia No. 5
6. Magnolia No. 18
7. Magnolia No. 17
8. Magnolia No. 15
9. Magnolia No. 1
10. Palm No. 12

markers. Facilities shared by Eagle Pines and Osprey Ridge include a driving range, a putting green, a pro shop, a restaurant, and a lounge. Course record: 60 (Bart Bryant, 1993).

LAKE BUENA VISTA: This Joe Lee design is a Rodney Dangerfield of sorts. One of the shortest of the five 18-hole courses, it features a good amount of water, and its fairways, hemmed in by stands of pine and oak, are Disney golf's tightest. Lake Buena Vista honors its reputation as a friendly course for less experienced golfers. But it is also well equipped to challenge more-skilled players. As golf writer Glen Waggoner once put it, Lake Buena Vista may be the weakest link in the Disney chain, but it's still head and shoulders above the number two venue at most other golf resorts in the U.S.

The course's toughest holes—the 11th and the 18th—were at one time counted among the ten most humbling tests in the history of the Funai Classic at Walt Disney World Resort. But perhaps no one has greater respect for the course than Calvin Peete, who, in the 1982 Classic, blitzed the Palm in a record-breaking 66 strokes, only to give it all back—and more—on little ol' Lake Buena Vista.

The course plays to 5,194 yards from the front tees, 6,264 from the middle, and 6,819 from the rearmost markers. Facilities at Lake Buena Vista include a driving range and a practice green. Course record: 61 (Bob Tway, 1989).

Tennis

Even if you can't quite picture Mickey with a midsize racquet in his hand, Walt Disney World can still serve up plenty of tennis action for players of any caliber. There is a total of about about 20 courts scattered around the World, including four located at the Dolphin hotel and shared with the Swan. You'll find one hard court at Yacht and Beach Club, two at BoardWalk, two more at Fort Wilderness (watch out for swinging toddlers), two at Saratoga Springs, and a nice, quiet trio at Old Key West.

The Grand Floridian resort's duo of courts boasts clay surfaces. Tennis courts lighted for night play are available at many Disney resorts; this is a big deal, given the daytime heat during much of the year. Disney's Contemporary resort courts should please even the pickiest players. The six courts, lighted for night play, are clay, with a subterranean irrigation system that keeps them evenly watered without sprinklers. They're not quite in the shadow of Cinderella castle, but they are in close proximity to the Magic Kingdom. The fee to play at Contemporary and Grand Floridian is $8 per person, per hour (all other courts are free).

The Contemporary (home of the Disney Racquet Club) and Grand Floridian serve as the tennis hub of Walt Disney World. In addition to independent play, both offer group and individual instruction. Experienced players may also take part in the "Play the Pro" program and participate in organized convention-style tournaments. For more information, or to book a court, call 407-WDW-PLAY.

KNOW BEFORE YOU GO: Courts are busiest during June and July, but they are first come, first served (so to speak). February, March, and April also tend to be busy, especially around holidays and spring break. January, October, and November should be considered prime time to play. The courts are generally open from 8 A.M. to 7 P.M., but hours vary seasonally. Equipment rentals are limited in availability. Courts are available on a first-come basis. Locker room facilities are available for use at no extra charge.

Dress: It's usually hot, so we recommend cool, loose-fitting tennis whites. As for footwear—opt for flat-bottomed tennis shoes (cross-trainers and running shoes tear up courts).

Fishing

Drop a line, it's promptly answered. That's typical fishing at Walt Disney World. Bay Lake, which adjoins man-made Seven Seas Lagoon, was stocked with 70,000 largemouth bass in the mid-1960s. A restrictive policy allowed the fish to swell in numbers and size.

On these waters you're not just likely to catch fish—you're apt to catch largemouth bass weighing

eight pounds or more. And it's not uncommon for a group to catch 15 to 20 fish over a couple of hours, or for a first-timer to reel in half a dozen good-size bass.

The official policy is catch-and-release, and no license is required for fishing on Walt Disney World waterways. Fishing guides know their territory well, keep close track of where the fish are biting, and serve in whatever capacity guests prefer—from straight chauffeurs to casting coaches and even all-out facilitators.

Reservations for all Disney fishing excursions must be made at least 24 hours in advance and may be made up to 90 days ahead. Call 407-939-7529 (WDW-PLAY) for reservations and pricing information.

Guided Fishing Trips

BAY LAKE & SEVEN SEAS LAGOON: Guided expeditions offering first-rate largemouth bass fishing depart from the Fort Wilderness marina at 7 A.M., 10 A.M., and 1:30 P.M. (hours vary seasonally) for two-hour trips on Bay Lake and Seven Seas Lagoon. Trips are made on pontoon-style boats and can hold up to five passengers.

The fee per boatload runs from $180 to $210 (tack on about $90 more for an extra hour) and includes guide, gear, and beverages. Guides will pick up guests at the Contemporary, Fort Wilderness, Grand Floridian, Polynesian, and Wilderness Lodge marinas. Call 407-WDW-PLAY (939-7529).

LAKE BUENA VISTA: Guided two-hour excursions plying Lake Buena Vista and adjacent waterways depart at 7 A.M., 10 A.M., and 1:30 P.M. from the Downtown Disney Marketplace marina. On 7 A.M. trips, anglers have the lake and the largemouth bass therein all to themselves (later, rental boats may infringe on prime fishing territory).

The cost for up to five people, including guide, gear, and beverages, is $200 to $225 for two hours. Guides will also pick up guests at Port Orleans French Quarter, Port Orleans Riverside, and Old Key West. Call 407-WDW-BASS (939-2277).

CRESCENT LAKE: Daily fishing excursions depart at 7 A.M. from the BoardWalk dock and 7 A.M. and 10 A.M. from the Yacht and

Beach Club marina. Cost is $200 to $225 for two hours (about $90 more for an extra hour) for up to five people, including guide, fishing gear, bait, and refreshments. Call 407-WDW-BASS (939-2277).

Fishing on Your Own

Resort guests who prefer to fish solo may do so on the canals of Fort Wilderness—catch-and-release only. Poles may be rented for about $4 per half hour at the Fort Wilderness Bike Barn. Rods and reels cost about $6 per half hour or $9 per day; bait runs about $3.50.

Port Orleans Riverside has a pond called the Ol' Fishin' Hole that's stocked with catfish, bass, and bluegill. Catch-and-release only,

Fishing Tips

Although the fishing is good here year-round, it's most pleasant from November through May, when temperatures are cooler. As for strategy, one local recommends going with plastic worms. To stack your odds, he suggests shiners (they're included). Also, top-water baits work well in spring and fall.

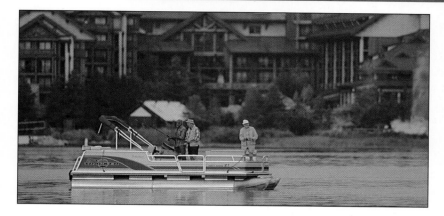

the quiet spot features a small dock among tall reeds where, from 7 A.M. to 3 P.M. every day (hours may vary seasonally), fishing is returned to its cane-pole-and-worm roots. Pole rental is $4 per half hour, including worms. Call 407-934-6000, extension 6278.

Pole fishing is also available at Coronado Springs, Saratoga Springs, and Downtown Disney (at their respective marinas). Rates are the same as at Fort Wilderness (see above).

Biking

While Fort Wilderness is certainly prime territory for some leisurely cycling, the World is filled with picturesque roads that wind within some of its most sprawling and scenic resorts.

Bikes are available (about $8 per hour or $22 per day, with some variation among locations) in precisely the spots where guests will want to ride them: Fort Wilderness, Wilderness Lodge, Old Key West, Port Orleans Riverside, Saratoga Springs, Caribbean Beach, BoardWalk, and Coronado Springs.

Boating

Guests looking to cruise, paddle, or even create a small wake on the pristine lakes and waterways of Disney World have nothing short of the largest fleet of pleasure boats in the country at their disposal. Resort marinas stand by with sailboats, pontoon boats, canopy boats, canoes, pedal boats, and minispeedboats, all of which are available for rent on a first-come, first-served basis.

On the World's most expansive boating forum, the 650-acre body of water comprising Bay Lake and the adjoining Seven Seas Lagoon, watercraft from

153

the Contemporary, Wilderness Lodge, and Fort Wilderness marinas converge with boats lighting out from the Polynesian and Grand Floridian. Other areas are more contained. Craft rented at the Caribbean Beach cruise around 45-acre Barefoot Bay. As boats on loan from the Downtown Disney Marketplace roam 35-acre Lake Buena Vista, small flotillas of rental craft drift in from the upriver marinas of Old Key West and Port Orleans French Quarter and Riverside. Meanwhile, watercraft from the Yacht and Beach Club make ripples on Crescent Lake, while pedal boaters, kayaks, canopy boats and speed boats ply the 15-acre Lago Dorado at Coronado Springs.

Resort marinas are usually open from 10 A.M. until early evening (hours vary seasonally). No privately owned boats are permitted on WDW waterways. Renters must present a WDW resort ID card, a driver's license, or a passport. Some boat rentals carry other restrictions.

CANOEING: Paddling among the narrow channels of Fort Wilderness during the peaceful morning hours, canoers pass through forest and meadows, encountering the occasional

154

quacking contingent along the way. Canoes (which run about $7 per half hour or $11 per hour) are available at the Fort Wilderness Bike Barn. Use of these watercraft is restricted to Walt Disney World canals.

CRUISING: For groups interested in taking a leisurely sunning, sightseeing, or party excursion on the water, motorized canopy boats and pontoon boats are the only way to go. Seventeen-foot canopy boats accommodating up to six adults (about $26.50 per half hour) and 21-foot pontoon boats holding ten adults (about $36 per half hour) are available for rent at most marinas. Guests must be 18 years old to rent a pontoon boat and canopy boat. For information on special-occasion cruises, see page 176.

PEDAL BOATING: For those who prefer pedal-pushing to paddling, pedal boats (accommodating two pedaling passengers and two freeloaders) are available for about $6.50 per half hour or $11 per hour at most marinas. WDW resort guests can rent the boats at the Caribbean Beach, Old Key West, Swan and Dolphin, and Coronado Springs. The Swan,

Dolphin, and Old Key West also rent Hydro Bikes (singles, $8 per half hour; doubles, about $16 per half hour), which resemble upright bicycles affixed to pontoons. Guests of Animal Kingdom Lodge, the All-Star resorts, Saratoga Springs, and Pop Century can rent boats at any of the above-mentioned locations.

SAILING: Bay Lake and Seven Seas Lagoon offer pretty reliable winds and unparalleled running room. Sailing conditions are generally best in March and April. Sailboats may be rented at the Grand Floridian, Polynesian, Contemporary, Wilderness Lodge, and Caribbean Beach marinas. Rental fees range from $20 to $25 per hour.

SPEEDBOATING: Among the most enjoyable ways to cool off at Walt Disney World is the legion of minispeedboats called Sea Raycers (which replaced Water Mouse boats). The boats' small hulls ride a choppy surface as though they were galloping steeds, maxing out at 22 miles per hour. (A bonus: Drivers must be at least 12 years old and at least 5 feet tall to pilot the boats.) Fort Wilderness Marina offers

one of the more uncrowded arenas at WDW. While the boats seat two, adult boaters will reach greater speeds going solo (and creating tiny wakes for one another). Sea Raycer boats are restricted to lakes only and are available for about $24 per half hour at the Grand Floridian, Polynesian, Contemporary, Wilderness Lodge, Fort Wilderness, Yacht and Beach Club, Caribbean Beach, Port Orleans Riverside, Old Key West, and Coronado Springs marinas.

WATERSKIING, WAKEBOARDING, AND TUBING: Guests interested in hitching a ride around Bay Lake and Seven Seas Lagoon pay about $140 per hour for a boat

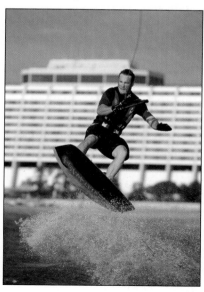

and instructor. Cost is by the boatload, and up to five people can be accommodated at a time.

Trips depart from the Contemporary. Reservations must be made at least 24 hours in advance and can be made up to 90 days ahead of time. Call 407-939-0754.

Jogging

Despite pleasant terrain that looks like it's been spread with a rolling pin, Walt Disney World can be a rough place to pursue the world's most mobile form of exercise. From late spring through early fall, comfortable running conditions are fleeting, with early birds getting the best shot at an enjoyable run. In the cooler seasons, joggers have greater freedom to explore the many compelling choices here.

Inquire about maps of the jogging trails and footpaths accessible from most WDW resorts at the hotel's Lobby Concierge desk. Courses range in distance. Port Orleans Riverside, Old Key West, and Fort Wilderness offer some of the most extensive and scenic venues.

Parasailing

If the notion of flying like a kite above Bay Lake with a panorama of the Magic Kingdom appeals to you, factor in a harness that allows you to sit in a reclined position and you have an idea of the parasailing experience as it exists at Walt Disney World.

The flight lasts seven to ten minutes, and the landing is exceptionally soft, thanks to the parachute and the two-person crew's skillful handling (as one reels in the cord, the other slows the boat to just the right speed). You won't even get wet! Parasailing excursions are offered at the Contemporary marina, with four-time World Overall Champion Sammy Duvall and his world-class instructors.

The cost is about $90 for single riders and $140 for tandem riders. Make reservations up to 90 days in advance by calling 407-939-0754. Guests must check in 20 minutes before departure. (If you're afraid of heights, this adventure will certainly scare you silly. If you're a non-acrophobe, we highly recommend the experience. The views of the Magic Kingdom are stunning.)

Swimming

As if it weren't enough to have an inside track to two massive water parks (see "Other Pursuits" in the latter part of this chapter), Walt Disney World resorts are themselves bursting at the seams with watery playgrounds. With no fewer than 60 pools spread throughout Disney's hotel grounds, guests at each resort can be assured of easy access to at least one pool. However, it is important to note that due to a policy initiated to prevent overcrowding, Walt Disney World hotel pools are open only to guests staying at that resort; pool-hopping is permitted between sister resorts (the Yacht and Beach Club; Pop Century resorts; Port Orleans Riverside and Port Orleans French Quarter; All-Star Movies, All-Star Music, and All-Star Sports; and the Swan and Dolphin).

Stock Car Driving

The drone of stock cars burning up a one-mile oval sets most anyone's mind to racing. Ergo a pumped-up driver's ed has been introduced at the WDW Speedway, near the Magic Kingdom parking lot.

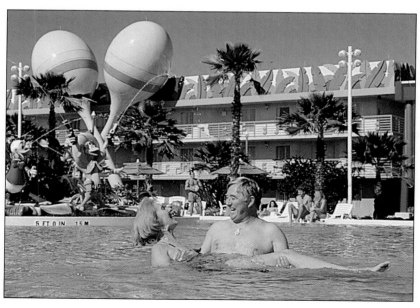

The Richard Petty Driving Experience even welcomes back-seat drivers. (Or passenger-seat drivers, as the case happens to be.)

Prefer to keep your sweaty palms off the wheel? Try the Riding Experience, about $100 for three laps; no reservations necessary.

Want your foot on that gas pedal? If you can drive a stick shift (and can prove it), consider reserving the three-hour Rookie Experience (about $380). It includes instruction and eight high-speed laps. If that doesn't sound like enough of a challenge, perhaps the 18-Lap King's Experience (about $750) is more your speed. Or, finally, ponder the Experience of a Lifetime

(about $1,250). It delivers three rounds of Petty practice. Prices quoted don't include tax.

To get in the driver's seat, call 800-237-3889.

Disney's Wide World of Sports Complex

Should your definition of paradise include slam dunks, screeching fastballs, and the intoxicating aroma of steamed weenies, welcome to nirvana. Disney's Wide World of Sports complex, which sprawls over 200 acres, is one agile place. Capable of hosting a dozen events at once, the facility has an archery-to-wrestling lineup that can make for compelling competition.

The complex serves as the spring-training ground for Major League Baseball's Atlanta Braves and the summer training camp of the National Football League's 2003 Super Bowl champion Tampa Buccaneers. It also hosts the Amateur Athletic Union (AAU) and a veritable turntable of tournaments.

Despite its large size, the complex somehow comes off as almost quaint. Its old-time Floridian architecture harks back to a simpler time and place. It recaptures the essence of a neighborhood ballpark, beckoning

Sports Complex Tips

• For a complete, updated sporting event calendar, call 407-828-FANS (3267) or pay a visit to www.disneyworldsports.com.

• WDW resort guests may take buses from the Disney-MGM Studios during park hours or from Downtown Disney. Note that transfers can take quite a bit of time.

• Tailgating in the parking lot is not permitted. (Parking is free.)

• Take an umbrella to outdoor contests (the area's prone to afternoon showers), and know that games may be canceled due to inclement weather.

• Want to be a part of the action? Volunteer to work at a Wide World of Sports event. Call 407-828-3267.

friends and families to spend a lazy afternoon together.

The complex, near the junction of I-4 and U.S. 192, has an armory of box and bleacher seats to accommodate all manner of spectators. Among the facilities to observe are the 7,500-seat baseball stadium; a field house that hosts basketball, wrestling, and volleyball; a track-and-field complex; 10 clay tennis courts; and nine multipurpose fields for football, soccer, lacrosse, and more.

About $10 (plus tax) will get you a general admission ticket on days when events are scheduled. It allows you to take in a number of nonpremium events—that is, competitions that are worth watching, but not quite major league. Tickets for all premium

Which Way to the Beach?

WDW resort guests need not set out for the coast to find pretty strands to sunbathe on and get sand between their toes. Between the resorts fronting Bay Lake (the Contemporary, Wilderness Lodge, and Fort Wilderness) and those alongside Seven Seas Lagoon (the Grand Floridian and Polynesian), there are over five miles of white-sand beaches. And that does not include the powdery white stretches at the Caribbean Beach, Yacht and Beach Club, Swan and Dolphin, and Coronado Springs resorts. The beach fronting the Polynesian's Tahiti guest building is among the more secluded shores. All beaches are reserved exclusively for guests staying at those properties. Note that swimming is not permitted.

events, such as Atlanta Braves games, are available through TicketMaster (407-839-3900; *www.ticketmaster.com*) and include license to roam the complex. Premium tickets can also be purchased at the complex's ticket office on the day of the event, if available.

For the whole lineup, visit the Wide World of Sports complex's website: *www.disneyworldsports.com.*

If an afternoon of cheering (pom-poms optional)

and rooting for the next-best-thing-to-the-home-team leaves you with a linebacker-style appetite, head straight for the All Star Cafe. The burgers are good, the atmosphere's festive, and as far as restaurants go, it's the only game in town. Vendors offer stadium snacks for those dining in their seats or on the run.

Health Clubs

Ten WDW resorts offer guests free access to health club facilities. They are: Animal Kingdom Lodge (Zahaniti Fitness Center), BoardWalk (Muscles & Bustles Health Club), Contemporary (Olympiad Fitness Center), Coronado Springs (La Vida Health Club), Grand Floridian (Grand Floridian Spa & Health Club), Old Key West (R.E.S.T. Exercise Room), Polynesian (guests use the Grand Floridian Health Club), Saratoga Springs (Saratoga Springs Spa & Fitness Center), Wilderness Lodge (Sturdy Branches Fitness Center), Yacht and Beach Club (Ship Shape Health Club). What if you're staying at one of these resorts? Provided that you are staying at another owned-and-operated Disney resort, you can use any health club facility (based on availability) for a $12 fee per day. Note that the Polynesian resort does not have its own fitness center. Guests who have a spa treatment may use the adjacent health club facility at no extra charge.

The bare-bones facility at the Swan is free for all Swan and Dolphin guests, and fine for on-the-road maintenance. Better equipped—more cardiovascular machines and saunas—are the

Contemporary Fitness Center, Muscles & Bustles at BoardWalk, La Vida at Coronado Springs, Sturdy Branches at The Villas at Wilderness Lodge, Ship Shape at the Yacht and Beach Club (which has a whirlpool, steam room, and sauna), and Zahanati Health Club at Animal Kingdom Lodge (which boasts a steam room plus spa services including massages, manicures, and pedicures). R.E.S.T. at Old Key West is free for DVC resort guests.

The best of the lot distinguish themselves by offering exceptionally pleasant environs and the likes of personal trainers and strength and cardio machines. The Dolphin ($10 per day; free for Swan and Dolphin guests) offers aerobics and Polaris equipment, and the Grand Floridian Spa & Health Club comes with frills; for details, see this chapter's "Spas" section.

The well-appointed Spa at Disney's Saratoga Springs Resort could be a Life Fitness warehouse if not for its airy

WDW's Most Striking Feature

Walt Disney World lies squarely within a band of Central Florida known as the Lightning Capital of the World. Prime striking season runs from May through September, peaking during July and August, when Mother Nature unleashes about 40 thunderstorms over just 62 days, according to National Weather Service figures. Most of these storms come and go rather quickly.

To protect yourself, seek shelter (the type with four walls and a roof) the moment you see a storm developing, and wait a good 15 minutes after the last rumble before resuming outdoor activity. Trees and umbrellas do not provide safe refuge. For a weather report, call 407-824-4104.

SHOPPING

In Downtown Disney Marketplace

THE ART OF DISNEY: If you skip this showroom filled with limited-edition art pieces, collectibles, and animation cels, you've missed out on some of the most spectacular ogling to be had in all of Walt Disney World. A Disney artist is on hand daily to draw personalized sketches of favorite characters, as well as answer questions about the animation process.

Downtown Disney, Defined

In addition to the World's best shopping, the Downtown Disney Marketplace offers restaurants, lounges, a marina, special events, and interactive fountains. Walkways link the Marketplace to its spirited neighbors: Pleasure Island and Downtown Disney West Side. The three locales (and the stockpile of clubs, shops, and restaurants therein) are collectively known as Downtown Disney—a district zoned exclusively for entertainment. Buses and boats service the area. Marketplace shops are described in this section (starting above), while Pleasure Island and West Side shops are summed up in the margin on the next page. See our "Restaurant Guide" and "Nightlife Guide" in the *Dining & Entertainment* chapter for further details on the restaurants and clubs located here.

BASIN: Scents make sense at this shop, which soothes body and soul with bath crystals, soaps, shampoos, lotions, custom candles, and gift baskets. Time seems to stand still here—the decor is reminiscent of a nineteenth-century shop.

DISNEY'S DAYS OF CHRISTMAS: This is the World's largest excuse to say "Ho, ho, ho." Rather than tick off the many delightful trimmings—both traditional and Disney style—proffered at this trove of decorative items, ornaments, and collectibles, we'll cut to the chase: Just add eggnog.

DISNEY'S WONDERFUL WORLD OF MEMORIES: In this nook, you'll find Disney World–branded scrapbook supplies (kits, glue sticks, scissors, and Disney stickers, etc.), plus a host of Disney books, stationery, and postcards—a wealth of materials to leave you with lasting memories of your Disney vacation.

EUROSPAIN: Presented by Arribas Brothers, this shop offers crystal keepsakes (engraved on-site by cutters who demonstrate the age-old art of glass sculpting), porcelain figurines, glass slippers, and more.

EARL OF SANDWICH: This Marketplace spot specializes in gourmet sandwiches and freshly made baked goods. Other savory snack items are available. (This shop occupies the space once filled by the Gourmet Pantry.) If you can't get a seat inside, know that there's ample outdoor seating along the waterfront.

GOOFY'S CANDY CO.: A shop that aims to satisfy every sweet tooth—from simple to sublime. Expect to find all things gooey and sugar coated. They even have a chocolate dipping kitchen. This makes us happy.

TEAM MICKEY'S ATHLETIC CLUB: This expansive shop specializes in sport-specific Disney character apparel, gear, and souvenirs

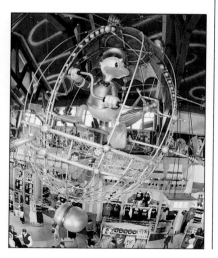

Beyond the Marketplace

The shops at Pleasure Island and Downtown Disney West Side are light on Mouse goods and heavy on offbeat items with adult appeal.

At Pleasure Island, Changing Attitudes sells funky fashions; Suspended Animation has cels; and Mouse House offers T-shirts and novelty items.

On the West Side, Starabilias peddles Hollywood memorabilia; Magic Masters offers crystal balls, linking handcuffs, and other magician's wish list items; and Magnetron is the place for umpteen magnets. Zen Zone is relaxation central; Virgin Megastore fills the music bill; and Sosa Family Cigars offers premium smokes.

that run the gamut from Goofy golf club covers to Minnie Mouse tennis whites.

WORLD OF DISNEY: The most comprehensive collection of Disney character merchandise available anywhere and a shopper's concierge desk equipped to locate any item in stock make this vast retail emporium an unbeatable venue for one-stop souvenir sprees.

As you make your way through the maze of displays, ranging from limited-edition watches to stuffed animals, from intimate apparel to office accessories, and from frames to photo albums, notice how each room has a different theme, replete with colorful murals and whimsical character sculptures. The villains room is one of our favorites.

In the Parks
Magic Kingdom
AGRABAH BAZAAR
(Adventureland): This open-air marketplace was designed to resemble a Moroccan port, where merchants from around the world come to sell their vases, brass, and other exotic wares.

BRIAR PATCH (Frontierland): The specialty of the house is merchandise that sweetly portrays Winnie the Pooh and cohorts.

CRYSTAL ARTS (Main Street): Presented by Arribas Brothers, his shop offers cut-glass bowls, vases, plates and clear-glass mugs and steins similar to those found at Eurospain in the Downtown Disney Marketplace. Items can be

engraved on-site, and guests have the opportunity to observe an engraver or glassblower at work.

DISNEY & CO. (Main Street): Victorian wallpaper and elaborate woodwork are the backdrop for this lovely shop. Among the wares: games and toys.

DISNEY CLOTHIERS (Main Street): Souvenir clothing earns big style points here, as various Disney characters appear on ties and leather goods, and are appliquéd on collared shirts, denim shirts, sweaters, jackets, and nightshirts. Selection is small but choice.

EMPORIUM (Main Street): The Magic Kingdom's largest gift shop offers an array of WDW logo and character merchandise (including lots of stuffed animals, T-shirts, sweatshirts, and hats) whose variety is eclipsed only by that found at the Marketplace. Be sure to get a glimpse of the display windows out front.

THE KING'S GALLERY (Cinderella Castle): You'll pay a king's ransom

164

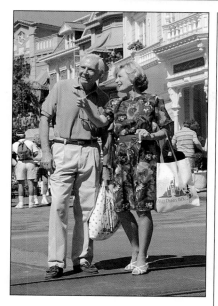

chocolate-covered Mickey-shaped pretzels, and creatively candy-coated marshmallows, this is the source. Who knows? You may even get to watch the candy-makers in action.

MAIN STREET MARKET HOUSE
(Main Street): Brass lanterns and oak floors provide the background for a selection of old-fashioned snacks and dishware. There's a small selection of candy, too.

to walk off with some of the treasures at this richly appointed shop with suits of armor and Spanish-made swords. But don't overlook the Cinderella keepsakes.

UPTOWN JEWELERS (Main Street): If you're shopping for a character watch, 14-karat gold or sterling silver jewelry, or souvenir charms, this elegant catchall is the place.

MAIN STREET ATHLETIC CLUB
(Main Street): A nifty stash of sports-related character apparel can be found here. If you want to score some great gear sporting classic Disney characters in action, don't pass.

YANKEE TRADERS IMPORT-EXPORT
(Liberty Square): A front porch with a rocking chair sets the tone for this cozy niche chock-full of kitchen accessories and candy.

MAIN STREET CONFECTIONERY
(Main Street): The sweet-toothed fall in line for peanut brittle, fudge, and marshmallow crispy treats made on the premises. For Pooh's Hunny Pots (chocolate filled with gooey caramel),

YE OLDE CHRISTMAS SHOPPE
(Liberty Square): Although smaller than Disney's Days of Christmas at the Downtown Disney Marketplace, this locale is a fine resource for traditional and character holiday decorations. Have a holly, jolly Christmas!

Epcot Standouts

THE AMERICAN ADVENTURE (World Showcase): Heritage Manor Gifts waxes patriotic with Americana. Highlights include decorative throws, history books, and American memorabilia.

THE ART OF DISNEY (Future World): The Art of Disney serves as the park's repository for Disney animation cels and limited-edition art pieces and collectibles. It is one of five such showrooms at Walt Disney World.

CANADA (World Showcase): A vast array of Canadian handicrafts and Indian artifacts puts the Northwest Mercantile on the essential-shopping circuit. But don't neglect the refined pottery and pewter candlesticks at La Boutique des Provinces.

CHINA (World Showcase): Yong Feng Shangdian is so huge, it's almost a province. The montage of paper fans, Chinese prints, silk robes, antiques, vases, and tea sets is truly something to behold.

FRANCE (World Showcase): Boutiques offering all things beautiful and French. Our favorites are Plume et Palette (collectibles), Les Vins de France (fine French wines, cookbooks, and some hand-painted dishes), and La Signature (Guerlain cosmetics and fragrances).

GERMANY (World Showcase): The little shops here are simply irresistible. Die Weihnachts Ecke is bursting with cuckoo clocks, nutcrackers, and wood carvings. Volkskunst features beer steins in all sizes, while Der Teddybär is simply a delightful toy shop. Weinkeller boasts about 50 vintage varieties and holds daily wine tastings. Kunstarbeit in Kristall offers steins, crystal, and assorted Christmas goodies. Finally, Glas und Porzellan is a boutique stocked with Goebel's M. I. Hummel figurines.

ITALY (World Showcase): When in this multishop pavilion, we gravitate toward Enoteca Castello for Italian wines, plus some chocolates, La Bottega Italiana for decorative ceramics and glassware, plus masks from Venice, and Il Bel Cristallo for Armani figurines, silk scarves, and leather purses and bags.

JAPAN (World Showcase): In the vast emporium known as the Mitsukoshi Merchandise Store, kimono-clad dolls (priced from $20 to $500) merit special attention, as do colorful kimonos, origami kits, bonsai, candy, and children's toys. You will also find a variety of items with which to set the table and decorate the home.

MEXICO (World Showcase): At the Plaza de los Amigos you can find all things South of the Border, including Mexican liquor, salsa and other hot sauces, sombreros, and a fine selection of ceramics and other handicrafts.

MOROCCO (World Showcase): At least half the fun of shopping in this pavilion's maze of Berber bangles, basketry, and clothing is never knowing just what awaits around the bend (we found a lovely little bottle filled with rosewater, known as *cortas*).

MOUSE GEAR (Innoventions, Future World): Epcot's best address for character merchandise also stocks a selection of souvenirs relating to surrounding pavilions (most notably, Spaceship Earth). This shop stays open about a half hour after the rest of the park. It's a great place to wait out the big exit crush.

NORWAY (World Showcase): The Puffin's Roost is undoubtedly Central Florida's best source for trolls and gorgeous, often hand-knit, Norwegian ski sweaters (bargains when compared to the cost of flights to Oslo). Wood carvings and hand-crafted jewelry add to the purchase panorama.

UNITED KINGDOM (World Showcase): Some of Epcot's finest shops lie within this pavilion's borders. There's The Toy Soldier (where Winnie the Pooh

167

Talk About an Eclectic Mix . . .

The unique array of merchandise found in shops at the Studios is best quantified by example. Recently, you could have filled the following unlikely shopping list:

- An end table once owned by Cecil B. DeMille
- Limited-edition Disney animation cel
- *I Love Lucy* silk tie
- *Austin Powers* movie lot crew ID badge
- A cocktail dress from Susan Lucci's closet

and Thomas the Tank Engine star); The Crown & Crest (a British free-for-all complete with intricately designed chess sets and pub glasses); Sportsman Shoppe (a bounty of cashmeres and sports apparel); The Queen's Table (with fragrances, soaps, and other collectibles); and The Magic of Wales (tartans). And there's a prime spot for fans of

fine bone china and English teas—The Tea Caddy.

Disney-MGM Studios

ANIMATION GALLERY: One of five Walt Disney World venues showcasing limited-edition art pieces, collectibles, and animation cels from a variety of Disney movies. The difference here: the chance to watch an artist creating and to buy the resulting artwork right on the spot. (Note that this service is not always offered and may not be available during your visit.)

KEYSTONE CLOTHIERS: Characters turn up on smartly styled men's and women's casual wear, luggage, and shoes, not to mention accessories of the character tie and boxer short sort.

Pin Trading

In the mood for some Olympic Village–style pin trading? You're in luck. A veritable bartering brouhaha has erupted at Walt Disney World. Here's how it works:

Simply purchase—or pack—some starter pins (available throughout WDW). Put the pins in a highly visible place (say, on your hat). Then keep your eyes peeled for pin-bearing park-goers or Disney cast members.

If your pin-trading etiquette is not up to snuff, ask a cast member for advice. Remember: If you're displaying a pin, it's assumed you are willing to trade it— so don't flaunt family heirlooms or other pins you can't part with. And when it comes to swapping with cast members, it's strictly Disney pin for Disney pin.

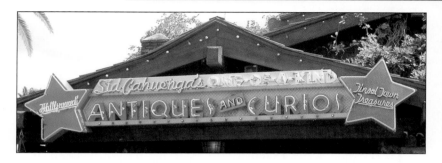

SID CAHUENGA'S ONE-OF-A-KIND:

Celebrity encounters abound in this den of movie and television memorabilia. There's lots of signed photos and movie posters and, if you time it right, very belated premiere invitations to Disney animated films.

There's also an occasional opportunity to snap up hand-me-downs direct from the stars, so when someone compliments your handbag, you can say, "Yeah, Mae West liked it, too."

MOUSE ABOUT TOWN: A well-heeled wardrobe of subtly mouse-infused jackets, sweat-shirts, and sports apparel in colors a human-about-town would also appreciate. Golf-related accessories and apparel abound.

ONCE UPON A TIME: . . . there was a little shop that offered a very classy souvenir collection—musical snow globes featuring artfully rendered Disney charac-ters and housewares.

The Mouse Delivers

- Prowling the property but can't find the object of your obsession? Ask a park employee, and if that must-have Donald Duck screen saver or Tinker Bell tea set exists, he or she should be able to find out where it's sold.

- Have a sudden, not-to-be-denied yearning for a certain music box, watch, or tie that you saw in a shop during your visit? Call WDW Mail Order at 407-363-6200.

- If your Disney cravings are still unfulfilled, call 800-237-5751 for the Disney Catalog or 818-265-4660 to find the Disney Store nearest you. Or browse through the Disney Store's offerings online at www.disneydirect.com.

- Theme park shoppers may arrange to send purchases to a location near the gates for later pickup. Walt Disney World resort guests can have purchases deliv-ered to their hotel free of charge. (Packages don't arrive until the next day, so don't ship anything for the day you plan to check out.) For an extra charge, shop-pers may arrange to have pack-ages shipped home.

SUNSET CLUB COUTURE: This purveyor of jewelry and limited-edition timepieces has the sort of incomparable selection that makes collectors' eyes widen. Consider gold pocket watches with conspicuous ears, marcasite pieces with stylized Mickey designs, and custom-made watches with tremendous face value (namely, your choice of characters, drawn and then sealed onto the watch's face).

THE WRITER'S STOP: A cozy commissary of cookies, cappuccino, stationery (and scrapbooking accessories), and Hollywood- and Disney-themed page-turners that provides a comfy pit stop (and shop).

Animal Kingdom

DISNEY OUTFITTERS (Discovery Island): Nature-themed apparel and gifts can be found here. Selections vary from everything you need to start your own backyard habitat to tinkling chimes, aromatic candles, and soothing fountains. Pal Mickey tour guides may be purchased here, too.

ISLAND MERCANTILE (Discovery Island): The park's largest shopping oasis in a nutshell: stuffed animals on safari. Certainly, this is the last word in safari hat style, as interpreted by every Disney character that ever saw the embroidered front of a sweatshirt.

MOMBASA MARKETPLACE/ZIWANI TRADERS (Africa): Take one of the striking Kenyan-made walking sticks for an in-store test stroll, and you may well receive raves on your carving skills while perusing the soapstone elephants, hand-painted boxes, raku animal figurines, straw hats, colorful apparel, and other traditional African wares—as well as a selection of Disney character–inspired items.

Conservation Initiative

As anyone who has ever given a gorilla a dollar could tell you, animals aren't great money managers. Which is why initiatives like the Disney Wildlife Conservation Fund come in handy.

This fund was established to support conservation efforts worldwide. You can help by tacking on a dollar for the Wildlife Conservation Fund when you make a purchase at any Animal Kingdom shop. If you're interested, pick up a brochure from a shop display for a list of nonprofit organizations assisted to date.

Expect a gentle solicitation at the cash register. Don't expect a gorilla looking for a handout.

OTHER PURSUITS

You're at Walt Disney World, but you're not in the mood for a theme park, don't feel much like swatting a little ball or sitting poolside, and have already shopped (and dropped). You're up for something, but lack inspiration. What to do? Don't despair. Disney's got it covered.

Water Parks

Typhoon Lagoon

The centerpiece of this 54-acre water park—ostensibly a small resort town transformed by a big storm—is a surf lagoon larger than two football fields that incites happy pandemonium with every five-foot wave that comes along. But there are also three speed slides (which drop 51 feet at 30

Did You Know?

Pontoon boats may be chartered for a cruise at any time of day. The cost for a one-hour excursion starts at about $150 for up to four guests. Each additional guest (with the maximum of 12) pays about $50. Call 407-WDW-PLAY (939-7529) for details.

miles per hour), three quick and curvy body slides, and a trio of raft rides that send tubers rollicking through caverns and waterfalls. Wanna know what your socks experience during the washing machine's spin cycle? Give Crush 'n' Gusher a whirl. It's the park's new "water coaster" thrill ride. For a calmer alternative, hop in a tube and float along the lazy river that encircles the park.

KNOW BEFORE YOU GO: Typhoon Lagoon is near Downtown Disney. Pools are heated during winter, and the park may be closed for refurbishment for about two months each year (call 407-WDW-PLAY [939-7529] for exact dates). During warmer months, the masses arrive early, often filling the parking lot before noon. When capacity is reached, no one is admitted until crowds subside, often around 2 P.M. (Typhoon Lagoon is usually the second water park to reach capacity. Blizzard Beach is first.)

HOW TO GET THERE: Direct buses from the TTC and all Disney resorts except the Grand Floridian, Contemporary, Polynesian, Wilderness Lodge, and Fort Wilderness (which may require transfers at the TTC until about 4 P.M.).

WHERE TO EAT: Of the two main snack stands, Leaning Palms offers a larger selection than Typhoon Tilly's. Picnic areas are close at hand. Outside food is welcome, but alcoholic beverages are not.

Typhoon Lagoon Tips

- Tidal conditions in the lagoon change every hour, alternating (with warning) between gentle waves and surf city. Call 407-WDW-PLAY (939-7529) for current conditions or to ask about early-morning surf lessons.

- For time checks, look to the shrimp boat marooned atop Typhoon Lagoon's makeshift mountain; it sounds its horn and shoots a 50-foot flume of water into the air every 30 minutes.

- Bad weather or capacity crowds can prompt the park to close.

- Women will find that one-piece suits fare generally better on the slides here.

VITAL STATISTICS: Hours vary, but are generally 10 A.M. to 5 P.M., with extended hours in effect during summer months (call 407-939-7529 for current times). Adult admission is about $34, not including tax. Entry to the Typhoon Lagoon water park is a "Water Parks and More" option (aka "plus" option) with the Magic Your Way ticket. It's included with a Premium Annual Pass, too. Dressing rooms are available, and lockers and towels may be rented. Singapore Sal's has beach basics.

Blizzard Beach

Disney legend has it that this 66-acre water park—Walt Disney World's largest—is the melted remains of a failed Disney ski resort. Call it a not-so-little white lie. The bottom line on this place built around a "snow-covered" man-made peak called Mount Gushmore: It has some amazing runs. Chief among them is a ski-jump-turned-speed slide that sends giddy riders down the watery equivalent of a double-black-diamond run (a 120-foot drop at a 66-degree angle, in which speeds reach 55 miles per hour). A second slide plunges from 90 feet. Less intimidating highlights include a raft ride accommodating five people per raft, side-by-side "racing" slides, and flumes that slalom. For cool yet calm, there's a lazy floatable creek that encircles the park (though it does at one point run through a cave dripping with ice-cold water) and a free-form pool with gently bobbing waves.

KNOW BEFORE YOU GO: Blizzard Beach is located near Animal Kingdom, adjacent to Disney's Winter Summerland miniature-golf course. All pools are heated during the winter; the park is

Blizzard Beach Tips

- The chairlift that transports guests to the summit of Mount Gushmore affords a wonderful view, as does an observatory located at the summit itself.

- Women will find that one-piece suits fare better on the speed slides here.

- Inclement weather or maxed-out crowds can cause the park to close early.

- The concrete pathways can get hot, making water shoes a coveted commodity.

typically closed for refurbishment for at least one month or two each year (call 407-WDW-PLAY [939-7529] for the exact dates). During the warmer months, the masses descend upon Blizzard Beach early in the day, and the parking lot frequently closes before noon. When peak capacity is reached, no one is admitted until crowds ease up, usually around 2 P.M. The park may also close due to inclement weather.

HOW TO GET THERE: Buses are available from Disney-MGM Studios and all WDW resorts.

WHERE TO EAT Of the four snack stands, Lottawatta Lodge is the largest and most centrally located. Picnic areas are nearby.

VITAL STATISTICS: Hours vary, but are generally from 10 A.M. to 5 P.M., with extended hours in effect throughout the summer months (call 407-939-7529 for current times). Adult admission is $34, not including tax. A Blizzard Beach/Disney's Winter Summerland pass, including Blizzard Beach admission and a round of mini golf, costs about $42. Entry to Blizzard Beach is a "Water Parks and More" option (aka "plus" option) with the Magic Your Way ticket. It's also included with a Premium Annual Pass. Dressing rooms are available, and lockers and towels may be rented. The Beach Haus stocks essentials.

Natural Distraction
Fort Wilderness

Simply put, no place on Walt Disney World property is better equipped to satisfy yens related to the great outdoors than this campground and recreation area, set on 700 forested, canal-crossed acres on the shore of the

World's largest lake. Between its scenic canals and its guided fishing excursions, Fort Wilderness gives anglers unparalleled access to Bay Lake's largemouth bass. Since the lake was stocked with over 70,000 bass in the sixties, this waterway is teeming with fish that are ready to tangle with your line.

A marina invites guests to rent all manner of boats for explorations of the lake. (See "Sports" earlier in this chapter for more details on fishing and boating excursions.) Escorted trail rides and a hiking path deliver nature lovers into peaceful areas where it's not uncommon to see deer, armadillos, and birds. Myriad pathways provide inspiring venues for joggers and cyclists (bikes are available for rent), and tennis, volleyball, and basketball courts are scattered about the property. There's also a goat-heavy petting farm (hey, grown-ups like animals, too), a blacksmith shop (where you can meet the man who shoes the horses that pull the trolleys on Main Street, U.S.A.), and a funky tree that has mysteriously

174

grown around a lawn mower. The two swimming pools are open only to campground guests. In the evenings, carriage rides and wagon rides (see pages 63 and 176 for more information), Mickey's Backyard Barbecue and the popular dinner show, the Hoop-Dee-Doo Musical Revue, keep things humming. Note that the beach is for sunbathing only.

HOW TO GET THERE: This isn't the easiest place to get to—but there are several travel options. The quickest way is generally by car. But know that guests staying at any Walt Disney World–owned property may take boat launches from the Magic Kingdom park, Wilderness Lodge, or the Contemporary resort. Buses also transport guests with a Disney resort ID or a multi-day admission ticket.

Fort Wilderness Tips

- You can survey the beauty of Fort Wilderness via bicycles rented from the Bike Barn for about $8 per half hour or $22 per day.

- Getting to and from this area can take a lot of time—inquire at the Lobby Concierge as to the most efficient route. Build in extra commuting time if you're planning to attend the Hoop-De-Doo Musical Revue.

GETTING AROUND: Only vehicles bound for campsites are permitted beyond the guest parking lot. Fort Wilderness is serviced by an internal bus system that links all recreation areas and campsites (buses circulate at 20-minute intervals from 7 A.M. to 2 P.M.). Guests who prefer greater independence may rent bikes or electric carts from the Bike Barn.

WHERE TO EAT: The Settlement Trading Post and the Meadow Trading Post stock a tiny supply of staples and prepare sandwiches; there's also Trail's End Buffet for all-day dining.

VITAL STATISTICS: Admission is free for Disney resort guests. The Bike Barn in the Meadow Recreation Area is the place to pick up trail maps and rent bikes (about $8 per half hour, $22 per day), canoes ($6.50 per half hour, $11 per hour), rods and reels ($5.50 per hour, $9.50 per day), fishing poles ($4 per hour, about $9 per day), and electric carts (about $46 for 24 hours; reservations necessary; call 407-824-2742). Wagon rides depart twice nightly at 7 P.M. and 9:30 P.M. from Pioneer Hall and last about an hour ($6; call 407-939-7529 to confirm times).

Fort Wilderness carriage rides depart every thirty minutes, from 6 P.M. until 9:30 P.M. Each 30-minute ride begins in front of Crockett's Tavern at Pioneer Hall and costs $30 (credit cards are not accepted; Disney hotel IDs, cash, and Disney Dollars are). Tickets are sold by the carriage drivers. Small carriages fit two guests, larger ones can accommodate four. For more information, call 407-824-2734.

Guided 45-minute trail rides depart four times daily from the Tri-Circle-D Livery near the visitor lot; reservations suggested ($32; call 407-939-7529 up to 90 days ahead).

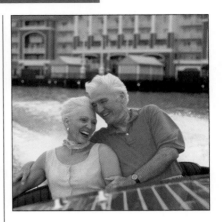

Romantic Excursions and Specialty Cruises

Breathless

Moored at the Yacht and Beach Club marina, the *Breathless* is a sleek 24-foot Chris-Craft reproduction of a 1930s mahogany runabout. The motorboat, named after the Dick Tracy character, is equipped with bench seats and fits up to seven. The boat escorts private parties on brief journeys around 25-acre Crescent Lake and adjoining waterways at speeds up to 50 miles per hour. But the most romantic outings are its dusk IllumiNations cruises, which zip by BoardWalk, the Swan and Dolphin, and the Disney-MGM Studios en route to providing prime views of the show (from beneath the bridge at Epcot's France pavilion).

RATES: The one-hour IllumiNations cruise starts at about $180. Cost is per boatload (up to seven passengers); driver is provided.

RESERVATIONS: Reservations can be made as far as 90 days in advance (up to 24 hours ahead) and are recommended for the *Breathless*. Call 407-WDW-PLAY (939-7529). Inquire about the length of the voyage when you book the reservation.

Grand 1

This striking 44-foot Sea Ray, completely furnished with two bedrooms, two bathrooms, kitchen, and living/dining room, is the sort of craft that escorts VIPs on private tours of the Seven Seas Lagoon and Bay Lake before nightfall, pausing in just the right spot as the Wishes fireworks show (when available) explodes above Cinderella Castle. But don't be misled: The *Grand 1* defines VIPs quite broadly, to encompass any group of up to 14 passengers lucky enough to snare a reservation. Although providing vistas of the Magic Kingdom fireworks is the *Grand 1*'s specialty, the elegant craft can be booked for most any hour, most any day. You may content yourself with feasting merely on the fireworks and the stars, or you may have your excursion catered, courtesy of chefs at the Grand Floridian. Thus, the possibilities extend from a private cruise for two, complete with dinner and champagne, to a cocktail party for 14, with as much shrimp, chips and salsa, chicken wings, beer, and wine as the boat can hold.

RATES: You'll pay $400 an hour (plus tax) to rent the *Grand 1*. Cost is per boatload (up to 14 passengers); driver and deckhand are included, refreshments are not.

RESERVATIONS: Reservations for excursions on the *Grand 1* should be made as far in advance as possible, preferably at the time you book your accommodations; they must be made 24 hours ahead. Call 407-824-2439 to book the *Grand 1*.

Pontoon Boats

No one will ever confuse a pontoon boat with a yacht, but when it comes to specialty cruises, no one's looking at the boat anyway. What matters: comfort, a great vantage point, and timing. So it is that Disney's pontoon boats, which accommodate up to ten people on private one-hour cruises, provide some of the best seats around for the fireworks and IllumiNations (when available). Wishes fireworks cruises ply the Seven Seas Lagoon and Bay Lake, making quiet ripples on the water just outside the Magic Kingdom. IllumiNations excursions prowl the waters of Crescent Lake.

RATES: Cost for Wishes (Magic Kingdom) or IllumiNations (Epcot) pontoon cruises, which both last about an hour, start at about $150 per boatload (for up to ten passengers); a driver is provided.

RESERVATIONS: Specialty cruises must be reserved at least 24 hours ahead; advance reservations, accepted up to 90 days ahead, are strongly recommended (especially during peak times of the year). Call 407-WDW-PLAY (939-7529).

Spas
Grand Floridian Spa and Health Club
Although more pocket-size than palatial, this simple peach-and-aqua-hued retreat has ample space to coddle 17 people at once—provided that there's a twosome being pummeled to contentment in the couple's treatment room. His-and-hers lounges, saunas, steam rooms, and whirlpools make worthy hangouts of the locker rooms. Signature services include baths steeped in native Floridian flowers and a deluxe facial complete with two masks and hand and foot massages. A cooling wrap incorporating lavender oil and calendula soothes the sunburned. Ultimate Relaxation pairs a traditional massage with a soak in a hydrotherapy. The facility is much less opulent than one might expect at this resort, but it certainly delivers a relaxing spa respite.

178

WORTH NOTING: The treatment menu includes aromatherapy; reflexology; shiatsu; Swedish, sports, deep tissue, and hydrotherapy massages; as well as a relaxing massage designed especially for expectant mothers. Massages last 25 to 80 minutes. Manicures, pedicures, and soothing hand and foot treatments are administered in the comfort of chairs that massage the lower back; feet are soaked in whirlpool baths. The spa offers a variety of body wraps (lavender and calendula, marine algae, clay, paraffin) and exfoliating scrubs (herbal, sea salt); an array of facials, including one especially for men; and several therapeutic and aromatherapy baths. Couples may receive side-by-side aromatherapy massages or a hands-on massage lesson in the couple's treatment room.

KNOW BEFORE YOU GO: The Grand Floridian Spa is located next to

Did You Know?
You're not only welcome, you are encouraged to show up at least 30 minutes before your scheduled spa service to lounge in the sauna, steam room, and whirlpool. Similarly, all three spas are linked to first-rate health clubs, which you can use before or (yeah, right) after your treatment.

The Spa at Disney's Saratoga Springs Resort

the health club at its namesake hotel, near the Magic Kingdom. Hours are from 6 A.M. to 9 P.M. (varies seasonally). Reservations may be made up to one month in advance. Call 407-824-2332.

HOW TO GET THERE: Monorail and boat transport is available to WDW resort guests from the Magic Kingdom. Similarly, guests may take the monorail from Epcot and the TTC, and buses from Downtown Disney, the Disney-MGM Studios, and Animal Kingdom.

RATES: Expect to pay about $57 for a 25-minute massage and about $115 for a facial. Prices do not include gratuity. We recommend a tip of 18 to 20 percent for quality service.

PACKAGES: Both half-day and full-day options are available. Packages range from the basic Spa Sampler (about $224; facial, manicure, and pedicure) to The Ultimate Day ($594; seven treatments, plus lunch).

This sweat-free zone within Sweat Central (aka the Saratoga Springs Fitness Center) is a realm of unaffected calm.

Services include the tingling Warm Seafoam Mud Wrap and Seaweed Hydro-Massage, a penetrating immersion in salt water and seaweed. The locker rooms are each equipped with a steam room, sauna, and whirlpool. Ordering a spa cuisine lunch is always an option in the spa's coed lounge. Specifics may change.

WORTH NOTING: The treatment menu includes aromatherapy, reflexology, sports, and Swedish massages, as well as couples treatments. Massages last about 25 to 80 minutes. The lineup of body wraps and scrubs includes several that incorporate soothing marine substances (seaweed, salt water, sea salt, and sea mud). In addition to a variety of specialty manicures and pedicures, this spa offers an array of facials, from seaweed to aromatherapy.

KNOW BEFORE YOU GO: The spa is tucked within the resort's fitness center. Treatment hours are from 8 A.M. to 8 P.M. daily. Reservations are taken up to one year ahead.

Spa Tips

- Reserve treatments well in advance; confirm your appointment before you arrive.

- Request a female or male spa therapist if you have a preference. The spa will honor your wishes, if at all possible.

- Drink plenty of water to counter dehydrating effects of treatments.

- Jewelry and spa treatments don't mix. Plan ahead and leave yours in a safe at your hotel.

- Don't forget to jump in the shower before receiving a treatment at the spa.

- If it's a body treatment, leave underwear in the locker. Robes provided are sized for modesty, and therapists are trained to discreetly cover your most private parts during treatments.

- Bathing suits are optional for the separate men's and women's saunas and whirlpools.

Health club hours are 6 A.M. to 9 P.M. daily. Call 407-827-4455.

HOW TO GET THERE: Buses transport WDW resort guests from the theme parks and Downtown Disney. There are footpaths to the spa from the Downtown Disney Marketplace and West Side. (It's about a five-minute walk.)

RATES: It costs about $110 for a 50-minute massage and about $115 for a facial (plus gratuity).

PACKAGES: Packages range from the basic "Relaxed Yet?" for about $295 to the "Adirondack Adventure," which is about $356.

The Spa at Wyndham Palace

Opposite Downtown Disney in more than location, this peaceful piece of the Wyndham Palace Resort offers a pampering repertoire that's about as deep and diverse as they come. Snazzy pedicure chairs with built-in whirlpool foot baths and back-massage capability overshadow the locker room saunas and steam rooms. Other appealing touches include landscaped outdoor whirlpools and use of one-way glass to provide views from the 14 treatment rooms. An herbal bath borrowed from Germany and Shirodhara (a hair and scalp treatment with Asian origins) are among the more esoteric specialties. The cool-mud Theme Park Leg Relief Wrap shows the spa's lighter side. Speaking of light, spa cuisine can be delivered poolside.

WORTH NOTING: Treatments include aromatherapy, sports, shiatsu, Swedish, deep-tissue, reflexology, and hydrotherapy massages lasting from 25 to 80 minutes. An adjoining full-service salon offers

New Spa on the Block!

At press time, the Dolphin resort announced the pending arrival of its very own Mandera Spa. The peaceful retreat is expected to reflect "the beauty, spirit, and traditions of ancient times, along with the soul and ritual of Asian culture."

The spa menu will showcase (among other things) Mandara's signature Balinese massage, an eclectic variation of the traditional Swedish massage developed in Bali. There's a hair and nail salon, tea garden, and a meditation garden, too.

For more information on the spa and how to book a treatment, visit *www.swandolphin.com*.

the usual services; normal pedicures and manicures are eclipsed by the likes of the 80-minute Sports Pedicure, complete with whirl-pool foot bath, heated mud pack, aromatherapy massage, paraffin dip, and reflexology.

The spa offers a variety of specialty baths (mineral, herbal, mud, seaweed) and facials, including one designed to relieve sun-stressed skin. Body scrubs and wraps incorporate cool and warm mud, sea salt, and Asia's ancient Ayurvedic therapies.

KNOW BEFORE YOU GO: The Wyndham Palace Resort & Spa is located on Buena Vista Drive, across from the Downtown Disney Marketplace. Hours are from 6 A.M. to 9 P.M. (varies seasonally). Call 800-981-1472.

HOW TO GET THERE: The resort is a short walk from Downtown Disney, which can be reached from the Magic Kingdom, Epcot, the Disney-MGM Studios, and Animal Kingdom via bus.

RATES: A 25-minute massage runs about $60, and facials cost about $92 (including 18 percent gratuity).

PACKAGES: The half-day and full-day options range from the Royal Sampler (about $160; body scrub, hydrotherapy massage, neck and shoulder massage) to the Man's Day Away ($325; personal training session, four treatments, plus lunch). Customized packages are also available.

Spa 101

As a rule, aromatherapy massages are the lightest (and most aro-matic); reflexology (all in the feet) and shiatsu involve precise pressure points rather than the (light or deep) kneading motions of Swedish massage; hydrotherapy massage (delivered by jets or a water-jet wand as you float in a tub) is as deep as it gets.

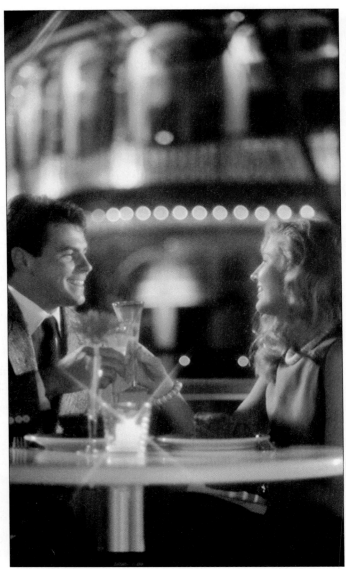

From casual to posh, Disney dining offers a delicious world of possibilities.

Dining & Entertainment

It's late in the book and we're sure you must be dying of hunger by now, so we'll begin by running through the food specials. But first, you'll be happy to hear that the outfit you are wearing at this moment, plus shoes, will be just fine for most any WDW restaurant (assuming that you didn't get all gussied up to read this chapter or that you're not in your pajamas). And second, atmosphere is a specialty of the house (you won't simply dine on seafood here, you'll do it cheek-to-cheek with a bustling coral reef or within the effervescent context of a New England clambake). Sampler platters include such unfamiliar cuisines as Norwegian and Moroccan. And if you're looking for some sophisticated eats, you're in luck.

In response to patrons' requests for fresher, more imaginative fare, Disney has given its chefs greater freedom. As an example of the quality of dining that can now be found at Walt Disney World, consider Artist Point restaurant, which features the likes of just-hooked king salmon, creatively prepared and served with hard-to-find pinot noirs from the Pacific Northwest. But we're getting carried away and you're hungry and need to make some decisions. Our "Restaurant Guide" will help. It cuts to the chase and describes the best dining spots for adults in the World.

Of course, you also need to be thinking about what you want to do later in the evening. Please, take your time, and when you're ready to think about after-dinner entertainment, know that this chapter's "Nightlife Guide" provides the complete scoop on Pleasure Island, the West Side, and BoardWalk, as well as compelling spots in the theme parks and resorts.

Enjoy!

RESTAURANT GUIDE

We're happy to report that Walt Disney World has more tempting cuisine for the sophisticated palate than ever before, as behind-the-scenes improvements—from fresher, more flavorful ingredients to stronger wine lists—have quietly pushed the epicurean envelope. Healthier, more interesting grazing options in the theme parks can provide inexpensive treats that help subsidize the sit-down meals.

To ease the task of deciding among the many eateries, we've whittled the list down to the full-service restaurants and more casual noshing spots we recommend as the best adult bets. Under the heading "Standouts,"

you'll find stellar places to grab a great bite on the quick, moderately priced restaurants with exceptional flair, and extra-special havens worth every hard-earned dollar for their distinctive food and setting. Under the designation "Good Bets," we've corralled additional locales, also highly regarded, that we've come to know as fine places to have a meal. Because Disney's theme parks are unique terrain calling for both firm arrangements and flexible eating plans, we have included recommendations for fast-food and full-service options.

THEME PARKS:
Table Service
Standouts

AKERSHUS (Norway, Epcot's World Showcase): The ambience of a medieval Norwegian fortress—marked by dramatic cathedral ceilings, stone archways, and iron chandeliers—is not to be denied. Nor is the delicious novelty of the Norwegian fare. This is your

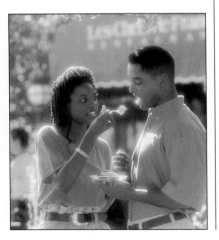

Reservations Explained

A Walt Disney World reservation is far from traditional. The system here was devised to minimize wait times, while allowing for walk-ins (who are willing to wait). When you make a reservation, you will receive a seating time, but it's not a guarantee that you'll get a table at that time. Instead, you'll be asked to check in at the restaurant at your reservation time and will then become eligible for the next available table. (Our advice: Arrive early.)

Here's how the system works: (1) Those with a reservation will be seated at or near their assigned time, and (2) walk-ins will have a shot at any open tables. To make arrangements, call 407-WDW-DINE (939-3463) up to 90 days ahead of your preferred dining date. Hours are daily from 7 A.M. to 11 P.M. It's best to confirm policies with 407-WDW-DINE. And be sure to bring your confirmation number.

you think the elegant decor, with its evocative interplay of brass sconces, milk-glass chandeliers, mirrors, and leaded glass, is convincingly French, wait until you swallow your first morsel. This is hearty dining, so you might want to stroll around the promenade to walk off your escargots, rack of lamb, and chocolate soufflé.

The impressive wine list is *très* French. Reservations suggested.
`D $$$-$$$$`

chance to sample well-prepared signature dishes that don't often leave Scandinavia. Breakfast is a character affair (hosted by Disney princesses). Wine selection is limited. Reservations suggested.
`B L D $$-$$$`

BISTRO DE PARIS (France, Epcot's World Showcase): An intimate bistro that puts on romantic airs rather than the usual bustle. If

THE CRYSTAL PALACE (Main Street, Magic Kingdom): A landmark of sorts, this restaurant—one of our favorites in the Magic Kingdom—could be a Victorian garden if not for the walls and ceiling. The airy atmosphere provides a pleasant escape from the crowds on Main Street, and the

---

B breakfast L lunch D dinner S snacks | $ $15 $$ $15-$25 $$$ $26-$46 $$$$ $47 and up

185

How to Book a Table

- In the theme parks: Reservations are suggested for nearly all table-service restaurants in the theme parks; simply call 407-WDW-DINE (939-3463). For same-day arrangements in the Magic Kingdom, report to City Hall; in Epcot, head to Innoventions Plaza; in the Disney-MGM Studios, go to the corner of Hollywood and Sunset; in Animal Kingdom, ask at Guest Relations in The Oasis (go to Rainforest Cafe for a table at the restaurant itself). Same-day plans can also be made at all park restaurants or by dialing *88 from a pay phone within a theme park.

- In WDW resorts: Reservations for Disney resort restaurants may be made by calling 407-WDW-DINE or by dialing *55 on any house phone.

- Elsewhere at Walt Disney World: Unless otherwise noted, reservations at Downtown Disney and the Hotel Plaza Boulevard resorts may be made by calling 407-WDW-DINE (939-3463).

that makes Crystal Palace a good spot to dine among Disney characters. Reservations suggested.
B L D $$-$$$

50'S PRIME TIME CAFE (Disney-MGM Studios): In a word: cool. This good-humored retreat to the era of *I Love Lucy* is an amusing amalgam of comfort food, kitschy 1950s-style kitchen nooks, and attentive servers of the "No talking with your mouth full" ilk. Expect Mom or her favored offspring to meddle in your affairs here ("Did you wash your hands? All right, then; what color was the soap?"). And recognize that the best fun is had by doing some regressing of your own. As for the fare, it's tasty

home cooking as it used to be (heavy on the meat and potatoes), served in generous-to-the-point-of-grandmotherly portions. Most guests find that it honors

all-you-can-eat buffet is easily the most bountiful spread of any meal in the park. It's driven by fresh produce, including a salad bar, and adds carved meats, fish, and creative sides for dinner. Friends from the Hundred Acre Wood wander about during all meals. It's the selection of fare their memory of fried chicken, meat loaf, s'mores, and peanut-butter-and-jelly milk shakes. A full bar is available. Reservations suggested. L D $$-$$$

GARDEN GRILL (The Land, Future World): When your assigned reservation time comes due at this lazy Susan-turned-dining area (it rotates slowly above the rain forest, desert, and prairie scenes visited by the Living with the Land boat ride below), you are politely informed by a "farm-hand" that you have chores to do. Bessie has been milked, apparently, but the table hasn't been set. And so it is that you are seated, only to have to stand and harvest your place setting from the center of the table. Chip, Dale, and pals make the rounds at each meal. The meals, which are served family style, feature vegetables grown in The Land's greenhouses, fried fish, chicken, and grilled flank steak. Reservations suggested. L D $$-$$$

HOLLYWOOD BROWN DERBY

(Disney-MGM Studios): The Studios' most gracious dining is found at this faithful revival of the original cause célèbre, which

opened on Hollywood and Vine back in 1926. Dressed to the nines in chandeliers and celebrity caricatures, the restaurant stokes the appetite with its finely chopped signature Cobb salad and fabulous grapefruit cake. The international wine list is excellent. Reservations suggested. L D $$$

Note: Guests who make reservations at their Disney resort or at any of the theme parks can take advantage of the Fantasmic! Dining Opportunity. Special seating for the evening's performance of Fantasmic! is included with a meal at no extra cost—except for tax, gratuities, and beverages, which carry an additional charge. (The Fantasmic! dinner package can—and should—be booked in advance; call 407-939-3463.)

B breakfast L lunch D dinner S snacks $ $15 $$ $15-$25 $$$ $26-$46 $$$$ $47 and up

Smoker's Alert

With the exception of designated areas, public parts of Walt Disney World are all nonsmoking. Same goes for the rest of the state, as it is now a Florida law. Check park guidemaps for areas where smoking is permitted, or inquire at your resort's lobby concierge desk.

LES CHEFS DE FRANCE (France, Epcot's World Showcase): "Bright lights, big dining room" describes this airy restaurant. With three of France's best chefs—Paul Bocuse, Roger Vergé, and pastry guru Gaston Lenôtre—keeping tabs on this nouvelle French kitchen, the broth is far from spoiled. We love the mere thought of the Lyon-style onion soup and the ways in which they fill a puff pastry. Wine pairings are suggested from the modest list. Reservations suggested. L D $$$-$$$$

L'ORIGINALE ALFREDO DI ROMA RISTORANTE (Italy, Epcot's World Showcase): Adorned with massive murals that evoke the Italian countryside, this restaurant inspires a "when in Rome" frame of mind from the outset. You suddenly hear an Italian grandma's voice in your head, urging you to "mangia." But do you go with the specialty of the house, fettuccine Alfredo? Or maybe lasagna is more to your liking? It's hard to go wrong at Alfredo's, as fresh pasta is made on the premises and Italian wines are in ready supply. This restaurant is a favorite for its atmosphere, which is at once romantic and festive. Reservations suggested. L D $$$

Good Bets

BIERGARTEN (Germany, Epcot's World Showcase): Prepare for the best of the wurst. A buffet of traditional German cuisine (don't miss the red cabbage, spaetzle, or sauerbraten) is the main attraction in this charming makeshift courtyard. Adding to the fun are communal tables, steins of beer, a selection of German wines and liqueurs and live entertainment (lunch and dinner). Follow it up with apple strudel. Reservations strongly suggested. L D $$-$$$

CINDERELLA'S ROYAL TABLE

(Cinderella Castle, Magic Kingdom): The grand renaissance setting provides a suitable backdrop for the equally grand American fare served here. Specialties have included roast prime rib, herbed chicken, and tuna. The majestic blue goblets, or the milady and milord salutations from our waiter always make us feel like queen and king for a day (or a meal). Long live the royal treatment! Reservations are strongly suggested for all meals, especially the daily character breakfast and lunch. (The toughest tickets in town. Call 90 days in advance, first thing in the morning, and keep your fingers crossed.) B L D $$$

CORAL REEF

(The Living Seas, Future World): It's all about sneaking bites of fresh fish under the watchful eyes of sea turtles, dolphins, and gargantuan groupers. Every table has a panoramic view of the living coral reef; some are right up against the glass. Menu items run the gamut from traditional seafood dishes such as broiled salmon. Grilled Black Angus rib-eye and pan-seared chicken

breast are also on the menu for those who are satisfied simply watching the fish. Reservations suggested. L D $$$

HOLLYWOOD & VINE

(Disney-MGM Studios): An Art Deco–style buffet restaurant with Tinseltown flourishes. Menu highlights have included citrus chicken and rotisserie turkey, as well as the catch of the day. Spirits are available, too.

Note: Guests who make dining arrangements at their Disney resort or at any of the parks can take advantage of the Fantasmic! Dining Opportunity. Special seating for the evening's performance of Fantasmic! is included with the meal at no extra cost—except for tax, gratuities, and beverages, which carry an extra charge. (The Fantasmic! Dining Opportunity should be booked in advance; call 407-939-3463.) D $$$

LE CELLIER STEAKHOUSE

(Canada, Epcot's World Showcase): We love retreating to this wine cellar-like spot, a favorite place for a hearty meal. The menu has featured stuffed filet, grilled veal chop, and New York strip steaks. Cheddar cheese soup is another

Dining Plan

If you are planning to book a Magic Your Way vacation package (see page 17), you may also purchase the Disney Dining Plan. Offered at regular and premium levels, the plan allows you to pre-pay for one counter-service meal, snack, and table service meal per day. The plans, which start at about $35 per day (including tax and gratuity) must be purchased for your entire trip. At press time, roughly 100 WDW eateries were participating in the program. Note that some menu items carry an additional surcharge, and "table service" doesn't necessarily mean high end. In order to dine at a "signature" spot (think California Grill or the Hoop-de-doo), you'll need to exchange two table ser-vice meals. We did the math—and, though the selection of venues is a bit restrictive—the Disney Dining Plan really can save you a chunk of change. (Though it takes a bit of work and patience.)

specialty. Then there's potential for crème brûlée. Microbrews from Quebec and Canadian lagers are served. Reservations suggested. L D $$-$$$

MARRAKESH (Morocco, Epcot's World Showcase): It's not every day that you can slip into an exquisitely tiled Moroccan palace and expect to be entertained by belly dancers and musicians as you polish off a sampler plate of distinctive Moroccan cuisine, such as couscous or kebobs. The music isn't always subtle. Reservations suggested. L D $$$

PLAZA RESTAURANT (Main Street, Magic Kingdom): Frozen desserts outnumber the fine burgers and sandwiches on the menu in this underappreciated-yet-ever-so-charming Main Street spot. Consider this ratio a hint to rope off some stomach space for one of the enormous sundaes or floats. Reservations suggested. (The dining area is rather compact.) L D S $$

RAINFOREST CAFE (Animal Kingdom and Downtown Disney Marketplace): Lush (and loud) as a jungle, this place is thick with tropical vegetation and fish-filled aquariums (not to mention the occasional thunderstorm). Dishes answer to names like Mogambo (pasta with shrimp), Plant Sandwich (veggies), and Mojo Bones (barbecued ribs). Appetizers and desserts can be shared. Reservations are suggested at the Animal Kingdom location;

B breakfast L lunch D dinner S snacks $ $15 $$ $15-$25 $$$ $26-$46 $$$$ $47 and up

No Reservations?

If you're caught without dining reservations in the theme parks, you can sometimes snag a place at one of these eateries (if you're willing to wait a bit):

- Hollywood Brown Derby (Disney-MGM Studios)
- Marrakesh (Morocco, Epcot's World Showcase)
- The Plaza (Main Street, Magic Kingdom)
- Rainforest Cafe (Animal Kingdom)
- Biergarten (Epcot's World Showcase)
- Hollywood & Vine (Disney-MGM Studios)

the Downtown Disney locale is on a walk-up basis only. **B L D S $$-$$$**

ROSE & CROWN PUB AND DINING ROOM (United Kingdom, Epcot's World Showcase): The menu ventures only a tad beyond (tasty) fish-and-chips, but we've never been disappointed. Out-door tables offer a front-row view of the lagoon (and the nightly presentation of IllumiNations), and the indoor pub is downright neighborly. A pianist occasionally provides live entertainment. Reservations suggested. **L D S $$$**

SCI-FI DINE-IN THEATER (Disney-MGM Studios): The huge salads, sandwiches, entreés, and desserts here are more creative than at your average drive-in, but the food takes a backseat to the campy setting. Parking attendants lead guests to their cars (the tables resemble 1950s-era convertibles). Science-fiction and horror trailers play in a continuous loop on a large screen. A full bar is available. Reservations suggested. **L D $$-$$$**

SAN ANGEL INN (Mexico, Epcot's World Showcase): The lights are low, the mood is romantic, and there is a smoking volcano poised tableside. If that's not enchantment enough, there's a mystical pyramid and a moonlit river. The menu? You might need to bring the table candle closer to read it, but you'll find Mexican fare from margaritas to chicken mole. Reservations suggested. L D $$$

TEPPANYAKI DINING ROOMS (Japan, Epcot's World Showcase): It's not exactly an authentic dose of Japanese cuisine (Tempura Kiku next door gives a closer approximation with its sushi, sashimi, and tempura), but it offers a good time.

Guests sit around a large teppan grill and watch as a nimble chef demonstrates just how quickly enough chicken, beef, seafood, and vegetables to feed eight people can be chopped, seasoned, and stir-fried. Entrées are sizzling and tasty. Small parties are seated together, making the meal a social affair. Reservations suggested. L D $$$

Fast Food
Standouts

BACKLOT EXPRESS (Disney-MGM Studios): Shady and inconspicuous (it's tucked away by the Indiana Jones Epic Stunt Spectacular), this sprawling spot has indoor and outdoor seating. Paint-speckled floors and movie prop debris give you an idea of the decor. Turkey paninis, grilled vegetable sandwiches, hot dogs, burgers, sesame chicken salad, chili, and assorted desserts are available. L D S $

BOULANGERIE PATISSERIE (France, Epcot's World Showcase): The chocolate croissants, blueberry tarts, apple turnovers, and such are timeless. Follow your nose, and don't neglect to notice the sweet temptation aptly known as the Marvelous. Kronenbourg beer and French wines are also offered. S $

CANTINA DE SAN ANGEL (Mexico, Epcot's World Showcase): Forget for a moment the *churros*, the frozen margaritas, and the Dos Equis drafts: this place has south-of-the-border charm. When the

Special Dietary Requests

Walt Disney World restaurants that accept reservations can accommodate special dietary requirements (such as allegies to gluten or wheat, shellfish, soy, lactose or milk, peanuts, tree nuts, fish, or eggs). Such establishments may cater to lifestyle dietary needs (such as no sugar added, low fat, low sodium, vegetarian, or vegan) as well. Similarly, guests who require kosher meals may also have their needs met. Make your kosher requests known at least 24 hours in advance. While a credit card is necessary to guarantee the order, it won't be charged if the reservation is cancelled at least 24 hours before the reservation time.

The following theme park fast food spots offer kosher selections: Cosmic Ray's Starlight Cafe at the Magic Kingdom; ABC Commissary at the Disney-MGM Studios; and Pizzafari at Animal Kingdom.

To make a special dietary request, call 407-939-3463.

weather cooperates, the outdoor lagoonside seating makes the experience even better. L D S $

COLUMBIA HARBOUR HOUSE (Liberty Square, Magic Kingdom): This spot distinguishes itself from the rest of the fast-food crowd by emphasizing things from the sea—among them, clam chowder, fried fish, salads, and harpoons (which are strictly for decor). If you get salad, request the dressing on the side (we do). For relative privacy, take your tray to the upstairs dining room. L D S $

FOUNTAIN VIEW ESPRESSO AND BAKERY (Innoventions Plaza, Future World): This ode to pastries and coffees is a veritable oasis any time of day. Wine and beer are also available. B S $

KRINGLA BAKERI OG KAFE (Norway, Epcot's World Showcase): Simply a super place for a sweet fix or a light lunch. Among the tasty morsels here are open-face sandwiches (roast beef, turkey, and salmon), sweet pretzels called kringles, and vaflers (heart-shaped waffles freshly made and topped with powdered sugar and preserves). Ringnes beer is on tap. The outdoor seating area is shaded by a grass-thatched roof. L D S $

MAIN STREET BAKE SHOP (Main Street, Magic Kingdom): This dainty spot is renowned for quick breakfasts (from bagels to warm cinnamon rolls) and enormous fresh-from-the-oven cookies (we

B breakfast L lunch D dinner S snacks $ $15 $$ $15-$25 $$$ $26-$46 $$$$ $47 and up

love the chocolate chip). The ice-cream cookie sandwiches make good use of flavors from the Plaza Ice Cream Parlor next door. B S $

SOMMERFEST (Germany, Epcot's World Showcase): Here, quick sustenance takes such classic forms as bratwurst, soft pretzels, Black Forest cake, German chocolates, beer, and German wine. The nicely shaded outdoor seating area sports a festive mural. L D S $

STARRING ROLLS CAFE (Disney-MGM Studios): Have croissant and cappuccino, will travel. This is the place to get the day off to a sweet start or to take a cookie or coffee break under umbrella-shaded tables. Added bonus for coffee connoisseurs: they roast their own beans! B L S $

SUNSHINE SEASONS (The Land, Future World): This bumper crop of food stands, located directly beneath the hot-air balloons on the pavilion's lower level, is the best place in Epcot to strap on the ol' feed bag and graze. For dining on the lighter side, select from fresh salads, soups, and handsomely garnished baked

Cheap Eats

Our suggestions for spur-of-the-moment fast food:

- Backlot Express (Disney-MGM Studios)
- Casey's (Main Street, Magic Kingdom)
- Columbia Harbour House (Liberty Square, Magic Kingdom)
- Pecos Bill Cafe (Frontierland, Magic Kingdom)
- Starring Rolls Cafe (Disney-MGM Studios)
- Sunshine Seasons (The Land, Epcot's Future World)
- Tusker House (Africa, Animal Kingdom)
- Wolfgang Puck Express (Downtown Disney West Side)

potatoes. Heartier fare comes in the form of pastas, sandwiches, and barbecued pork. Baked goods, ice cream, and libations round out the options. The eating's more peaceful here outside prime dining hours. B L D S $

TUSKER HOUSE (Africa, Animal Kingdom): Wild elephants could not keep us away from this, the park's most civilized grazing option. Consider fried or rotisserie chicken, turkey wraps, and grilled chicken salad in a bread bowl, and you may wish your safari vest came with Tupper-

B breakfast L lunch D dinner S snacks $ $15 $$ $15-$25 $$$ $26-$46 $$$$ $47 and up

ware attachments. We dig the carved chairs inside, but somehow the Safari Amber beer tastes better outside, under the thatched roof. L D S $-$$

Good Bets
COSMIC RAY'S STARLIGHT CAFE
(Tomorrowland, Magic Kingdom): Burgers, veggie burgers, salads, and rotisserie chicken are among the offerings here. Oddity of note: It isn't one-stop shopping. You may have to stand on several different lines to fill your order. Open seasonally. L D S $

FLAME TREE BARBECUE (Discovery
Island, Animal Kingdom): Take a good gander and you'll see fingers being licked at the riverfront tables bounding this pulled-pork and barbecued-brisket hut. Open seasonally. L D S $

PIZZAFARI (Discovery Island,
Animal Kingdom): When the name of the craving is pizza, consider a spot that still prefers plain old pepperoni to funky nouveau toppings. The menu strays a bit more than the average pizza place (with the likes of grilled chicken Caesar salad), but we stick to the basics. Seasonal. L D S $

PLAZA ICE CREAM PARLOR (Main
Street, Magic Kingdom): Simply the park's most bountiful stash of ice cream. Head here when you'd like to have a choice of flavors. S $

YAKITORI HOUSE (Japan, Epcot's
World Showcase): This pleasant spot (named for the specialty of the house, a savory skewered chicken) is set beside one of the most relaxing settings in all of Epcot for a quick and satisfying bite. Sake and Kirin beer are available. L D S $

In the Resorts
Standouts
ARTIST POINT (Wilderness Lodge):
The Pacific Northwest theme of this restaurant is announced in landscape murals, while tall red-framed windows look out to Bay Lake. The cavernous dining room is by no means intimate, but it's not without a certain charm.

Artist Point's hallmark is its knack for translating fresh seasonal ingredients from the Pacific Northwest into flavorful creations. An excellent example is the wild king salmon marinated in maple whiskey, then roasted with apples and herbs and served on a smoking cedar plank, accompanied by winter squash. If the signature tomato salad is in season, by all means give it a try.

The desserts are worth making room for, no matter how full you think you are. It's just the fork-licking finale you'd expect from a restaurant of this caliber. The wine list features some of the best pinot noirs coming out of Washington and Oregon right now. The cumulative effect is an artist's palette for the sophisticated palate. Reservations suggested. D $$$

BIG RIVER GRILLE & BREWING WORKS (BoardWalk): A standout for its fresh-brewed ales alone, this unassuming place delivers huge portions of pub grub. The straightforward menu runs from burgers and steaks to lobster pot pie and yellowfin tuna.

This restaurant tends to be more low-key than the other BoardWalk eateries, and makes for a peaceful retreat during the day. Seating is available outside on the boardwalk. First-come seating. L D S $$

CALIFORNIA GRILL (Contemporary): The fresh, seasonal ingredients credo gets an artistic interpreta-

Coffee Talk

For java as main course, skip the usual cup of Nescafé and head to one of these coffeehouses—they know double lattes from skim mocha cappuccinos.

- American Adventure (Epcot's World Showcase, a stand in the front of the pavilion)
- Contemporary Grounds (Contemporary resort)
- Kona Cafe (Polynesian resort)
- Sleepy Hollow (Liberty Square, Magic Kingdom)
- Starring Rolls Cafe (Disney-MGM Studios)
- Kusafiri Coffee Shop & Bakery (Africa, Animal Kingdom)
- Ghirardelli Soda Fountain and Chocolate Shop (Downtown Disney Marketplace)
- The Writer's Stop (Disney-MGM Studios)

tion at this casual feast for the eyes (as well as the stomach) on the Contemporary resort's 15th floor. Chefs at this acclaimed restaurant keep no culinary secrets as they prepare dishes in an exhibition kitchen.

The West Coast theme shines through in such dishes as alderwood-smoked salmon with whole roasted onions, and grilled-pork tenderloin with

B breakfast L lunch D dinner S snacks $ $15 $$ $15-$25 $$$ $26-$46 $$$$ $47 and up

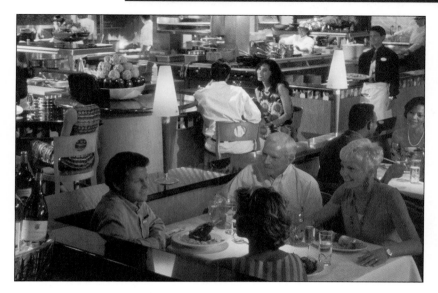

balsamic vinegar-smothered mushrooms and polenta. If there's a bit of a din in the dining room, it's partly because of unsuppressible raves and the waitstaff's collective ability to elaborate on any dish, ingredient, or wine.

The star-studded wine list is a striking mix of greatest hits and good finds. (At press time, six vintages were available by the glass, but that may change.) Also drawing a crowd: the Grill's divine California-style pizza, fine sushi bar, and a host of vegetarian choices. The goat-cheese ravioli appetizer is a crowd favorite.

Fresh desserts along the lines of butterscotch crème brûlée provide the finishing touches, as do sweeping views of the Magic Kingdom (from select seats). Reservations are strongly suggested. The restaurant's only real drawback? It's usually quite chilly. Bring a sweater, just in case. **D $$$-$$$$**

CAPE MAY CAFE (Beach Club): The ever-popular all-you-can-eat New England-style clambake held nightly in this beach-umbrella-decked dining area is among the best values at Walt Disney World. The tasty line-up includes mussels, fish, clams, oysters, peel-and-eat shrimp, corn, ribs, red-skin potatoes, chowders, and salads; lobster is available for an extra charge. If you like, dessert can be milk and cookies. Breakfast is a character affair. Reservations suggested. `B D` `$$-$$$`

CITRICOS (Grand Floridian): From the aromas wafting from the open kitchen, it's clear that the chef has vowed to wow you with cuisine from the southern Europe herb by fragrant herb. Even if the kitchen were sealed off from view and scent and there were no pastry chefs at work in the dining room, no loaves of bread baking, no private party room or artful wine pairings or potential for a plate of seared jumbo sea scallops with asparagus, shiitake mushrooms, and wine butter, we'd still . . . Strike that. There's no changing the essence of Cítricos. Reservations suggested. Closed Monday and Tuesday. `D` `$$$-$$$$`

FLYING FISH CAFE (BoardWalk): Expect an earful when you ask about the catch of the day at this compelling eatery bound and determined to serve seafood "so fresh it has an attitude." Fun, sophisticated decor from the designer of the Contemporary's California Grill elevates the

appeal. As an example of the (exhibition) kitchen's knack for light, creatively prepared dishes, consider barbecue-glazed salmon with sweet-corn pudding and potato-wrapped yellowtail snapper. The menu items vary daily, but steaks and vegetarian choices are usually offered. Make sure you save room for dessert. Note that the fare tends to be more impressive than the service. Reservations are suggested. `D` `$$$-$$$$`

JIKO—THE COOKING PLACE (Animal Kingdom Lodge): One of the most unusual Walt Disney World dining experiences, Chef Anette Grecchi Gray's cuisine is inspired by the tastes of South Africa, with influences from around the globe. Start with

We (Almost) Never Close

The following hotel eateries offer limited menus 24 hours a day during busy seasons (hours may change):

Captain Cook's Snack Co. (Polynesian)

Food and Fun Center (Contemporary)

Gasparilla Grill & Games (Grand Floridian)

Tubbi's (Dolphin)

B breakfast L lunch D dinner S snacks $ $15 $$ $15-$25 $$$ $26-$46 $$$$ $47 and up

one of the paper-thin flatbreads, like kalamata olive with five cheeses, or the unusual cucumber, tomato, and red onion salad with a watermelon vinaigrette. Pan-roasted monkfish is a signature dish, but you'll always find filet mignon and braised lamb shank on the menu, too. End your meal with a fabulous cheese course or the Jiko Dream-sicle or Tanzanian chocolate candies. The impressive wine list is exclusively South African, one of the most extensive collections in the U.S. The ethereal dining room was designed by Jeffrey Beers, a nod to the opening scenes of *The Lion King*. D $$$-$$$$

NARCOOSSEE'S (Grand Floridian): Within the conspicuous octagonal building that looks out over Seven Seas Lagoon, you'll find a casual restaurant whose open kitchen presents such not-so-casual fare as filet mignon and garlic-stuffed Maine lobster. Yet on the seasonal menu, you may also discover wild salmon, lamb chops with garlic mashed potatoes, and penne pasta with sautéed vegetables. The food is excellent, and the international wine selection is quite good—you might even enjoy a predinner glass on the veranda. Reservations suggested. D $$$

VICTORIA & ALBERT'S (Grand Floridian): Indulgent without being too haute to handle, this is considered by many to be the grande dame of the Walt Disney World dining scene. The seven-course prix fixe menu changes daily, always offering a selection of fish, poultry, beef, veal, or lamb selections as well as a choice of soups, salads, and desserts. The $95-per-person adventure begins with the arrival

Dinner in Bed

Sometimes it doesn't matter how great a restaurant's ambience is. You want the next knock on the door to be a person with a platter. Room service at Disney's deluxe hotels is as grand as you want it; ask nicely and your appetite for most anything on a house restaurant menu can be sated. With the exception of Wilderness Lodge and the Polynesian (last knock: midnight), the deluxe hotels will rustle something up around the clock. Even at moderate and value hotels, room service isn't just about breakfast; from 6 P.M. to 11 P.M. you can order sandwiches, pizza, salads, and the like. Note that deliveries generally, but not always, come within an hour.

B breakfast L lunch D dinner S snacks $ $15 $$ $15-$25 $$$ $26-$46 $$$$ $47 and up

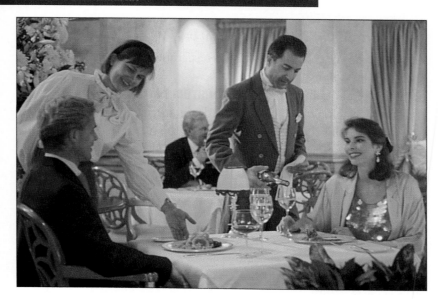

of hors d'oeuvres. As an example of what could follow, consider Oriental shrimp dumplings, chicken consommé with pheasant breast, poached Maine lobster with passion fruit butter, mixed field greens with raspberry–pinot noir vinaigrette, and a dark chocolate and strawberry soufflé. Perfect portions keep it all surprisingly manageable. The strains of a harp or violin provide a romantic backdrop. The wine list is encyclopedic. At the end of the meal, guests are presented with a souvenir menu and a red rose (ladies only). In sum, though the experience is an extremely expensive one, for many it is also quite special. Did we mention that every host and hostess here is named Victoria or Albert? Jackets are required for men. Reservations are necessary. D $$$$

Cook Nook

You're on vacation from cooking, but you still might relish some time in the kitchen. No stirring, roasting, or chopping is required. Victoria & Albert's Chef's Table in the Grand Floridian lets you chat up the masters in the kitchen as they prepare culinary delights. To book this aromatic roost, call 407-WDW-DINE six months in advance. The Chef's Table costs $125 per person (plus tax); with wine pairings, it's $185 per person.

OLIVIA'S CAFE (Old Key West): We thoroughly enjoy the Key

| B breakfast | L lunch | D dinner | S snacks | | $ $15 | $$ $15-$25 | $$$ $26-$46 | $$$$ $47 and up |

Secrets to Success

Hungry and in no mood to wait in line? To avoid the crunch, plan to eat an early (or late) meal. Table service restaurants are usually less crowded at lunch than at dinner, so you might want to make lunch the main meal of the day. But if it's a dinner spot you relish, choose a place where reservations are available (see page 185 for details). Know that Disney's reservations system does allow for walk-ins. But, because there's often a wait involved, show up before you're starving.

Western manner with which Olivia's approaches its theme; certainly, the laid-back setting and menu convey the spirit of the leisure-centric locale. Menu items include salads, conch chowder, baked mahimahi, conch fritters, and seven-layer fudge cake. Wine, beer, and cocktails are served. The menu changes seasonally. Reservations suggested. B L D $$

YACHTSMAN STEAKHOUSE (Yacht Club): Quite simply, a carnivore's paradise. The generous portions begin with massive rolls and continue with the imperative spicy fried onion skillet and the Yukon gold mashed potatoes. Of course, there's no skimping on the excellent and expertly prepared aged beef entrées (prime rib, filet

mignon, and chateaubriand, to name a few), so good luck finding room for crème brûlée. The menu also includes chicken and seafood dishes. This restaurant is filled with dining nooks suited for special occasions. Reservations suggested. B L D $$$

Good Bets

BOATWRIGHT'S DINING HALL (Port Orleans Riverside): Reasonably priced Southern specialties are the big draw at this unique eatery, where the centerpiece is a riverboat under construction, boat-making tools are mounted on the walls, and tables are set with condiment-filled toolboxes. Try the baby back ribs and Cajun dirty rice. Full bar. Reservations available. B D $$-$$$

CONCOURSE STEAKHOUSE (Contemporary): If filet mignon stuffed with mushrooms speaks to you or you'd like to sample some of the best mashed potatoes in the World or you just want a quick, civilized bite one step removed from the Magic Kingdom, here you have it. The "Stickey Mickey" is a breakfast bonus; individual pizzas and salads are good for lunch. The atmosphere isn't much to speak of, but the food is. Reservations suggested. `B L D $$$`

GRAND FLORIDIAN CAFE (Grand Floridian): Wall-length windows incorporate the hotel's central courtyard into this inviting restaurant's potted-palm greenery. A pleasant spot any time of day, it's a reasonably priced way to check out the World's poshest resort.

Seasonal dishes feature traditional American comfort food; past selections have included fried chicken and sea bass. Try the citrus french toast with cinnamon or the crab cakes with Key lime remoulade. Excellent wine selection. Reservations available. `B L $$$`

Dining Guide

This is not a comprehensive listing of the World's eateries—for that, we immodestly recommend *Birnbaum's Official Guide to Walt Disney World Dining 2006.* Instead, this chapter is a selective roundup of the best adult dining and snacking venues.

Those restaurants designated as "Standouts" are dining rooms and fast-food places whose exceptional flair, distinctive fare, and/or terrific setting have earned our highest recommendation. "Good Bets" are additional locales that offer consistently rewarding dining experiences.

KIMONOS (Swan): This is the place for good sushi and tempura in a lounge styled with bamboo and kimono accents. A wine selection is complemented by sake, Japanese and domestic beers, and cocktails. The calm is occasionally interrupted by a cacophony of karaoke (a big draw at night). Reservations accepted. `D S $$-$$$`

'OHANA (Polynesian): The beauty of 'Ohana's family-style dining experience—a South Pacific feast prepared in the restaurant's prominent open-fire cooking pit—is that the hickory-grilled skewers of turkey, pork, shrimp, chicken, and beef just keep coming. Lo mein noodles, rice, and dumplings are among the accompaniments, and the fresh pineapple dipped in caramel sauce is a fine dessert.

To make the most of 'Ohana's setting, which features exotic wood carvings under a vast thatched roof, request a table that's right up against the windows overlooking the Seven Seas Lagoon. (The number of tables there is limited, but it's worth a shot.) This puts you a comfortable distance from the grill and

B breakfast L lunch D dinner S snacks $ $15 $$ $15-$25 $$$ $26-$46 $$$$ $47 and up

the route where the coconut-rolling contest is held, but still in prime position to be serenaded by Polynesian songs. Breakfast is a character affair. Reservations suggested. `B D $$$`

PALIO (Swan): A sleek Italian trattoria that's a trusty source for imaginatively prepared homemade pasta, pizza baked in wood-fired ovens, and traditional veal and seafood dishes. (It's also one of the rare WDW spots where you'll see candles on the table.) Beers and Italian wines are also served. Reservations available. `D $$$`

WHISPERING CANYON CAFE (Wilderness Lodge): For savory eating that does not stop until you say "when," consider this family-style restaurant a good candidate. (Don't be fooled by the name. This place can be downright rowdy.) At dinner, menu items such as apple-rosemary rotisserie chicken, barbecued pork spareribs, and smoked barbecued beef brisket are sure to satisfy. Homemade desserts come with an extra charge. (Breakfast, lunch, and dinner selections are also available à la carte.) Reservations suggested. `B L D $$$`

Other Options in the World
Standouts

FULTON'S CRAB HOUSE (Downtown Disney Marketplace): Walk the gangplank onto this would-be riverboat and with one glance around you're prepared to book passage. Still, the polished woods, brass detailing, and nautical nostalgia of the restaurant are secondary to the fresh seafood served therein.

The extensive (albeit pricey) dinner menu changes with the day's arrivals. It's not unusual for Hawaiian albacore tuna (accompanied by, say, crab bordelaise and corn-whipped potatoes) to be seen next to Great Lakes walleye pike (with garlic

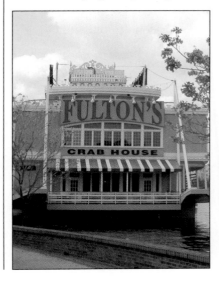

chips and herb rice). Standbys include crab cakes; cioppino, a San Francisco style stew with seafood in a tomato broth; garlic chicken; crab and lobster platters; and filet mignon.

For a quicker fix, visit the ravishing raw bar at the adjoining Stone Crab lounge suits. For a reasonably priced lunch, it's lounge or bust. Reservations suggested. L D S $$$$

HOUSE OF BLUES (Downtown Disney West Side): An eclectic menu with New Orleans taste buds (think étouffée, jambalaya, barbecue, and crispy catfish nuggets) distinguishes this folk art–studded restaurant.

It's a good spot for a late-night bite. Air conditioning–phobes

will enjoy the atmospheric, lakeside Voodoo Garden. The lively Sunday gospel brunch is a winner. Reservations are suggested. L D S $$

PORTOBELLO YACHT CLUB (between Pleasure Island and Downtown Disney Marketplace): Menu standouts at this polished yet casual piece of nautica include thin-crust pizzas baked in a wood-burning oven, farfalle primavera, and spaghettini á la Portobello, a seafood medley served over pasta in a light tomato and wine sauce.

Portobello also offers desserts, coffees, and an impressive wine list. Smoking permitted on the patio only. Reservations are suggested. D $$$$

Knockout Views

California Grill (Contemporary)

Cantina de San Angel (Mexico, Epcot's World Showcase)

Cap'n Jack's Restaurant (Downtown Disney Marketplace)

Cinderella's Royal Table (Magic Kingdom)

Coral Reef (The Living Seas, Epcot's Future World)

Fulton's Crab House (between Pleasure Island and Downtown Disney Marketplace)

Garden Grill (The Land, Epcot's Future World)

Matsu No Ma Lounge (Japan, Epcot's World Showcase)

Narcoossee's (Grand Floridian)

Rose & Crown Pub Dining Room (United Kingdom, Epcot's World Showcase)

B breakfast L lunch D dinner S snacks $ $15 $$ $15-$25 $$$ $26-$46 $$$$ $47 and up

WOLFGANG PUCK CAFE (Downtown Disney West Side): This eatery marks the Los Angeles chef's Florida debut and brings trendy California cuisine to the fore.

There are actually three dining arenas here—an express counter, a cafe, and a formal dining room on the second floor—plus a sushi bar. All feature the famous chef's signature gourmet pizzas, rotisserie chicken, and other specialties prepared in the display kitchen.

The **Wolfgang Puck Express** counter here (there's also one at the Marketplace) offers wood-fired pizzas, Chinois chicken salad, and focaccia sandwiches that defy most definitions of fast food. First-come seating. L D S S

At **Wolfgang Puck Cafe**, the menu includes (excellent) sushi, Thai chicken satay, and penne with wild shiitake and oyster mushrooms. Reservations suggested. L D S $$-$$$

Wolfgang Puck Cafe—The Dining Room puts hunger pangs happily to rest with such dishes as baby vegetable risotto and roast Cantonese duck with plum sauce, plus a wine list well suited to the cuisine. Reservations suggested. (Note that The Dining Room may undergo a name change in the near future.) D $$$

Scenic Cocktail Spots

Atlantic Dance
(BoardWalk)

California Grill Lounge
(Contemporary)

Cap'n Jack's Restaurant
(Downtown Disney Marketplace)

Matsu No Ma
(Japan, Epcot's World Showcase)

Narcoossee's
(Grand Floridian)

Outer Rim
(Contemporary)

Stone Crab
(Fulton's Crab House between Pleasure Island and the Marketplace)

Top of the Palace
(Wyndham Palace)

Good Bets

CAP'N JACK'S RESTAURANT (Downtown Disney Marketplace): This pretty pier house perched over Lake Buena Vista is the place to socialize over cold drafts and fresh seafood. The strawberry margarita is tops, as are the clam chowder, and crab cake starters. Or try the pan-seared Ahi tuna and seafood pasta entrées. First-come seating. L D S $$

OUTBACK (Wyndham Palace, Hotel Plaza Boulevard; 407-827-3430): Despite its similar meat-and-potatoes inclinations, this establishment has no relation to the chain of the same name. Go for the baby back ribs, shrimp, and steak. Reservations suggested. D $$

PLANET HOLLYWOOD (Downtown Disney West Side): This casual restaurant is ensconced inside a 120-foot-diameter sphere and surrounded by a three-dimensional collage of movie memorabilia. The menu has simple, creative flair and depth (consider the blackened shrimp, a Shanghai chicken salad, or the good old reliable hamburger and french fries). Reservations suggested. L D S $$-$$$

NIGHTLIFE GUIDE

Downtown Disney Pleasure Island

In the pages that follow, we present the best nightlife in Walt Disney World. You'll receive a thorough orientation to Pleasure Island; next, an introduction to Downtown Disney West Side; and a briefing on the clubs found along the BoardWalk.

The final section of this guide completes the nightlife picture with our report on other recommended clubs and lounges located on WDW property. Cheers!

This bustling metropolis is a six-acre island consumed entirely by clubs, stage shows, and live entertainment. Guests must be 18 or joined at the hip to a parent to be admitted to clubs. Mannequins is strictly 21 and up on Fridays and Saturdays, and BET SoundStage Club sets a minimum of 21 on Thursdays, Fridays, and Saturdays. While the main draw here is certainly the clubs, Pleasure Island's shops are a draw in and of themselves. There is no longer an admission fee (doors usually open at 7 P.M.).

At press time, some venues charged a cover, but the admission prices and policies have been known to change. Admission to Pleasure Island venues is an option with the "Water Parks and More" add-on for the Magic Your Way Ticket and is included with a Premium Annual Pass. The legal drinking age in Florida is 21, and a valid photo ID is required. While clubs close down at 1 A.M. or 2 A.M., last call is generally sounded about a half hour before closing time.

A Walking Tour

As you make your way through the main entrance, you pass (limbo if you like) under a neon archway and into the pleasure-dome itself. The first building on the left houses Mannequins, a pulsating den of special effects and techno-pop tracks that puts a unique spin on the standard club scene with a huge, rotating dance floor. Mannequins adds contemporary decor and an edgy air to its no-holds-barred scene. It takes its name from the many mannequins found throughout. Reserved strictly for patrons 21 and older, Mannequins is a club in the urban mold, and it attracts a dressed-to-impress crowd.

The music here is cranked so

Pleasure Island Tips

- It's fun to club-hop, but you can't do it with a glass in hand. Plan ahead, and ask that your last drink be served in a plastic cup. Most places keep some by the door.

- Caught with your pockets empty? There's an ATM located out front at the Rock 'n' Roll Beach Club.

- Adventurers Club and Comedy Warehouse are the island's only entirely nonsmoking venues.

- At the end of the night, if your feet are too tuckered to wait for a bus, consider taking a cab back to your resort. The fares for authorized cabs usually range between $10 and $20, depending upon your WDW destination.

- If you buy a bucketful of a specialty drink such Pleasure Island Punch, know that the second bucket comes at a discount. Of course, by the time you're ready for it you may not care.

---

loud that a jet could pass through virtually unnoticed, yet somehow the place is packed all night long with revelers who actually employ verbal communication in their flirtations. If you can stand the volume, you may take pleasure in the fact that the circulating dance floor gives a little boost to your dance skills and allows for exceptionally easy scoping, whether you're dancing or on the sidelines.

As for drinks, Mannequins offers a full bar. This club is

popular with locals and visitors, so be prepared to encounter a line at the door, especially on weekends.

Directly across from Mannequins you'll see what appears to be an authentic Irish pub. And, you know what? It is! It's Raglan Road. The cozy-yet-rollicking pub, which opened in the summer of 2005, is a meticulously decorated Emerald Isle oasis—complete with freshly prepared Irish cuisine and live entertainment. Oh, and of course, pints of stout and other spirited beverages. An evening here leaves most eyes—Irish or otherwise—smiling. Top o' the evenin' to ya.

Onward. When you leave the Raglan Road, you're on course for the Rock 'n' Roll Beach Club. At the top of the surfboard stairway, you enter a rollicking dance spot that is substantially more laid-back than Mannequins (perhaps due to its surfer sensibility and live bands).

While dancing is definitely a big deal here—the dance floor is generally jam-packed with twentysomethings—there's more to do than twist and shout the night away.

Many guests enjoy the three-story club's music and casual

atmosphere without so much as stepping onto the lowest level. They shoot pool, play air hockey and pinball, and hang out at tables overlooking the dance floor to people-watch and sip a cold beer. Roving souls should note that some of the specialty drinks here

More Reasons to Go West

Downtown Disney West Side has more than just restaurants, nightclubs, and movie theaters. It's also home to interesting shops (open until 11 P.M.; see page 163 for details) and DisneyQuest (see page 215). Most notably, it has a permanent tent for a Cirque du Soleil show called La Nouba. Wipe out all thoughts of Bozo-style antics; this circus ensemble is not your typical ringmastered, big-top production. Cirque features a cast of 60 performing a mix of acrobatics and modern dance. Wild costumes and dramatic original music add to the fun. Cirque fans consider it The Greatest Show in Downtown Disney. Call 407-939-7600 for tickets (up to six months in advance).

Two for Tea

Teatime with all the trimmings—scones, tiny sandwiches, and pastries served on bone china—is 2 P.M. in the Garden View lounge at the Grand Floridian. A large selection of teas and tasty accompaniments are offered every day until 6 P.M. (reservations recommended).

are available in portable 16-ounce squeeze bottles.

From the Rock 'n' Roll Beach Club it's on to 8TRAX—a place so seventies and eighties that "YMCA" is a scheduled event (12:30 A.M.). Suffice it to say that the *Saturday Night Fever–* style dance floor is not only an extraordinarily popular destination but an infinitely fascinating eyeful. Decor tends toward the psychedelic.

Moving along, the next club on the horizon is Pleasure Island's biggest enigma—the Adventurers Club. This elegant and eccentric parlor takes after the salons of nineteeth-century explorers' clubs, and is decked out with photos, trinkets, and furnishings that document the awfully far-reaching (and far-fetched) travels of its card-carrying members.

On the surface, it's a quiet place, filled with comfortable chairs. But penetrate the recesses of the Adventurers Club and you'll notice some pretty odd characters milling about, stumble upon some rather curious corners and goings-on, and, ultimately, be invited into a hideaway library (where those odd characters put on a curious show, complete with haunted organ). This is a nonsmoking venue.

Next door to the Adventurers Club is the BET Sound-Stage Club. This urban den for rhythm and blues and hip-hop has the cool aura of an unstoppable after-hours party.

Reserved strictly for patrons 21 and older, it's the kind of place you'd like to think Aretha Franklin might frequent, with all due respect (pun intended). A mix of music videos keeps the energy level high and the crowd pumped to dance all night long.

Our next order of business is not a club, but a forum known

209

as the West End Stage, which provides much of the juice for Pleasure Island's street party; live bands perform here nightly. Unless you are allergic to confetti, this is the place to be when the nightly New Year's Eve countdown reaches its pyrotechnic climax (showtime is 11:45 P.M.). Note that the New Year's Eve festivities may not be presented during your visit.

In any case, the most strategic spot to take it all in (since you'll be standing anyway) is the queue for the Comedy Warehouse located right across from the BET SoundStage Club. Get there no later than 11:30 P.M. (the last show is at 12:05 A.M.) to get a jump on any New Year's revelers

who might have the same idea. The Comedy Warehouse is the sort of club in which you prop yourself on a stool and hope to fall off laughing. The troupe of improv comedians does funny things with suggestions from the audience. The zingers come when you least expect it.

Every improvised performance is a little bit different, but you can expect the audience to provide some pretty challenging raw material ("We need an occupation" nets the likes of "rutabaga farmer"), and count on the troupe to rise to the occasion with amusing songs and skits. The show can be hit and miss, but if the line is short, give it a whirl.

Beer, wine, and cocktails are served (only to guests older than 21 brandishing a valid photo ID); popcorn is the preferred snack. Comedy Warehouse is a nonsmoking venue.

Downtown Disney West Side

The West Side forges with the Marketplace and Pleasure Island to make a triple-header of the distraction zone known as Downtown Disney. It's a colorful lakeside strip of restaurants, shops, and energy. Here, guests pay as they play, springing for cover charges only at places they patronize.

Puffer's alert: Smoking is allowed in designated areas only. Ask at the venue for the nearest spot. Night owl's alert: Whereas Planet Hollywood takes orders up to 1 A.M., Bongos and House of Blues serve until 1:30 A.M.

The easternmost spot at the West Side is the AMC Theatres complex, a colossal celebration of the silver screen (make that screens—there are 24 of them).

The marquee is au courant, the seats are roomy and plush (not to mention stadium style), and the sound system, developed by George Lucas, is first-rate.

Call 407-298-4488 for showtimes, the earliest of which are about 1 P.M. And bring a sweater. The air-conditioning here is powerful, to say the least.

If you prefer a diversion with an added dimension, start a conga line and head for the

After-Dark Dazzle

- The Magic Kingdom's extended curfew during busy seasons (generally summers and holiday periods) means the relaxed atmosphere and romance of the park in the early-evening hours are more accessible. After-dark also means nightly fireworks and performances of the nighttime parade.

- The fireworks show is a pyrotechnics display worthy of a Fourth of July finale. And the evening parade is not to be missed; if there are two performances, aim for the later one, when the prime viewing spots (anywhere on Main Street) are easier to snare, thanks to the little ones' need to go beddie-bye.

- Epcot's World Showcase, which stays open until at least 9 P.M. year-round, assumes a sparkling beauty at night. For this reason, Disney presents a special show, IllumiNations. This simulation of our planet's evolution features a three-story globe, intense fireworks, and stirring music. The 13-minute show, typically ignited at closing time, is visible from any point along the promenade.

- Sure to top the after-dark A-list is Fantasmic!, served up in an amphitheater behind The Twilight Zone Tower of Terror at the Disney-MGM Studios. The 26-minute show takes you inside Mickey's dreams as he conducts dancing fountains, swirling stars, and a delightful musical score. Animation projected onto water screens on the lake helps tell the story, which climaxes with a visit from Disney villains. A battle powered by flaming special effects leads to a character-filled finale.

- The Electrical Water Pageant, a 1,000-foot-long string of illuminated floating creatures, makes its way around Bay Lake each night. You can usually view the pageant at 9 P.M. from the Polynesian, 9:15 P.M. from the Grand Floridian, 9:35 P.M. from Wilderness Lodge, 9:45 P.M. from Fort Wilderness, and 10:05 P.M. from the Contemporary. Times may change.

three-story pineapple directly across the promenade. Bongos Cuban Cafe, created by singer Gloria Estefan and her husband, Emilio, is a bright, boisterous restaurant that parades the flavors and rhythms of Cuba and other Latin American countries.

When you've had your fill of the fruit-fly fandango, plot a moonlight stroll along the peaceful shore of Lake Buena Vista. Melt away the Miami mentality with a dose of cool: House of Blues. It has capacity for 2,000 soul men and women. Inspired by one of America's proudest musical traditions, the club also serves up country, with an occasional mix of R & B, gospel, or rock.

You may buy tickets through TicketMaster (407-839-3900; *www.ticketmaster.com*) or at the

Information, Please

For more on Downtown Disney happenings—from retail to concerts to the AMC 24 movie lineup—call 407-WDW-2-NITE (939-2648).

box office up until showtime; the cost is $5 to $30, depending on the act.

BoardWalk

While merely strolling the boards of this nostalgic entertainment district a short walk from Epcot provides a delightful escape to simpler times, the temptations en route are tough to resist. Cotton candy vendors, savory dining, and surrey bike rides aside, BoardWalk gives the World things it has long needed— a sports bar, a brewpub, a sing-along piano bar, and more. In addition to being an appealing resort (see *Checking In* for a complete description), BoardWalk is a great adult hangout. Although there's no general admission fee, Jellyrolls charges a cover after 7 P.M. (about $7–$10), while Atlantic Dance is usually cover-free. You must be 21 or older to enter both venues. Valet parking ($7) is available. All of the bars and clubs described below stay open until 2 A.M. With the exception of Atlantic Dance, which is open Tuesday through Saturday, all bars and clubs are open seven days a week. Smoking is permitted in designated spots only.

High on the hit list is ESPN Club, a sports bar so over-the-top it practically has referees. Between the live sports commentators, the ballpark fare, and the more than 100 televisions (some in the restrooms) broadcasting any number of games, no unnecessary time-outs are taken. Professional athletes tend to drop by on occasion to engage in a little Q&A with diners (from a stage, with a moderator; no autographs, please). Ask a host what's on the lineup for your stay. And try those chicken wings.

Several first downs away, the Big River Grille & Brewing Works invites you to bend the ol' elbow right under the brewmaster's nose. Five specialty ales,

including two that change with the seasons, are crafted on the premises. It's a tough job, but someone's got to polish off the beer bread and raise a glass to the brew maestro. After trying the beer sampler (tastes of all five ales for about $5), we heartily waved on the Tilt Pale Ale house brew. Hot beer pretzels and other appetizers from the restaurant menu are available at the bar until the kitchen closes around 11 P.M., providing fitting accompaniments to tastings.

Walk a few short strides into the dueling-pianist realm of Jellyrolls and you're soon crooning and swaying along with the rest of the congregation to songs from the 1970s to the present. As an example of the musicians' versatility,

Virgin Daiquiri, Anyone?

Soft drinks, fruit juices, and tasty specialty drinks *sans* alcohol are available at all Walt Disney World clubs. Just ask the bartender.

consider this sampling of one set: "King of the Road," "Joy to the World," and a rousing medley of TV theme songs—including odes to *The Brady Bunch* and *The Jeffersons*. The music comes uninterrupted (except by the wisecracking pianists themselves). Soon you're wondering how you got so hoarse.

So you head next door to Atlantic Dance, an elegant club which is perpetually reinventing itself. A deejay supplies a sound track to groove to, with a live band filling in on auspicious nights. You're free to dance, and, if you like, enjoy a specialty drink on a balcony overlooking the water. From this perspective, the game highlights on ESPN Club's monitors seem miles away. But they're not, and so, when your mood shifts, you can easily venture back to check the scores. Such is an evening at BoardWalk.

214

Other World Options
Standouts

CALIFORNIA GRILL LOUNGE (Contemporary): The popular, if tiny (and ever-shrinking) companion lounge to the California Grill restaurant offers what amounts to box seats for the Magic Kingdom fireworks. You can order from the California Grill menu, too. Doors close: 1 A.M.

CREW'S CUP (Yacht Club): When it comes to beer, the Crew's Cup runneth over with 35 international brews. Consider the warm copper-accented decor, the scintillating aromas wafting in from the neighboring Yachtsman Steakhouse, and the potential for four-cheese garlic bread and New England clam chowder, and you have an even better idea of why we are putty in this lounge's hands. Doors close: midnight.

THE LAUGHING KOOKABURRA GOOD TIME BAR (Wyndham Palace, Buena Vista Drive): At what is affectionately known as "The Kook," a band plays Top 40 music Wednesday through Saturday for a crowd in the 25-to-40 age range. If you'd rather not dance, snag a spot in one of four seating areas. Some 80 beers are on hand. Daily happy hour. Doors close: 2 A.M.

MARTHA'S VINEYARD (Beach Club): Although appetizers and desserts are served, the main reason you're here is the wine. Selections from a real Martha's Vineyard winery, as well as those from California, Long Island, and European vineyards, make for tough decisions, but it helps to know that wine can be ordered in sample sizes, as well as full glasses. Doors close: 11 P.M.

MATSU NO MA (Japan, Epcot's World Showcase): A quiet setting where—in addition to sake, beer, cocktails, and green tea—you can drink in a stunning vista of Epcot. Sushi and edamame are among the items served. Doors close: at park closing.

ROSE & CROWN PUB (United Kingdom, Epcot's World Showcase): We've always loved this cheeky classic—for its polished-wood and brass decor; its rich Irish, Scottish, and British drafts; and its neighborly feel. So we weren't too surprised during one of many visits to overhear a gentleman asking a fellow behind the bar to please let Jerry (a bartender not present) know that he was sorry he'd missed him. "Next time," he said hopefully. You needn't be a fan of shandies or black and tans to appreciate that. Doors close at park closing. Note that specifics are apt to change.

STONE CRAB (Fulton's Crab House, Downtown Disney Marketplace):

DisneyQuest: A Virtual Toy Box

Call it a virtual-reality check. An ode to flippers and joysticks. A bumper-car blast from your arcade past. DisneyQuest at Downtown Disney West Side is five stories of rampant interactivity that could test the supple wrists of The Who's Pinball Wizard. A sampling: You paddle a buoyant raft around rugged rocks, not to mention dinosaurs, on the Virtual Jungle Cruise. After rediscovering Centipede, you ride a simulated self-made roller coaster—a hair-raising excuse for a Virtual Makeover at Magic Mirror. Disney-Quest is open from 11:30 A.M. to 11 P.M. Sunday through Thursday, 11:30 A.M. to midnight Friday and Saturday. One-day admission is about $32, not including tax (prices may change).

Like the local heartthrob who happens to be loaded, this gorgeous riverboat bar stacks the odds even more in its favor with an excellent raw bar, prime water views, and a honey-wheat house brew. It doesn't just make Bloody Marys from scratch (as in hand-squeezed tomatoes and fresh horseradish), it garnishes them with shrimp. Doors close: 2 A.M.

TERRITORY (Wilderness Lodge): This scenic spot is marked by wood-carved grizzlies and a muraled map of the western frontier that "unfolds" over the ceiling.

While this spot can be swamped with diners-in-waiting during prime mealtimes, it more often inspires lingering. Appetizers and snacks add to the appeal. But the true toast of the Territory is Lodge House Brew, a microbrewed light beer with a hint of honey that's a Wilderness Lodge exclusive. Doors close: midnight.

TUNE-IN LOUNGE (Disney-MGM Studios): This Formica-laden spot, the family den to 50's Prime Time Cafe, serves Dad's Super Snacks and spirits from Dad's Liquor Cabinet, while vintage television sets show clips from the decade's most popular sitcoms (all food related). A baby-

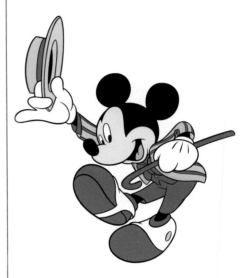

boomer's paradise, it's a great spot to cool off and regroup. Doors close: at park closing.

Good Bets

CAP'N JACK'S RESTAURANT (Downtown Disney Market-place): This pier house jutting out over Lake Buena Vista scores with a convivial atmosphere and strawberry margaritas. It also offers reasonably priced sunsets and beautiful seafood (or is it the reverse?). If there's a line for a table, sit at the bar. Doors close: 10:30 P.M.

RIVER ROOST (Port Orleans Riverside): This one's nothing fancy. Just your average, unassuming nook that happens to have a fireplace and ready access to chicken wings and spicy Cajun onion straws. Drinks stop at midnight.

MIZNER'S (Grand Floridian): If you look past the house orchestra that sets up shop nightly outside this second-floor alcove, you'll find a mahogany bar with fine ports, brandies, and appetizers. It's popular with the business set. Doors close: 1 A.M.

NARCOOSEE'S (Grand Floridian): You've got to love a lounge that's thoroughly steeped in Victoriana on the inside, and framed by a lake that lies like a picnic blanket beneath the Magic Kingdom fireworks on the veranda. Worldly wines by the glass, as well as traditional cocktails and specialty drinks. Doors close: 10 P.M.

RAINFOREST CAFE (Two locations: Downtown Disney Marketplace and Disney's Animal Kingdom. The latter has two entrances: one outside the park entrance, and another inside the turnstiles. When the restaurant is mobbed, we like to take in the thunderstorms and waterfalls from the central mushroom-capped bar. We simply saddle an unwitting zebra or giraffe (the animal bar stools are strictly hooves-to-hips) and

chase our tails. The festive, if bustling, "natural" ambience is intoxicating. Doors close: 11 P.M., weekdays; midnight, weekends.

SHULA'S (Dolphin): Enjoy your cocktail of choice in either the bar or cozy lounge areas of this restaurant that proclaims itself to be "one of the Top 10 steakhouses in America." Who are we to argue? Former Miami Dolphins coach Don Shula scores big with appetizers ranging from barbecued shrimp to steak soup. There's a TV in each room, too. Expect the big sporting event du jour to be playing. Doors close: 11 P.M.

Dinner Shows

If you're looking for a side of entertainment to complement your meal, consider a Disney dinner show. Reservations are required and may be booked up to one year in advance by calling 407-WDW-DINE (939-3463). Special dietary requests are honored with advance notice. Cancellations must be made at least 48 hours prior to showtime to avoid paying full price. Prices are subject to change.

The most popular of the lot is the Hoop-Dee-Doo Musical Revue, held in Pioneer Hall at Fort

Wilderness. The show incorporates whoopin', singin', dancin', and audience participation in a frontier hoedown. Vittles include ribs, fried chicken, salad, corn, and strawberry shortcake. There are three seatings, at 5 P.M., 7:15 P.M., and 9:30 P.M.; adults pay $49.01, including tax and tip.

At the Polynesian resort, Disney's Spirit of Aloha Dinner Show—complete with hula skirts, ukuleles, and fire—dancers takes guests on a whirl-wind journey from New Zealand to Samoa. The meal is served family style and features, chicken, spareribs, rice, and a fruit dessert. The outdoor show is presented in Luau Cove. It is a rain-or-shine affair and is canceled only when temperatures drop below 50 degrees. Adults pay $49.01, including tax and tip.

It's not a dinner show per se, but the nightly Oktoberfest celebration at the Biergarten in the Germany pavilion at Epcot's World Showcase makes for an entertaining experience. It features performers in lederhosen or dirndls yodeling and playing everything from accordions to cowbells. Seating is family style (eight to a table), and the buffet includes bratwurst, chicken, spaetzle, red cabbage, and potato salad.

Adults pay $19.99 for dinner, plus tax and tip; beer costs extra (though the beer selection is a tad limited for a place that fancies itself a beer hall). The cost for lunch is $14.99. Note that entertainment comes with lunch and dinner.

A lower profile dinner show, Mickey's Backyard Barbecue, is one of our favorites. Think of it as a Fourth of July–type picnic, fortified by live entertainment. As an instructor gives line-dance lessons, a country band whoops it up Nashville style. Disney characters kick up their heels on the dance floor. The chow includes chicken and ribs, corn-on-the-cob, baked beans, corn bread, and other reminders of summer, plus as many cold drafts as you need to wash it all down. This seasonal show, presented at Fort Wilderness, costs $39.01 for adults (with tax and tip). For reservations, call 407-939-3463 up to a year ahead.

INDEX

A

accommodations, 39–79
  check-in and check-out times, 40
  cost–cutting tips, 14, 39
  Deluxe resort properties, 41–61
  Disney Vacation Club and Camping, 41, 42, 61–65
  Moderate resort properties, 41–42, 66–71
  packages, 15–16
  ranking system for WDW resorts, 42
  rates, 44
  reservations, 40, 45
  room service, 199
  seasonal rates for 2006, 44
  special room requests, 45, 54
  Value resort properties, 41–42, 71–74
  WDW resort properties, 40–74
  amenities, 41
  resorts on Hotel Plaza Boulevard, 76–79
  special occasion (made-to-order) surprises, 52
  special room requests, 45, 54
admission passes and tickets, 16, 17, 18–20, 84, 93, 118, 130, 172, 174–175, 206
  Disney's "Ticket Tag" System, 18
  Fastpass, 83, 87, 97, 122, 131
  multi-day tickets, 16, 17
Adventurers Club, The, 29, 207, 209
All-Star Movies, 39, 71–73
All-Star Music, 39, 71–73
All-Star Sports, 39, 71–73
AMC Theatres, 34, 208, 211
American Adventure, The, 94, 108, 113–114
  shopping, 166
Animal Kingdom. see Disney's Animal Kingdom
Animal Kingdom Lodge, 42–45
Atlantic Dance, 213, 214
ATMs, 17
  in the Disney-MGM Studios, 119
  in Downtown Disney, 207
  in Epcot, 96, 106
  in the Magic Kingdom, 84
  in WDW resort hotels, 41

B

banking. see ATMs; money matters
basketball, 49, 174
Beach Club, 59–61
  fishing trips from, 152
  lounges, 215
  restaurants, 197–198, 201
  snacks, 197
beaches, 55, 58, 66, 76, 160, 173
BET SoundStage Club, 206, 209–210
Big River Grille & Brewing Works, 47, 213–214
biking, 47, 58, 62, 63, 65, 66, 68–71, 76, 153, 174, 175
Birnbaum's Official Guide to Walt Disney World Dining 2006, 202
Blizzard Beach, 172–174
BoardWalk, 29, 35, 45–48, 58, 183, 206, 212–214
  fishing trips from, 47, 152
  lounges, 205
  restaurants, 196, 198
boating, 49, 51, 53, 55, 58, 60, 62–63, 66, 68–69, 71–72, 76, 153–156, 174, 176–178
Bongos Cuban Cafe, 212
Breathless (boat), 60, 176

C

campsites, 63–64
Canada, 94, 108–110
  restaurants, 189–190
  shopping, 166
canoeing, 154
car, traveling by, 21–22
  driving from the airport, 22
  rentals, 21–22
  tips for drivers, 23
Caribbean Beach, 66–67
carriage rides, 29, 63, 69, 175–176
cash machines. see ATMs
Castaway Cay, 75, 76
CentraCare (for nonemergency medical care), 20
check-in and check-out times for WDW resorts, 40
China, 94, 108, 112, 115–116
  shopping, 166
Christmas festivities, 14
  extended hours, 11
Cirque du Soleil, 13, 208
coffeehouses, 196
Comedy Warehouse, 207, 210
Contemporary, 48–50
  guided fishing trips from, 152
  lounges, 205, 214

  restaurants, 196–198, 201–202, 204
convention centers, 48, 51, 55, 68
Coronado Springs, 67–68
couples, 34–37
credit cards, 17
crowd patterns, 11, 81, 83, 87, 95, 97, 109, 120, 122, 131,–132
cruises, 154
  romantic excursions and specialty cruises, 176–178
  See also Disney Cruise Line

D

dinner shows, 29, 30, 217–218
disabilities, guests with, 28–31
  accommodations for, 29, 54
  wheelchair rentals, 30–32, 96, 109, 119, 131
Disney Adult Discoveries programs, 102, 116, 139
Disney Cruise Line, 16, 39, 58, 74–76
Disney Dining Plan, 190
Disney-MGM Studios, 81, 82, 118–129
  admission prices, 18–20, 118
  entertainment, 129, 211
  fireworks display, 129, 211
  getting oriented, 118–119
  hot tips, 120
  hours, 118
    Extra Magic Hours, 15
  quiet escapes, 123
  restaurants
    fast food, 192, 194, 196
    snacks, 196
    table service, 186–187, 189, 191
  sample schedule, 26
  shopping, 168–170
  Tip Board, 120
  touring priorities, 122
  walking tour, 119–129
Disney Vacation Club, 46, 57–58, 62
Disney Visa Card, 17
Disney Wildlife Conservation Fund, 135, 170
DisneyQuest, 34, 208, 215
Disney's Animal Kingdom, 81–82, 130–139
  admission prices, 18–20, 130
  Africa, 136–139
  Asia, 134–136
  behind-the-scenes tour, 139
  Camp Minnie-Mickey, 139
  Dinoland U.S.A., 133–134
  Discovery Island, 132–133
  entertainment, 138
  getting oriented, 130–131

hot tips, 132
hours, 130
 Extra Magic Hours, 15
The Oasis, 131–132
quiet escapes, 136
restaurants, 191, 194–195,
 198–199, 217
 snacks, 138, 196
sample schedule, 23
shopping, 170
Tip Board, 132
touring priorities, 131
walking tour, 131–139
Disney's Fantasia Fairways
 (mini golf), 145
Disney's Hilton Head Island
 Resort, 58
Disney's Magical Express, 21
Disney's Magical Holidays
 (December), 14–15
Disney's Old Key West Resort,
 58, 61–63
 guided fishing trips from, 152
 restaurant, 201
Disney's Share a Dream Come
 True parade, 92
Disney's Spirit of Aloha Dinner
 Show, 218
Disney Stars and Motor Cars
 Parade, 129
Disney's "Ticket Tag" System, 18
Disney's Vero Beach Resort, 58,
 78
Disney's Wide World of Sports
 complex, 13, 32, 141,
 158–160
Disney's Winter Summerland
 (mini golf), 145
DiveQuest, 102
Dixie Landings. *see* Port
 Orleans Riverside
Dolphin, 39, 54–56
 lounges, 217
 restaurants, 198
Dolphins in Depth (3-hour
 program), 102
Downtown Disney Marketplace, 162
 guided fishing trips from, 152
 lounges, 205, 216, 217
 restaurants, 190, 196,
 203–205
 shopping, 162–164
Downtown Disney Pleasure
 Island, 29, 183, 206–210
 lounges, 205
 restaurants, 204
 shopping, 162, 163
Downtown Disney West Side,
 29, 183, 208, 210–212
 DisneyQuest at, 34, 208, 215
 restaurants, 194, 204–206

shopping, 162–63, 208

E

Eagle Pines (golf course), 144,
 146, 148
Easter festivities, 12
8TRAX, 29, 208
Electrical Water Pageant, 53, 211
Electric Convenience Vehicles
 (ECVs), 30–32, 96, 131
Epcot, 81–82, 93–117
 admission prices, 18–20, 93
 behind-the-scenes tours, 102,
 116
 drinking spots, 117
 entertainment, 94, 211
 getting oriented, 96
 hot tips, 95
 hours, 93, 95, 109, 211
 Extra Magic Hours, 15
 IllumiNations, 94–95, 109, 211
 International Gateway, 109
 lounges, 205, 215
 quiet escapes, 108
 restaurants
 fast food, 192–196
 snacks, 196
 table service, 184–185,
 187–192, 204–205
 romantic spots, 111
 sample schedule, 25
 shopping, 166–168
 Tip Board, 97
 touring priorities, 97
 walking tours, 96–97, 116
 See also Future World; World
 Showcase
Epcot Seas Aqua Tour, 102
ESPN Club, 34, 46, 213
Extra Magic Hours, 15

F

Fantasia Garden (mini golf), 145
Fantasmic!, 120, 129, 187
Fantasmic! Dining Opportunity,
 187
fast food. *see* restaurants; snacks
Fastpass, 81, 83, 87, 97, 122, 131
fireworks displays, 12, 15, 51,
 92, 109, 120, 129, 177, 187,
 211
 sunset cruises and, 176–178
First Aid Centers, 20
fishing, 30, 47, 49, 51, 53, 58, 60,
 62, 63, 69, 71, 151–153, 174
fitness centers. *see* health clubs
Fort Wilderness, 42, 63–64,
 174–176, 218
 fishing trips from, 151–152
 hayrides from, 29
France, 108, 111

restaurants, 185, 188, 192
 shopping, 166
Funai Classic at Walt Disney
 World Resort, 13, 142, 145
Future World, 97–106

G

Germany, 94, 115
 restaurants, 188, 194, 218
 shopping, 166
golf, 30, 33, 65, 70, 142–150
 instructions, 144
 reservations, 30, 143–144
 tournaments, 13, 142, 145–146
Grand Floridian, 34–35, 39,
 50–52
 afternoon tea, 34, 209
 guided fishing trips from, 152
 lounge, 205, 217
 restaurants, 198–200, 202, 204
 spa, 51, 161, 178–179
Grand 1 (boat), 176–177
*Guidebook for Guests with
 Disabilities*, 28
guided fishing trips, 151–152
guided tours, 116, 127-128, 139

H

Harambe (African Village), 137
health clubs, 47, 49, 51, 58, 60,
 62, 67–68, 77, 79, 160–161
Hilton, 77
holidays, 11–15
honeymoons, 37, 51
Hoop-Dee-Doo Musical Revue,
 29, 30, 63, 175, 218
horse-drawn wagon rides, 29,
 63, 69, 175, 176
Hotel Plaza Boulevard (resorts
 on), 39, 76–79
 lounges, 205, 215
 restaurants, 205–206
 reservations, 186
 See also Hilton; Royal Plaza;
 Wyndham Palace Resort & Spa
hotels. *see* accommodations
House of Blues, 13, 29, 33,
 204, 212

I

IllumiNations: Reflections of
 Earth, 94, 95, 109, 176,
 177–178, 211
Imagination!, 101–102
Innoventions Fountain, 94
Internet. *see* Web sites
Irish pub, 208
Italy, 108, 111, 114–115
 restaurant, 188
 shopping, 166–167

J

Japan, 94, 108, 112–113
  lounge, 205, 215
  restaurants, 192, 195, 204
  shopping, 167
Jellyrolls, 213
jogging, 47, 49, 53, 58, 65–66,
  68–69, 71, 156, 174

K

Kilimanjaro Safaris, 137–138
kosher meals, 193

L

Lake Buena Vista
  fishing trips on, 152
  golf course, 144, 146,
  149–150
Lost and Found, 32

M

Magic Kingdom, 81, 82–92
  admission prices, 18–20, 84
  Adventureland, 91–92
  entertainment, 92, 211
  Fantasyland, 88–89
  fireworks displays, 92, 211
  Frontierland, 90–91
  getting oriented, 84
  hours, 84, 211
    Extra Magic Hours, 15
  Liberty Square, 89–90
  Main Street, U.S.A., 85
  Mickey's Toontown Fair,
    87–88
  quiet escapes, 90
  restaurants
    fast food, 193–194, 195
    reservations, 186
    snacks, 196
    table service, 185–186,
      189–190, 204
  sample schedule, 24
  shopping, 164–165
  Tip Board, 84
  Tomorrowland, 85–87
  touring priorities, 87
  walking tour, 84–92
Magic Your Way Premium
  Package, 16, 190
Magnolia (golf course), 144,
  146–147, 149
Mannequins, 206, 207–208
massages, 34, 160–161,
  178–179, 181
medical matters, 20
Mexico, 108, 111–112, 117
  restaurants, 192–193, 204
  shopping, 167
Mickey's Backyard Barbecue
  (Fort Wilderness), 175, 218

Mickey's Jammin' Jungle
  Parade, 138
Mickey's Very Merry Christmas
  Parade and Christmas Party, 14
miniature golf courses, 145
money matters, 17–18
  cost-cutting tips, 14, 39
  seasonal rates for 2006, 44
Morocco, 94, 112
  restaurant, 190
  shopping, 167
movies, 34, 208, 211
multi-day tickets, 17

N

New Year's Eve celebration, 15
nightlife guide, 29, 206–218
  BoardWalk, 29, 212–214
  dinner shows, 29, 30, 217–218
  Downtown Disney Pleasure
    Island, 206–210
  Downtown Disney West Side,
    208, 210–212
  movies, 34, 208, 211
  other World options, 214–217
  scenic cocktail spots, 205
  in the theme parks, 211
  wine spots, 29, 117
Norway, 108, 112, 116–117
  restaurants, 184–185, 193
  shopping, 167

O

Oak Trail (golf course), 144, 147
Oktoberfest, 218
older travelers, 32–33, 96, 131
Orlando International Airport
  getting to WDW from, 22
  Disney's Magical Express, 21
  shopping, 164
Osprey Ridge (golf course),
  142, 144, 146, 147–148

P

package tours, 15–17
  Magic Your Way Premium
    Package, 16, 190
Palm (golf course), 144, 146, 149
parades, 14, 15, 92, 129, 138
parasailing, 49, 156
pedal boating, 154–155
pets, 33, 63
pharmacies, 20
picnic areas, 172, 173
pin trading, 168
Planet Hollywood, 206
planning your trip, 9–37
  admission options, 18–20
  multi-day tickets, 17
  convention centers, 48, 51,
    55, 68

crowd patterns, 11, 81, 83, 87,
  95, 97, 109, 120, 122, 131–32
  customized tips, 28–37
  engagements, 34–36
  getting around Walt Disney
    World, 20–22
  holidays and special events,
    11–15
  honeymoons, 37
  hot tickets, 13
  medical matters, 20
  money matters, 17–18
    cost-cutting tips, 14, 39
    seasonal rates for 2006, 44
  package tours, 15–16, 190
  packing, 12
  sample schedules, 24–27
  weather, 10, 32, 34, 161
  weddings, 36–37
  when to go, 10–15
Pleasure Island. see Downtown
  Disney Pleasure Island
Polynesian, 35, 52–54
  guided fishing trips from, 152
  restaurants, 198, 202–203, 218
pontoon boats, 171, 177–178
Pop Century Resort, 73–74
Port Orleans French Quarter, 41,
  70–71
  guided fishing trips from, 152
Port Orleans Riverside, 41,
  68–70
  guided fishing trips from, 152
  lounge, 216–217
  restaurant, 201
prices. see admission prices
reservations at Walt Disney
  World restaurants, 30, 32,
  184–186, 201

R

rainy day activities, 34
religious services, 37
renting a car, 21
reservations
  for WDW dinner shows,
    29–30, 217
  for WDW resorts, 40, 45
  tips, 30, 45
resorts. see accommodations
restaurant guide, 184–206
  Birnbaum's Official Guide to
    Walt Disney World Dining
    2006, 202
  booking a table, 186
  coffeehouses, 196
  cost-cutting tips, 14
  dietary needs, 193
  dining with the chefs (in their
    kitchens), 200
  dinner shows, 29–30,

217–218
Disney Dining Plan, 190
picnicking, 172–173
  without reservations, 191
reservations, 30, 186, 217
room service, 199
smoking regulations, 188
in the theme parks, 184–195
  fast food, 192–195
  table service, 184–192
  24-hour resort eateries, 198
in WDW resorts, 195–203
other WDW options, 203–206
See also snacks
Rock 'n' Roll Beach Club,
  207–208
Royal Plaza, 77–78
RV camping, 63, 64

S
sailing, 155
sample schedules, 24–27
Saratoga Springs Resort & Spa,
  58, 64–65
  spa, 160, 179–180
Sassagoula River Cruise, 69–70
shopping, 162–170
  in the Disney–MGM Studios,
    168–170
  in Disney's Animal Kingdom,
    170
  in the Downtown Disney
    Marketplace, 162–164
  in Downtown Disney Pleasure
    Island, 162, 163
  at Downtown Disney West
    Side, 162–163, 208
  in Epcot, 166–168
  made-to-order surprises, 52
  in the Magic Kingdom,
    164–165
  WDW Mail Order, 169
single travelers, 33–34
smoking regulations in WDW
  parks and resorts, 188
snorkeling, 76
spas, 34, 51, 58, 65, 79, 161,
  178–181
special events, 11–15
  engagements, 34–36
  honeymoons and weddings,
    36–37
  romantic excursions and
    specialty cruises, 176–178
  special occasion (made-to-
    order) surprises, 52
SpectroMagic (light parade), 92
speedboating, 155
sports, 142–161
  basketball, 49, 174
  biking, 47, 58, 62–63, 65–66,

68–71, 76, 153, 174–175
boating, 49, 51, 53, 55, 58,
  60, 62–63, 66, 68–69,
  71–72, 76, 153–156, 174,
  176–178
Disney's Wide World of Sports
  complex, 13, 32, 141,
  158–160
fishing, 30, 47, 49, 51, 53,
  58, 60, 62, 63, 69, 71,
  151–153, 174
golf, 30, 33, 65, 70, 142–150
health clubs, 47, 49, 51, 58,
  60, 62, 67, 68, 77, 79,
  160–161
jogging, 47, 49, 53, 58, 65,
  66, 68, 69, 71, 156, 174
parasailing, 49, 156
sailing, 155
snorkeling, 76
speedboating, 155
swimming, 47, 49, 51, 55, 58,
  60, 62–63, 65–66, 68–69,
  71–74, 77–79, 157, 174
tennis, 29- 30, 47–49, 51, 55,
  60, 62–63, 65, 78–79,
  150–151, 174
volleyball, 49, 51, 55, 60, 68,
  76, 79, 174
wakeboarding, 155–156
waterskiing, 49, 155–156
Star Wars Weekends, 12
stock car racing, 157–158
Swan, 39, 54–56
  restaurants, 202–203
swimming, 47, 49, 51, 55, 58,
  60, 62– 63, 65–66, 68, 69,
  71–74, 77–79, 157, 174

T
taxis, 22
telephone numbers, 30, 32
tennis, 29–30, 47, 48–49, 51,
  55, 60, 62–63, 65, 78–79,
  150–151, 174
tickets
  multi-day tickets, 17
  See also admission passes
tours (guided tours), 116, 127,
  128, 139
transportation, 20–22, 110
traveler's checks, 17
Typhoon Lagoon, 171–172

U
United Kingdom, 94, 108,
  110–111
  lounge, 215
  restaurants,
    191, 204
  shopping, 167–168

V
VIP program (guided tours), 127

W
wagon rides, horse-drawn, 29,
  63, 69, 175–176
wakeboarding, 155–156
Walt Disney Travel Company,
  16, 32
Walt Disney World Golf Classic.
  see Funai Classic at Walt
  Disney World Resort
Walt Disney World Golf
  Instruction, 146
Walt Disney World Guest
  Communications, 28
Walt Disney World Information
  (phone number), 32
Walt Disney World Marathon, 11
water parks, 171–174
  Blizzard Beach, 172–174
  Typhoon Lagoon, 171–172
water taxis, 110
waterskiing, 49, 155–156
WDW Mail Order, 169
weather, 10, 32, 161
Web sites:
  www.disneycruise.com, 76
  www.disneydirect.com, 169
  www.disneyhoneymoons.com
    37
  www.disneyvacationclub.com,
    58
  www.disneyweddings.com,
    37
  www.disneyworld.com, 11,
    16–18, 30–31, 84, 93
  www.disneyworldsports.com,
    160
weddings, 36–37
wheelchair rental, 30–32, 96,
  109, 119, 131
Wilderness Lodge, 34–35, 39,
  56–58
  guided fishing trips from, 152
  lounges, 216
  restaurants, 195–196, 203
World Showcase, 93–95, 107–117
  quiet escapes, 108
Wyndham Palace Resort & Spa,
  78–79
  lounges, 205, 215
  restaurants, 205–206
  spa, 79, 180–181

Y
Yacht Club, 59–61
  fishing trips from, 152
  lounge, 214–215
  restaurants, 201

Disney's Visa® Card

Earn *Disney Rewards*℠
No Annual Fee
No Block-out Dates

FREE $50

Walt Disney World®
Gift Certificate*

*You must apply for the card, be approved,
and use your card to receive your free gift.

APPLY TODAY — Call 1-877-273-7139
or Visit **www.disneyworld50certificate.com**
and be sure to mention key code **6M3L01**.

Subject to terms and conditions on reverse side

10% OFF

AT PLANET HOLLYWOOD

food, non-alcoholic beverage, or merchandise
(excludes taxes, gratuities, and alcoholic beverages) at
Planet Hollywood at DOWNTOWN DISNEY® West Side.

Subject to terms and conditions on reverse side

WITHDRAWN TERMS AND CONDITIONS

Disney Rewards℠ are subject to the terms and conditions of
the Disney Rewards℠ Program.

This offer is limited to a one-time award of $50 Gift Certificate upon
approval of your application for a Disney's Visa Card and first use of your card.
You must use the phone number, website, or application (if provided) contained herein
to be eligible for this offer. New cardmembers applying for this offer may not be
eligible for other new cardmember premiums. Please allow 4 to 6 weeks for delivery of
your $50 Gift Certificate after your first purchase, balance transfer, convenience check,
or cash advance. Gift Certificate is redeemable at participating locations at the Walt
Disney World® Resort in Florida for Food, Beverage, Merchandise and Recreation.
You may also apply it towards any portion of your room account at any Walt Disney
World® owned-and-operated Resort in Florida. Must use card to receive your free gift.

Florida law prohibits the purchase, possession or consumption of
alcoholic beverages by any person under the age of 21. Legal proof of age is required.
Not valid for purchase of Disney Dollars. May not be exchanged for cash.
Not valid at The Disney Stores.
Must redeem $50 Walt Disney World® Gift Certificate by 12/31/06.

Disney's Visa Card available to U.S. residents, 18 and older
(19 in AL and NE) and subject to credit approval.

**Offer valid at Planet Hollywood restaurant in
Downtown Disney® West Side.**

Not valid with any other offers.
PH Tracking Code: 1017 0000 0649

Valid through 12/30/06